REVIVE ME

CHARITY FERRELL

FOREWORD

This is for those who've lost someone without getting the chance to say goodbye; for those who've lost the one they love, their best friend, and the person who made them feel whole. This is for you. The ones who choose to mask the pain by numbing yourself.

Things will get better.

Things will look up.

You can be brought back to life.

PROLOGUE

My head fell back as dark spots crept from the corner of my lids before my sight grew blurry. My breathing labored, every exhale taking all of my energy, and I caught a glimpse of bright red before the pain seeped through my veins and everything went black.

This is what I'd wanted.

This is what I'd craved.

This is what I'd planned.

I'd wanted all the pain to fade away.

And that's exactly what I was getting.

CHAPTER 1

TESSA

Loss. That one word is so short. One syllable. Four letters. Yet, the meaning is massive. One word, one million feelings. We don't only mourn the loss of the person as we're grieving. We mourn the memories sweeping through and reminding us of the plans that are never going to happen. Pain seizes our body, runs its never-ending course, and takes us over.

We become a part of the loss.

We become lost.

When I lost him, I lost myself.

I was a planner. My parents insisted I had an agenda book with me in the womb, the time and date sketched in for when I was ready to be released into the world. Everything in my life was previously drafted; social events, meals, outfits, everything.

And he'd been a fixture in every one.

That was when I had the naïve belief that plans actually

worked out in my favor. That they didn't go astray. That was before reality bitch-slapped me in the face. Someone else's plan ambushed mine, went to war, and mine lost brutally. His plan took the most important person away from me, and I was trying my damnedest to come up with a backup. A Plan B. I was searching for anything that would help me recover from my loss. But my search always came up short. I had nothing.

Every morning, I'd wake up and slowly my recovery slipped further and further away from me. Nothing worked. My body ached like an essential organ had been ripped away from my flesh. It had survived the wound, operating with its daily functions, but it would always be ruptured.

I'd never be the same.

I pushed the rim of my black sunglasses up my nose to block out the hot Indiana sun beaming through the windows as I swerved my Honda Civic into the first parking space I spotted. I turned the key to shut off the ignition, grabbed my cell phone from the cup holder, and tapped my finger against the second name in my favorites.

Please answer.

I needed her with me today. A heavy ache pulled at my chest at the thought of going through this alone. No, that couldn't happen.

I put the call on speaker, allowing my head to fall back against the uncomfortable headrest as I listened to the resonating ringing coming from my lap until the familiar greeting picked up. *"You have reached the voicemail box of..."*

I shut the automatic recording off without leaving a message and tossed my phone into my bag sitting in the passenger seat.

Dread and anger surged through me. Why did I waste my time trying when I already knew what the result would be? It was the same every damn time. All of my calls and texts went unanswered. We'd been best friends since we were in diapers, but now she couldn't stand the sight of me. I reminded her too much of him.

I slammed my eyes shut, took a few breaths, and struggled with the urge to break down in tears. I wanted to shift my car into reverse and bury myself in the comfort of my bed. But that wasn't an option for me. I had to do this for Derrick. I had to walk through those doors every day for nine months. I snagged my bag, hoisting it over my shoulder, before stepping out of my car and kicking the door shut behind me. I just needed to get this over with.

The sun continued its assault on me, the warmth reflecting off the black pavement as I walked toward the double front doors to the brick building sitting in the middle of the parking lot. I wanted to swat the bright sunshine away and tell it to go to hell. I hated the sun now. I preferred the somberness of my quiet and dark bedroom.

I hadn't stepped into a school since that day. And it scared the ever-loving shit out of me. My heart pounded faster with every forced step as I eyed a small group of people gathered at the entrance doors. They were sitting on the ground, lounging on wooden benches, or leaning against each other as they laughed and joked amongst each other. Shit, I was so jealous of them.

Laughter. It had seemed so effortless then, but now it took every ounce of my strength and energy to force a smile for the sake of my younger brother. Every time I saw someone enjoying themselves, I was reminded that the grieving process was long and drawn-out, and I wasn't sure when it would stop. Or if it ever would.

I veered to the right, my feet feeling heavy as I maneuvered around the bodies and headed straight to the entrance doors. I jumped when a firm hand wrapped around my upper arm to stop my movement.

"Hey," I know you," a raspy voice called out from behind me.

I froze, every muscle in my body locking up, and nausea filled my stomach. He whipped me around to face him before I had the chance to smack his hand away and flee. I blinked a few times, staring at him through the thin lenses of my glasses, but there was no recognition.

He was standing at the edge of the crowd with the majority of everyone's attention on his tall, skinny stature. He had at least six inches on my five-foot-eight frame. Jet-black hair curled around his ears and peeked out from under a backward ball cap. A silver hoop looped around his eyebrow with a matching one caught on the bottom of his lip. His nose was crooked like it had been broken a few times. A baggy, wrinkled shirt covered his lean torso, and ripped jeans hung low along his waist.

A thick lump formed in the base of my throat. I knew people would have assumptions as to why I was there. There were a few others, but I knew they didn't want to be revealed, either. The truth would put all of us in an even more fragile state.

"You have the wrong person," I said, attempting to pull my arm out of his grasp, but he was stronger than me.

His long fingers tightened around the thin, long black sleeves that covered my bony arm. He took a few more steps, dipping his head down, and the smell of smoke and cinnamon smacked me in the face.

I shivered when his mouth hit my ear. "No, I saw you on the news. I know what happened to you. I know where you're from."

My throat tightened against the lump and made it difficult for me to tell him to leave me the hell alone.

"Awe babe," he cooed, his hand loosening before beginning to stroke my arm gently. "My bad, I didn't mean to bring that bad shit up." Oh really? "I just never forget a pretty face."

I cringed. I wasn't in the mood to deal with this guy's cheesy pickup lines. "Good for you," I bit out, pulling away and heading toward the doors before I took my anger or tears out on him. I couldn't handle that being brought up. I couldn't talk about it. It was always a green light for my turmoil emotions. Anger for what had been taken away from me and tears because I knew I'd never be getting it back.

He followed me, angling the front of his body as he took his steps before stopping in front of the door and opening it for me. "No doll, not fucking good for me. You see, if that shit didn't happen, your beautiful face would be lit up with a smile. You wouldn't be on the verge of bursting into tears or possibly punching me in the face."

And I wouldn't be here at all, dumbass.

"You have no idea what I'm on the verge of," I said, pointing to the lenses covering my near-to-tears eyes. I stepped forward quickly and let the door shut in his face. He quickly caught up and kept following me as I picked up my pace. My irritation heightened when his hand wrapped around my arm again, and he spun me around to face him.

He reached out, and his rough palms stroked the apples of my cheeks. "But you are, love."

"You know nothing," I rushed out, swiping his hand away from me for what felt like the millionth time and storming down the hallway. He yelled incoherent words from behind me, but I ignored him and pulled out the crumpled paper from my pocket as I went in search of my locker.

I squeezed myself into the tiny space when I found it as bodies bumped into me. I opened my bag and began transferring books into the slender compartment. My bag vibrated, and I pulled out my phone with anticipation.

She was calling me back.

Halle-freaking-lujah!

The excitement died, and my shoulders dropped when I eyed the name flashing across the screen. I tapped the ignore button and tossed the phone back in my bag. I didn't have the patience to deal with his shit right now.

"You can't keep ignoring me, Tessa," the husky voice growled behind me, causing every book in my hand to collapse onto the ground. Ignoring him, I bent down, picked them up, and tossed them onto the top shelf. "Tessa." His voice was deeper this time – more dominant.

I sighed loudly. "I haven't been ignoring you." I kept my eyes on the locker as I balanced my bag on the clip to hold it up.

"Will you please look at me?"

I turned around, leaning half of my body against the open locker, as I grabbed onto the edge of the door to support my weight. Dawson wouldn't leave me alone until I heard him out. I knew him too well to think otherwise. His six-two-frame lingered over me while his deep-set blue eyes zeroed in on mine. His muscled arms were folded across his broad chest as he studied me. His ash-blond hair was damp and had grown out since I'd last seen him, and a few days worth of scruff was spread over his cheeks.

"That's bullshit," he went on. "Your car is sitting in the driveway every damn time I come over, but no one will answer the door, except for Derrick, and he tells me you're holed up in your bedroom sleeping. I know your number hasn't changed, considering I just watched you look at my name and hit the fuck-you button."

I narrowed my gaze at him. "You of all people should understand how hard this day is going to be for me. I'm just trying to get it over with, and I don't need any more stresses." I averted my eyes back to the floor to avoid his reaction. I was acting like a bitch, I knew it, but I didn't have the energy to do anything else. I couldn't help him when I was barely holding myself up.

"Any more stresses? You think this day is going to be happy

go fucking lucky for me? We were all supposed to stick together, remember? He was my best friend. I miss him, too. I feel your pain, so why won't you talk to me about it?"

He was right. The three of us had made a pact at his funeral. We'd always be there for one another. Rain or shine, day or night, tomorrow or in a decade. But Daisy had bailed on the promise, giving me permission to do it next, and we left Dawson in the dust. With Tanner gone, our support chain had rusted – the links falling off and releasing us all on our own.

The bell ringing saved me from having to keep our conversation going. "You can call me tonight," I breathed out, grabbing a book and closing my locker. "We'll talk."

"If you don't answer your phone, I'm coming over and banging on your door until someone opens it."

He was telling the truth. He'd do exactly that. "Fine," I said, nodding. "Just let me get to class. You know how I am about being late."

⚜

I SET MY TRAY ON AN EMPTY, ROUND TABLE AND PULLED OUT a chair to sit down. My first three classes had been a dull and tedious affair. I already knew the material. I could've probably taught it better than the teacher. I'd taken the same classes my junior year and had planned on taking college courses this year but changed my mind when it came time to actually choose my schedule. If I already knew the material, all I'd have to do is show up to class, and that was it. No studying, no stressing, nothing.

I opened a bottle of water and looked around the busy lunchroom. Tables were packed with people yelling at each other and shoving food down their throats. My eyes scanned the room and fell on Dawson. He was at a table with his friends, Cody and Ollie. They'd gone to our old school and played football together.

I saw a small conversation happening between them, but there were no smiles or laughs. It was a rough day for all of us.

"Well, if it's isn't the prettiest girl in the room." I looked away from Dawson to find the guy from this morning tossing his tray onto my table and pulling out the chair next to me.

"Please don't call me that," I grumbled. What did this guy want from me?

I pulled my fork from the plastic wrapper, tried my hardest to act like he wasn't there, and poked at something that looked like macaroni and cheese. I didn't have an appetite but playing with my food sounded more appealing than having a conversation with him.

He opened up his milk carton, took a long chug, and wiped his mouth with the back of his hand. "You're not a very talkative one," he said, taking another swig while waiting for me to say something.

I glared at him. "What's your name?" My eyes briefly looked away in time to notice Dawson staring our way.

The guy grinned and held out his hand. "Reese, and you never mentioned yours, gorgeous." I rolled my eyes and ignored his hand. He looked down at it, shrugged, and kept smiling.

"Tessa, and please, spare me the ridiculous pick up lines."

I was a far cry from looking gorgeous. Shit, I wasn't sure if I was even treading the line of looking decent. My slim body now carried extra weight around my hips and thighs. The blonde hair that was once full of shine and bounce from the curls I'd spend hours perfecting were now straight, dull, and pulled into a sloppy ponytail. My face was clear of make-up, not even a hint of mascara, and I'd spotted a few blemishes around my chin when I woke up this morning. I wasn't wearing a mini-skirt or my best back-to-school outfit like most of the girls. I'd thrown on a pair of jeans and a black, long-sleeve scoop neck top. Nothing about me screamed beauty.

"They're not ridiculous if they're true."

Cue eye roll number two.

I didn't have time for this shit, either. I pushed my tray forward, settled my elbows on the table, and looked directly at him. "Look, I appreciate you trying to be friendly to the new girl and all, but I'm really not in the mood for the welcome to the new school gig you're playing. I'm sure you can find someone else who will appreciate your attention." I was sure girls fell at his booted feet and right into his arms.

His dark eyes widened in amusement. "Oh babe, trust me. I'm far from being on the welcome committee." He laughed deeply from the bottom of his throat. "I'm the last person they'd want new kids to be around in this shithole. I'm what they refer to as a bad influence and a delinquent," he paused, "their words, not mine." He grabbed the pizza slice on his tray and took a giant bite. "Look, we don't even have to talk. How about I stay here and keep you company? If you feel like striking up a conversation, we'll talk. If not, we don't have to. I'll sit here quietly and eat my grub."

I shook my head. "I don't need company. I'd like to be left alone."

"I get it. I get it." I raised a brow. He didn't get shit. He didn't get anything about me. If he did, he'd be running for the hills. "You're sad and want to be left alone. You hate everyone. You're isolating yourself, but that only makes shit worse."

"Didn't you just say you'd sit here quietly?"

"I will, just let me say one more thing." He didn't wait for me to answer or give him permission. He just kept talking. "After awhile, you're sucked in, and it's too late for you to find your way back. Trust me." I stayed silent, and he perked up in his chair. "Look, there's this party tonight. Come. I recognized you crying on the news at your brother's funeral. I know what happened to you."

A daunting memory smashed into my brain. The news vans, I'd lost count of how many, had been parked in front of our house for weeks. Cameras and microphones were shoved into our faces as the reporters begged for any comment they could get. The American people loved victims of tragedy. Those people who sat in front of their TVs, bought magazines with the appealing headlines, or tweeted about our loss had no idea. We wanted to crawl into a hole and hide, not showcase our pain nationally.

"I promise it will help get your mind off all your crazy shit going on. At least for a night," he added. I'd practically told him I hated people and now he was inviting me to a party?

"Thanks for the invite, but I'll pass." I probably sounded like a total bitch, but I couldn't help it.

He fished a pen from his pocket and clicked it open. "Here's my number." He grabbed the napkin from my tray and began scribbling down numbers. "And here's the address," he added, pointing to the sloppy handwriting. "I hope you come out. I give you my word it will help you get out of this funk. The longer you allow yourself to stay this way, the harder it is to get out. I can't say I know how to get rid of your pain, but I can make you immune to it for awhile." I stayed quiet. "It was a pleasure to meet you, Tessa."

He picked up his tray without saying another word, walked away, and joined a full table in the center of the room. He ignored the chaos of the people surrounding him and kept his eyes on me like I was the most interesting thing in the room.

But those eyes also looked predatory, like he wouldn't stop until he had me in his grasps. I quickly looked away, my eyes meeting Dawson's, before picking up my tray and dashing out of the lunchroom.

CHAPTER 2

TESSA

My knees hit freshly grown grass as I settled down onto the ground. I took a deep breath before slowly opening my eyes and staring at the stone in front of me. Panic coursed through my veins every time I saw it. I re-lived the sound of gunshots as I read the words. Seeing his name etched in the rough stone was like living the nightmare over and over again.

In Loving Memory of Tanner Benson
God called him home to Heaven.
1996-2013

I pushed the long sleeves of my shirt up my arms as sweat began to build around my hairline. "Today was hell without you," I said, warm tears pricking at my eyelids. "Daisy was a no-show." I snorted. "But that doesn't surprise me." I traced a finger against his name, back and forth against the rough, gravely stone, until I was sure I had every curve, slant, and space memorized. "Why did you leave me all alone?" I cried out into the emptiness of the cemetery. I was surrounded by the whispers of the trees, the still of the evening, and the hundreds of dead bodies buried around me. It was the most serene place I'd been to in months.

"You should've stopped him," went on, bending forward and smacking my palm against the gravestone. The tears fell faster, his name growing blurry through my vision, and I hit it harder.

It had been three months, three long, excruciating months, since he'd been murdered. I fell back down, wrapped my hands around my head, and shut my eyes.

My body had jerked in my chair at the sound of the first gunshot. I suddenly became alerted, along with everyone else in the classroom, and flinched as another shot reverberated. I shifted in my chair to turn around and look at the wall behind me. I was sure they were coming from the room next door.

"What the hell was that?" Dawson asked, getting up from his chair.

Everyone's attention moved away from the wall to him like he had all the answers. The stutter of gunshots seared through me. Something wasn't right. We lived in a small town full of hunters. Guns weren't out of the ordinary, but they were usually heard in the woods, not classrooms.

Mr. Higgins' shoes squeaked when he stormed to the front of the room. "This is code red!" he said urgently.

I watched everyone jump up from the chairs and perform the actions of the drill we'd been practicing for years – incase anything like this ever happened. I remembered how we'd goofed around during the procedure like it was a joke. Something like this would never happen around here.

We were so wrong.

He went directly to the door, twisted the lock with trembling fingers, and the room went dim with the flip of the light switch. He stumbled into empty desks while making his way to the other side to draw the blinds.

I froze in my chair when another round of shots fired and more screams erupted. How many was that? I tried to keep up, counting the number of shots and the different tones of screams, but there were too many.

"Remember the drill," Mr. Higgins directed.

Everyone ducked underneath their desks.

"What's happening?" a girl asked, tears streaming down her face.

"I'm not sure," he answered. "We need to make this room appear to be empty. If there's a dangerous person out there and they attempt to come in, do not scream."

The loud blast of alarms throttled through the room. I finally got up from my chair and dipped down under my desk as my hands went to my ears.

That's when it hit me.

That's when my heart was ready to pound out of my chest, and I went into full panic mode.

"Dawson," I whispered urgently, waving him over.

He scurried over, got down on his knees, and looked at me. Grabbing my hand, he interlocked our fingers and pressed his lips against my forehead.

"Everything is going to be okay, babe," he said, stroking my hair.

I shook my head, swallowing a few times as I tried to force the words from my mouth, but they were giving me a hard time. If I said them out loud, they would be true. They'd be real. It reminded me of the nightmares I had as a child, where my mouth would open wide to scream for my parents, but I suddenly had no voice. I'd struggle, cry, and push, but my throat was incapable of sound.

But it was real this time.

I was living a nightmare.

"Tanner's in that room," I finally managed to get out.

His hand tightened in mine while his body locked up. He stayed silent, but I saw the pain passing over his face. I quickly pulled my hand out of his, crawled out from under my desk and darted across the room, praying I'd make it to the door before he got to me. He was faster. I screeched when my body was gridlocked, a pair of hands attached to my waist, and I was pulled away from my destination.

"Tessa, stop!" he hissed into my ear. His hold tightened on me as I fought against him. I'd tear down every desk and chair in my way. I had to save him, or I'd never forgive myself.

"He's in there!" I shouted, my arm flying towards the door. My voice pierced through the room as I tried to scream louder than the alarms. I didn't care if anyone heard me. I glanced around the room, noticing the looks of shock and dread on peopls' faces.

Why weren't they doing anything?

Why weren't they trying to save him?

I pushed against Dawson with all my strength. "If you're not going to do anything, I will."

"Tessa, get down and lower your voice," Mr. Higgins demanded, stalking our way.

I clutched my hands to my chest. "You don't have to do anything," I desperately begged. "Just let me go in there and help. You can lock the door behind me, and none of you will be in harm's way." I had no idea what I was going to do when I got out of there, but I'd figure it out. No one moved, and Dawson's hold didn't loosen. "Please!" I screamed, kicking my feet against his legs as his hand shot up to cover my mouth.

"Tessa," he whispered. "Stop it."

"I'll stop it when you let me go!" I gave him another kick.

"Please shut up," a girl whispered from the floor. Her feet were pushed against her chest, and a strand of black mascara streamed down her swollen face.

"I'll be quiet when my brother's life isn't in danger. Now let me out!" I was being selfish, but I didn't care. Saving him was all that mattered at that moment.

I screeched when my body was lifted and dragged to the back of the room. I kept fighting him, my shoes dragging against the floor, as I whipped back and forth in his arms. I was pushed against a wall in the corner of the room, and his hands went to my shoulders to push me down until I hit the floor. I glanced up to see him standing in front of me. His nostrils flared, and the veins in his neck engorged. He crossed his arms, and stood in front of me like a barrier between the door and me.

"Please let me go," I pleaded, tears rolling down my cheeks.

"No!"

"Please!"

He bent down on his heels, and an arm went to each side of my head. "Baby, there's nothing we can do. Help is on the way." I took a deep breath and realized sirens were ringing out around us. "But you can't leave this room." I attempted to do a lame crawl underneath his arms, but he slammed his hand into the wall to stop me. "Quit, just fucking quit it." His palm pounded against the wall again. "Tanner is a fighter. He'll be okay. But if I let anything happen to you, if he knows I allowed you to put yourself in danger, he'll kick my ass and never forgive me. I couldn't forgive myself, either. I told him I'd always protect you if he wasn't around and that's what I'm doing. Now get the hell over it and stop fucking fighting me!"

Tears poured down my face as my body shook. Dawson's arm went around my back, and my face hit the soft cotton of his t-shirt.

"Okay," I sobbed. "I'll stop."

Tanner was a fighter.

He'd get through this.

I knew it.

I wiped away the tears rolling down my cheeks and stared at the sunset before leaving him. He was gone, and we were all left broken without him. Losing him was the worst pain I'd ever gone through. He was my other half. We'd been best friends before we were born. He was my confidant, my protector, my best friend, and my twin brother.

I pulled myself up, passing the rows of headstones as I made my way back to my car, and that's when I noticed it. I visited Tanner every day, but I'd never paid attention to the other headstones. I stopped, and my eyes burned with hate as I stared at the name.

Rodney Avila.

"Burn in hell," I seethed. I picked up a rock from the ground and tossed it at his name. "You stupid bastard!" I shrieked, throwing another, this one with more force. "I hate you! You killed all of them! You got what you deserved!" The tears streamed faster down my face, and I didn't even attempt to get rid of them this time.

I threw one more stone, flipped off the tombstone, and walked away. I'd never take that way through the cemetery again. Seeing his name was like poison bring dripped into my eyes. All of this was his fault.

He'd brought the gun to school. He'd hunted down his ex-girlfriend because she couldn't deal with his psychopathic tantrums and abuse anymore. She was moving on, and it wasn't with him. He grabbed his dad's gun before going to school, went to her first-period class, and killed everyone in the room. Then he pulled the trigger on himself.

I gripped my steering wheel tightly when I made it back into my car. Why did he have to kill everyone? If he was so unhappy, why couldn't he just do it to himself?

In the past, I would've never wished suicide on anyone, but this someone took my brother from me. He'd taken my family away from me. And I'd never forgive him, dead or not. I would hate him until I took my last breath.

Forgiveness wasn't an option.

CHAPTER 3

TESSA

I walked through the front door to find my younger brother, Derrick, on the couch with a video game controller in his hand. His fingers tapped the buttons quickly as he shouted at the TV.

"Are mom and dad here?" I asked, interrupting him by standing in front of the TV.

He paused the game and let out a snort. "You seriously asking me that?" He tossed the controller onto the coffee table and shook his head. "Even when they're here, they aren't." My brother was strikingly similar to Tanner. His thick, blonde hair was cut short, and he was getting taller and more muscular with each passing day.

"They'll get better, just give them time," I said, wishing I believed my words. After Tanner's funeral, they'd tapped out and forgot they had two living children to take care of. I was old enough to deal with the neglect. But Derrick was too young. So I took on the role of taking care of him.

He rolled his eyes. "Yeah right. You've been saying that for months. They don't even come home after work until midnight."

"Come on," I called, heading into the kitchen. "I'll make you something to eat. I'm sure you're starving."

"I'm always starving," he said, laughing lightly. "But I've already eaten." I twisted around to look at him. Derrick was fourteen, but the boy couldn't cook. He'd starve himself before figuring out how to make a grilled cheese sandwich. "Dawson fed me. He stopped by looking for you. We waited for a while, played a few levels, but you never showed. So he took me out for ice cream before going to work."

Shit! I'd turned off my phone and forgot about calling him. At least I'd gotten out of having that dreaded conversation.

"Ice cream isn't dinner." I walked into the kitchen, turned on the light, and peeked at him from around the corner. "Now get your butt in here so I can feed you some real food."

He groaned but did as he was told. I threw some easy-mac in the microwave and made us sandwiches. Derrick devoured his dinner while I picked at mine, listening to him ramble about school and his upcoming field trip to a football game. He might've been a teenager, but he was still young, and I didn't want him corrupted. I shielded him from my parent's problems the best that I could. My bond with my brothers, even when they're cutting my doll's hair off, was strong. Sibling friendships were something that would stayed with you forever.

"I'm going to go watch some TV in my room," he said, getting up from the table after we finished his homework. "Goodnight, sis."

I nodded and started to clean up. I heard his bedroom door

click shut upstairs at the same time the front one opened. I walked into the entryway to find my mom stumbling in and nearly falling face first against the staircase. I could smell the alcohol lingering on her breath from across the room. Her blue eyes took one look at me and turned cold. Muttering something underneath her breath, she shook her head and wandered up the stairs to her bedroom. I painfully watched until she disappeared and the door slammed shut. Thirty minutes later, my dad came home and repeated the same motions.

I sat down and slammed my hands down on the kitchen table. Taking a deep breath, I reached for the pile of mail sitting to the side. A large white envelope stuck out from the stack, and I pulled it out. My stomach fell when I noticed the letterhead.

I drug the rest of the pile to me, sorting through it, and noticed another white envelope. I pushed the others away, set the two in front of me, and focused on them. They both had the same address, just sent to different people.

One had his name. The other mine.

Both were from my dream college.

Tanner hadn't wanted to go to college on the East Coast, but he'd applied for me. He'd follow me anywhere to make sure I was safe.

I grabbed both envelopes, stormed across the room, and threw them into the trash.

Screw it.

I grabbed my bag and stepped out into the night. Maybe Reese was right. Maybe I needed to numb myself.

❧

I PARKED MY CAR ACROSS THE STREET FROM A ONE-STORY house that was in need of some serious TLC and double-checked my GPS to make sure I was at the right place.

Yep, it matched the address on the napkin. I squinted my eyes, noticing people standing on the front porch, the front lawn, and the small driveway. Bodies trickled in and out of the open doorway to the house. I tucked my wallet underneath my seat, ran my hands down my jeans, and got out of my car. My steps followed the loud music until I walked into a room full of people with cups in their hands, cigarettes between their fingers, and sweat running down their face.

A few pieces of furniture were pressed against the walls as people were scattered throughout the place. There were no familiar faces and most of them looked too old to be in high school. I kept walking, taking only a few steps and landed in the kitchen. The cabinets hanging on the walls were either broken or open. Alcohol bottles were strewed along the countertops and floor. A group of people surrounded a circular table in the middle of the room. I stood up on my tiptoes, and my eyes widened as a guy dropped his head down to a rectangular mirror and snorted a line of a white substance. He finished the line, shook his head, and threw his hands up in victory as a few others cheered and clapped his back.

I walked backward, ready to flee, when a pair of hands stopped me. I stilled as a splash of liquid smacked into my hair, and someone pushed me from behind.

"Damn pretty girl, you showed," a deep voice growled into my ear. I turned around to find Reese standing in front of me. He grabbed my hand. "We've got some kick-ass shit here. Can I get you something from the keg?" I stared at him, debating with myself whether to stay or leave. "Or something harder? Vodka? Whiskey? Whatever you want, love, I got you." His wiry lips gave me a sly smile.

A red, plastic cup was gripped in his hand, and he took a drink while waiting for my answer. I gave him a weak smile, noticing the bloodshot eyes and dilated pupils. I glanced around the room, observing everyone's carefree behavior with envy.

That's how I wanted to be.

That's how I wanted to feel.

That's why I was there.

My eyes zeroed in on a guy across from us. He sat slack against the wall, his body settled on the floor, as his head bobbed from side to side. A line of drool was dripping from his mouth onto the stained carpet.

"I'll have whatever he's having," I said, gesturing to him.

Cold lips kissed my cheek. "That's my girl. I'll hook you up real good, I promise. Be right back." *His girl?*

I nodded, running my teeth along my lower lip, and watched him disappear into the kitchen. I slouched back against the wall and shut my eyes. What was I doing here? Reese wasn't my type. He was a bad boy, and a bad boy had never been in my plans. They weren't my type. But he was giving me attention and wasn't treating me like I was the sister of the murdered football star. He was going to help me ... or at least that's what I was trying to convince myself.

My eyes shot open as something hard collided into my side. My head turned to find two people practically dry-humping each other. Their mouths were connected, their tongues and spit sliding against one another's, as their hands clawed at bare skin. I covered my mouth, turning away, and scurried off to find an open chair at the corner of the living room. Where the hell was I?

"Here ya go," Reese said, stopping in front of me and handing over a plastic cup that resembled his. "You're going to love this shit."

I glanced into the cup to see an unrecognizable brown liquid. Slowly bringing the rim to my chapped lips, the liquid hit my tongue, causing me to cringe. Gagging, I brought my hand to my chest, forcing myself to swallow down the repugnant concoction of licorice, sugar, and what I'd imagined Drano would taste like if I ever took a go at it.

"Holy shit!" I gasped, grabbing my throat, coughing, and pulling the cup away from me. I shook my head and stuck my tongue out as it began to feel fuzzy. "Why are you feeding me turpentine?"

He chuckled, pushing a hand into the pocket of his pants. "It's a Jagerbomb in a cup, love." I looked up at him and blinked a few times. Was I supposed to know what that meant? He smiled proudly like he'd invented the drink and was about to receive some award for it. "My specialty and favorite. It'll take you a few sips to get used to the taste, but after that, you'll be addicted. I promise."

I coughed again. "I highly doubt that."

"Give it a chance."

I held in a breath, exhaling slowly, and forced myself to take another drink. I wasn't new to drinking, but I'd always stuck to the beginner drinks; wine coolers, rum with fruit juice, or wine on holidays, definitely nothing this potent.

His hand shot towards me. "Come on." I grabbed it, giving him the power to pull me up from my chair. "I've got some people I want you to meet."

He tucked me into his side and guided me back into the kitchen. The idea of meeting new people felt more nauseating than the drink. The old Tessa was a people person, but now, I loathed social interaction.

"Hey guys," Reese called out. I curled closer to his side as everyone's attention turned to us. "This is my girl, Tessa. Be sure to make her feel at home, or you'll have to answer to me." He pointed to a few guys, "And hands off, assholes."

The guys laughed while a few greetings and waves came my way. "Aren't you a cute thing?" a soft, patronizing voice sang out.

I caught a glimpse of a skinny frame jumping off the counter and sauntering over like she was walking the runway. Her dark hair draped down her shoulders and stopped at the peak of her full cleavage. A tight top covered the outside of her boobs and dipped down into her bellybutton to expose the dips in between her cleavage and stomach. I blinked, watching her get closer, her smoky eyes narrowing my way, but her bright red lips smiled. I looked down, noticing the ripped jeans hanging loose on my waist and my long-sleeve top. I looked homeless compared to her.

"Alexa, play nice," Reese warned.

Her smile expanded. "I am playing nice. I was giving the girl a compliment. She's cute."

I looked away from her and decided not to thank her for the backhanded *compliment.* She waited a few seconds for my reaction but shrugged when she realized I wasn't giving her the reaction she wanted.

I moved my eyes to the floor as Reese's hold tightened on me. "Don't fuck with her. You do, you'll deal with me, and I know you don't want that shit," he snarled.

She laughed in his face. "Whatever, you know I'm not scared of you." She waved goodbye to everyone and ran her hand down Reese's arm before leaving the room.

"You'll have to excuse Alexa. She takes a minute to warm up to you," a guy with black dreadlocks said. I recognized him as the one snorting his victory earlier. "I'm Bobby, by the way, and this is my girl, Maya." He nuzzled the girl's neck sitting on his lap, and she giggled loudly before turning around and kissing him full on the lips.

"Hey girl," she said, waving. Her eyes were covered with a pair of cat-eye framed glasses, and her bright red hair was dyed blue at the tips.

Reese slid out an empty chair from the table and plopped down. Grabbing the drink from my hand, he set it down, grabbed my waist, and pulled me onto his lap. The weight of his arms wrapped around me, his hands landing high on my thighs, and I reclined against him. His chin sat in the crook of my neck as his hands began to roam higher. I moved forward, trying to deter his touch but not look uncomfortable at the same time.

"Did you just move here?" Maya asked. "I've never seen you around." My stomach rolled as I stilled. I didn't want them to know. They couldn't know. Or they'd treat me differently.

"She did," Reese said, coming to my rescue. He clapped his hands together. "Now, how about we take some shots, fuckers? Get this party started!" I let out a breath of relief. "I got you love," he whispered into my ear. His lips hit my neck, moving across my bare skin, then back to my ear as I shivered in his arms. "I got you," he repeated, his rough hand moving along the hem of my shirt.

"What's your poison, baby girl?" a guy with a bright purple mohawk asked, walking forward with a bottle of alcohol in each hand. He showed me a row of crooked teeth when he grinned and tipped both bottles my way.

"Uh, vodka?" I answered, reading the label on the clear bottle.

Vodka, I'd had that before. I could handle that.

"Hell to the yeah!" the guy shouted, grabbing a stack of shot glasses and filling them up to the rim with the clear liquid.

Reese swiped two glasses and handed one to me. "Drink up, pretty," he said, raising his glass in the air. "Cheers, bitches!"

Everyone, except for me, repeated his words and downed their shots. I hesitated. My glass stayed full while everyone smacked theirs against the table. I gripped it in my hand firmly and rested the edge at the top of my mouth before slowly tipping it forward. The alcohol flowed from the glass slowly and smacked into my tongue. The taste of my first drink still lingered in my mouth, and my throat screamed as I mixed it with the vodka. It burned its way down and started a fire in the pit of my stomach. I coughed a few times and instantly knew why Tanner had refused to let me take shots.

"Let's do another!" I yelled, the alcohol changing its course to my head. The shot hurt, but was exhilarating, giving me an adrenaline rush.

I flinched when Reese's hand elevated up my shirt and cupped my breast over my bra. My gut screamed at me, telling me this was not something I wanted, but my brain ignored it. I shivered uncomfortably at his caresses. He squeezed harder, taking it as the opposite of the signal I was trying to send. I slammed my eyes shut and slowly opened them as my head started to spin lightly. If anyone noticed him groping me, they didn't act like it. They just continued their drinking and chain smoking.

"You heard the girl," he shouted. "Pour us another damn round!" Another shot was shoved in my hand, and I swallowed it down with everyone else this time.

"Is this helping to get your mind off shit?" Reese asked, his cold hand still roaming my bare skin. I trembled, leaning back into his chest, and he took that as an even further invitation. "I knew it would." His hand groped my boob one more time before venturing its way to the back clasp.

I froze, the high of my night started to dissolve, as dread and reality kicked in. I didn't want his hands on me. I'd come here to get wasted and clear my head.

Sex wasn't my numbing agent.

Alcohol was.

"How about another?" I asked promptly, shouting the words without thinking. I needed him to slow down. If his hands were busy taking a shot, they wouldn't be on me.

The next shot tore straight through me. It was working. I felt weightless, dazed, and empty. This time when Reese touched me, I allowed it, sinking deeper into his chest and out of my head.

"You're skin is so soft," he rasped, his hands going to the waistband of my jeans. "You have no idea how incredibly sexy you are when you let yourself be free. Be free, Tessa, and I promise you the hurt will stop."

I quivered, chills breaking out along my arms. My eyes drifted open, and I noticed everyone's attention was now focused on us. My stomach did a somersault as bile crept its way up my throat.

"I need to use the bathroom," I said, pulling away from him and pushing up to my feet. He caught me before I fell on the floor and helped me balance myself. Why did I feel like I was riding on a Merry Go Round?

"Fuck babe, I'm sorry. I'm not trying to move too fast with you. I swear it. You were just sitting here on my lap, your ass rubbing against my cock, and I couldn't help myself." He swept a hand over his tortured face.

"No!" I quickly corrected. My stomach rumbled again. "You're, uh, fine, with whatever you were doing. I just really need to go to the bathroom."

"Down the hallway to the left, sweetheart," Bobby said, pointing a finger in the direction.

"You want me to go with you?" Reese asked.

I shook my head. "I'll be fine." I cautiously turned around and walked down the hallway, using the walls to help me walk in a straight line, or at least hold me up. I stopped in front of two girls standing outside the door laughing as they showed each other something on their phones.

I pointed to the door. "Is this the bathroom?"

"Sure is," one of the girls answered. "But it's probably going to be awhile."

The other laughed as I tilted my head at them. That's when I heard it. The loud grunts and heavy moans coming from the other side of the door. Just freaking great. Weren't there bedrooms around here?

"Is there another bathroom?" I asked, leaning against the wall to keep my balance. She shook her head. "Thanks." I left them and did my best to shove through the crowd.

My stomach continued its assault on me, and I stumbled down the porch steps to the side of the house just in time. My throat burned as bile swept up, and my head spun faster. I rolled it in circles, feeling the sweat begin its journey down my forehead, and bent forward again to empty my stomach until there was nothing left to dispel.

I collapsed onto the dirty ground and settled my back against the siding of the house while wiping my mouth with the back of my arm. That extra shot wasn't such a great idea. Actually, none of the shots was a good idea. I needed to find a way to keep the detached feeling without suffering the vomiting aftermath.

"I just want to go home," I cried out to the night.

There was no way I was getting behind the wheel of my car or asking Reese to take me home. He was in worse condition than me. I pulled my phone from my front pocket, practically tipping over in the process, and dialed Tanner's number without thinking. I used my shoulder to help balance the phone against my ear as I listened to the booming sound coming from the other end. The call kicked into voicemail, and more bile seeped up at the sound of his voice. I ripped the phone away from my ear, slammed my finger against the end button, and pounded it against the ground. I jerked to the side, gagging, as my body tried to heave up anything left in my stomach. None of us had the strength to disconnect his phone, so I kept paying the bill each month.

My throat scorched like fire when the tears started. I couldn't keep up with all of the sensations swirling through my body, through my mind, that created the chaotic mess that was me.

"Damnit!" I cursed, gripping my phone, and hitting the one name I dreaded to call.

"It's about time you called back," the sleepy voice answered on the second ring.

"Dawson!" I cried out, my voice breaking on the last syllable of his name.

"What's wrong?" he asked, suddenly panicked.

"I ... I don't know," I answered honestly. I didn't know how to explain to him what was wrong. I was drunk. I was sad. I was sick. I was lost. I couldn't pick one.

"Where are you?"

"I, uh." I paused to try and remember the address or route I'd taken to get there. I searched my pockets for the napkin but it wasn't there.

"Tessa baby, you've got to talk to me before I lose my shit. Tell me where you are."

"A party. I'm at a party."

"A party where?"

"I don't know. A party at a house," I answered in frustration.

I heard movement on the other line. "Give someone the phone."

"What?" He couldn't be serious. "What if they steal it?"

"Find someone who looks decent enough and give them your phone so I can get to you."

I crawled across the ground until I reached the front corner of the house. I peeked over the edge, noticing the yard wasn't as crowded as it had been.

"No one here looks like a decent person." If I lost my phone, I'd be stuck there with no ride *and* no form of communication.

"Goddamnit, give someone your phone or repeat directions back to me so that I can get you the hell out of there."

I continued my crawling movement and managed to hold my balance long enough to lift myself up. I walked ... or stumbled ... my way to the front of the house and found a guy sitting on the porch steps. He had a beer in his hand and a cigarette between his lips. I glanced around the yard but didn't see anyone else. He was my only option unless I wanted to go back inside, and that wasn't happening. I'd just puked my guts out, and I was sure there were particles of it lingering on me. What a lovely sight.

I headed over to him warily while Dawson bitched at me through the phone. If I weren't so desperate, I would've hung up. My pounding head couldn't handle his lecturing.

"Not feeling so good there?" the guy asked me.

"Will you give someone directions to come get me and not steal my phone?" I asked, getting straight to the point.

He laughed, flicking ashes from the cigarette onto the grass. "Sure, but only because you're cute." I stumbled up the steps, and he jumped forward to help me sit down. "You sure you're okay? I can drive you home if you'd like?" He ran his hands through his thick, dark hair and looked down at me with concern.

"I'm fine. I have someone on the way." I held the phone over to him, and he gave Dawson directions before handing it back to me.

"You stay on the line until I get there, okay. It should only take about ten minutes," Dawson said when I put the phone back to my ear.

"Okay." I heard the faint sound of his old, pick-up truck starting in the background.

"What's a girl like you doing around here?" the guy asked, looking over at me.

"A girl like me?"

"A girl like you. You look all put together. A goody-two-shoes who wants a ride on the wild side. You seem too pure for this shit. You don't get shit-faced on the regular, I can tell. Pre-warning, darlin', all of us are fucking tainted around here. You don't need to be around this shit. It will wipe off and stain you. And trust me, it ain't easy to get it off once it's there." I kept my attention on the ground, holding the phone up to my ear, and not saying anything. "Just make this party your last, okay? I'll consider it payback for not jacking your phone."

I nodded, wrapping my arms around me as I shivered. He flicked his cigarette onto the ground and unbuttoned his flannel shirt before pulling at the sleeves and wrapping it over my shoulders. I glanced over at him, the porch light illuminating his face, and his now bare chest. His arms and stomach were covered with colorful tattoos, works of art, and a cross necklace fell directly in between his breastbone.

I pulled the shirt tighter around my body. "Thank you."

"I'll wait with you until your ride gets here."

We both stayed silent while Dawson kept telling me how much closer he was getting with every passing second. Our heads shot up when the truck pulled in front of us, and Dawson jumped from the driver's side with the ignition still running. Before I knew it, my hand was in his and I was being pulled to the street, almost falling while trying to keep up with him.

"Shit!" I yelped when I was picked up and tossed into the seat. He slammed the door shut behind me, circled around the truck, and got in. I looked out the window, too terrified to face him, and noticed porch guy give me a wave as we pulled away. I started to pull at a sleeve of the flannel and gasped.

"What?" Dawson asked.

"I'm still wearing that guy's shirt," I answered, pulling it off my body. I bunched it up into my lap. "We need to take it back."

"Too late. We'll throw it away," he said, grabbing the flannel and throwing it out of the window before I had the chance to say anything.

"What the hell!" I shrieked. "What's the matter with you?"

"What's the matter with you?" he fired back. "Why were you even hanging out at a party like that?"

"A party like what? We go to school with those people," I kind-of-lied. Okay, maybe a few of those people went to school with us. "And don't act like you've never gotten drunk and stumbled around a few parties before. Don't be a hypocrite."

He snorted, turning at a stop sign. "That was different, and you know it. I wasn't around strangers. You couldn't even trust someone enough to hold your phone."

I rolled down the window, needing some fresh air. "So what? Now all of a sudden you give a shit about me? Now you're worried about the guys I hang out with?"

He winced, clenching his hands around the beat-up steering wheel. "Don't start that bullshit. You know I've always," he clenched his hands tighter, "always cared about you. Yeah, we've had some arguments, and some shit has happened that I regret, but that doesn't mean for one second I've quit giving a shit about you. So stop trying to make bullshit excuses for your childish behavior."

I scoffed. "You regret it, but how many times has it happened? You can't keep doing the same thing and then think shit is okay because you say you regret it."

"*Fuck.* I hate it when you have alcohol in your system. You know damn well why it couldn't happen. All it would've done is complicate shit."

I threw my hands up. "Oh, so hurt me to make everyone else happy and keep your life uncomplicated." I was sick of his crappy excuses. He'd indirectly pained me too many times. It wasn't anything big, but with each compromising situation we'd find ourselves in, the hurt built up every time he'd pull away and say it couldn't happen again.

The truck went silent until we pulled in front of my house.

"Selfish asshole," I muttered, opening up the door to get out, but falling to my knees instead.

Well, shit. That's not how I'd planned my landing.

"Jesus Christ," he said, and I heard his door slam shut.

I fell back, sinking against his truck, and began swatting at the small, dirty pebbles covering my jeans at the knees. He bent down in front of me, grabbed my arm, and tried to find a good angle to get me up.

I swatted at his hands. "Get away from me!" I was acting immature. I knew that. But I was drunk, and I'd never been one to get sloppy drunk, so I was blaming it on the alcohol and inexperience.

He tipped his head back and cursed to the sky. "Quit behaving like a damn child. You're better than this shit." His hands gripped my wrist as I continued my struggle against him.

"I'm not doing anything," I yelled, finally giving up to my losing fight. "I'm nobody now. I have nobody now." My eyelids began to feel heavy as tears pricked at them.

He knelt down again and grabbed my face with both hands. "Look at me," he said, lifting up my chin. Our eyes met, our lips only a few inches away. "Don't you dare say that shit. You're somebody to me. You're somebody to Derrick and your family. You're the reason he's happy. You're the reason I've had a happy life. You're the reason Tanner had a happy life. And we're all here for you."

"You know nothing." Tanner wasn't here for me anymore. My parents gave up once their golden, football star son died. I did well in school, but I didn't shine at any sports. I didn't have colleges looking at me because I could run a touchdown in record time.

"I know you're the reason I'm where I'm at now. You know all the shit I've been through. Who knows where I'd be if it weren't for you talking to me because I was too ashamed to tell anyone else my problems. Who knows where I'd be if you weren't packing my lunch because you knew I was low on money and couldn't afford food."

He brushed away my tears with his thumb and kissed my forehead. His mouth moved down to the tip of my nose and then to my lips. It was so quick. I was certain my inebriated mind had imagined it. I touched my lips with a finger and blinked. Was he even here?

All of a sudden, my breathing grew ragged. I felt like my heart was ready to pound out of my chest and fall onto the ground in front of me. "What is happening to me?" I gasped out, panting. My heart continued its assault on my rib cage, begging to be let loose, and my blood began boiling, my body feeling like an oven. I wrapped my hands around my neck, moving them up and down to try and catch my breath. A thousand tingles spread over my body, feeling like they were burning my skin off, and my throat began to close up. "Holy crap, I'm dying." I knew I was. If I wasn't, I was getting pretty close to it.

I felt the tips of his fingers massage my hair. "Tessa, baby, you've got to calm down."

I shook my head quickly. "I ... I can't."

"Yes you can. Take deep, large breaths," he instructed, his voice soft as he rubbed my arms.

"I don't know what's happening to me!"

"You're having an anxiety attack." I kept shaking my head. An anxiety attack? I didn't have anxiety. No, I was dying. "Look at me." I ignored him, trying to catch my breath. He pulled my chin back up with a single finger. "Look me in the eyes." I finally did as I was told because I had no idea what else to do. I was going to die anyways, so I might as well not spend my last breaths arguing with him. "Good job, baby, now keep them on mine."

My eyes focused on his, and his hands went to my shoulders as he began to massage them. "Now, let's breathe together. One big breath for me. Ready, go." My hands balled into fists as I took a deep breath and my stomach tightened up. "Good job baby, now let it out." I breathed out, and my stomach deflated. "Now again." I repeated the same exercise over and over again as Dawson talked me through each one until I felt like I could control breathing on my own.

"You feel better now?" he asked, the streetlight flickering above us.

I brought both of my hands up and covered my face. "Oh my God, this is beyond humiliating."

He chuckled, grabbing my hands one by one and picking them off my face. "Hate to break it to you, babe, but I've seen you in much worse states than this. Well, minus the drunken part. You should be embarrassed about that." I narrowed my eyes at him. "Remember when you got the chicken pox and no one would talk to you at school for two weeks because they thought you were still contagious and it was airborne?" I kept my eyes narrowed. Tanner, Dawson, and Daisy were the only ones who played with me at recess because everyone else thought I had the plague. Other kids wouldn't even touch the same pencil as me. "Or when you tried that new at-home facial you saw online? You practically burned all of the skin off your face."

I kept taking deep breaths and letting them out like we'd practiced when my stomach began to grumble. "Oh crap," I called out, turning to the side to get sick again, but nothing came out. I heaved again but nothing. I spit the nasty taste of alcohol out of my mouth.

His hands ran down my arms and over my back. He wiped my mouth with the bottom of his t-shirt when I got back up.

"Feel better?" he asked, and I nodded. "Good, now you need to sleep this shit off. I can't believe you of all people decided to go out and party on a school night." He pulled me up from the ground effortlessly, holding my elbow to keep me steady as we headed to my front door.

"Don't act like you've never done it before," I replied, remembering how he and Tanner would go out with the guys on the football team on school nights to have *night practices*. Then they'd call me late at night to sneak them through the back door. Tanner would always wobble to his bedroom, and I'd usually make Dawson something to eat to help sober him up before he crashed on our couch.

He laughed and fished a key from his pocket to unlock the door. I forgot he had a key to our place. I was surprised he wasn't walking in when no one would answer the door.

The door squeaked open, and we walked up the stairs to my bedroom without turning on any lights. My bedside lamp turned on, and I fell onto my bed without pulling down the blankets. I grunted when I was suddenly rolled over. Dawson brought down my blankets, turned me back, and tucked me in tightly.

"Be right back," he whispered and disappeared into my adjoined bathroom. He came back with a small glass of water and two white pills. I grabbed the pills, looked down at them, and then back at him. "What? You didn't have any aspirin in there, so I figured these would do the job, too. It helps with pain and moodiness, right? You'll need both of those tonight and tomorrow."

"Do you even know what Midol is?" I asked.

"It said relief for menstrual symptoms on the bottle, so yeah, it's for pain and moodiness."

"Menstrual means your period."

"I know that. You complain about headaches when you're on your period," he argued, handing over the glass of water. "And you're moody as hell. It's also better than nothing. I checked the ingredients. They'll help you not be as hung over in the morning." I popped the pills into my mouth and swallowed them down. "I'll be here in the morning to take you to school." He kissed my forehead and turned off the light.

I blinked against the sudden darkness, wanting to stop him and beg him to stay with me. I didn't want to be alone, but I bit my tongue to keep the words from falling out of my mouth. I was terrified of his rejection. I'd been able to handle it before, but I was too fragile now. I only needed one more hit with the hammer before I completely shattered.

CHAPTER 4

DAWSON

I'D BEEN PISSED OFF A LOT. I COULDN'T COUNT THE TIMES I'd wanted to shove my fist through the drywall in my bedroom or scream out in frustration for the irresponsible choices my mother made. I had a pretty shitty childhood, so those moments, those pissed off, dry-wall hitting moments, were endless. But the most heart wrenching was seeing Tessa's drunken, disheveled body collapse onto the ground as an anxiety attack forced her to tears.

That was by far the worst. And I wanted to kill whoever let her drink that much and then let her wander off alone. They hadn't even gone looking for her. I grinded my teeth together, feeling my jaw tick, and I was certain I knew who the culprit was. That douchebag from the lunchroom. Why was she even talking to that asshole? I didn't know the guy, but I knew *of* him, and while I usually wasn't one to pre-judge someone, what I'd heard wasn't good. It was dark. He was known for his partying, womanizing, and drug dealing. He was the last person Tessa needed to get involved with. He'd use her, rip her apart, and then leave her on the side of the street to rot.

The horn on my steering wheel blared when my fist slammed into it. Flashes of her defeated, lonely face seared through me. The pain she was going through killed me. I wanted to help her, and I was so pissed she wasn't letting me do it. I wanted to stay with her tonight, smooth her messy hair away from her face, and hold her until she fell asleep.

But I couldn't. I couldn't do that to my best friend. I'd made the promise to protect and look out for her. I'd also made the promise never to date or touch her. That was the dumbest fucking pact I'd ever made in my life. If there were anything I could take back, it would be the day I agreed and shook on that promise.

Tanner was my best friend. When I'd first moved to Indiana, things weren't going great. My mom was having a hard time finding a new job, and she was depressed about having to move to follow my dad. My new school was small and not very accepting of new kids, but Tanner stepped in and took me under his wing. He'd introduced me to Daisy, the girl he'd been dating since they were practically toddlers, and his twin sister, Tessa. But I could only meet his sister under one condition, and that was to keep my hands to myself, but the instant I laid eyes on her I wished I could take it back.

The bright, blue-eyed girl sitting at the lunch table mesmerized me. Her eyes reminded me of water reflecting on the pond I'd fished on in Illinois, clear with beautiful blue shades peeking through. I'd gone there every week with my friend Wyatt and his dad, yearning for my own dad to fish with. Curls the color of dandelions fell along her shoulder blades, and she smiled wide – even with a mouthful of colorful braces. She was in her awkward stage but still breathtaking.

I got to know her and found out there was more than just the mini-skirt, books, and blonde hair. Her parents were loaded, but she wasn't stuck up about it. She was nice and spent her Saturdays volunteering. She laughed at my lame jokes and always made me food when I came over to hang out with Tanner. She stayed up with me late at night to help me cram for tests and ace midterm papers. She was brilliantly intelligent, and the temptation to make her mine hurt like a bitch every day I saw her. I'd wanted her for years, and now it was too late to even ask Tanner to give me leniency on my promise.

I twisted the broken dial of my radio, and music began to pour through my cab. Blake Shelton's *"Mine Would Be You,"* sounded more like static than music through my nearly blown-out speakers. I took the long way home, cruising through the country roads, and passed the miles of cornfields before stopping at a dead end.

I stepped out of my truck and pulled down the rusted tailgate before plopping down. I had to clear my head. Whenever Tessa was involved, I had to clear my head. She was the most complicated yet intriguing person I knew. And that was saying a lot – considering my family was screwed up enough for a month-long special on Dr. Phil.

I leaned back and my elbows hit the cold metal as I cursed at the duskiness. My mom had dragged me to this small town to follow my deadbeat dad. He'd traveled to Indiana to commit his crime, and now we were stuck here because of it. She'd always follow him. No matter how shitty he treated and used her, she'd always be there and drag me along for the ride.

I had to stand by her and painfully watch her get excited about his once a month call – only to find out he wanted money. When I met Tanner and his family, they took me in as their own and showed me what it was like to feel loved.

Now all of that was gone. The people I cared about and cared about me was gone as fast as a gunshot ringing through the air.

☙❧

"WHERE THE HELL HAVE YOU BEEN?" SHE SCREAMED WHEN I walked through the front door. I stopped in my step and blinked until I made out the silhouette of my mother sitting in the dark.

"I had an emergency," I answered, pushing my truck keys into my pocket and flipping the lock to the door behind me. She leaned forward, and the lamp beside her flickered on.

"You're in high school, what possible emergency could you have?" she mocked. "A little slut wanting to get laid? You better be safe Dawson Thomas. I ain't raising no grandkids, and you know your father won't either."

I shook my head and took a good look at her. My mom had once been a beautiful woman, inside and out. She graduated from high school and enrolled in the local community college in our small town. She'd wanted to be a nurse and help deliver babies. Enter my dad. He came ripping through her life like a hurricane and destroyed everything that was her. She lost her scholarship, her job, and every ounce of confidence she had. My grandparents turned their backs on us when she'd taken jewelry from my grandma's room and gave it to my dad to pawn it. Apparently, he needed a new TV and a casino trip with the guys.

Some people do really stupid shit for love. She was his puppet, allowing him to dictate everything that happened in our lives. Strands of gray weaved into her dirty blonde hair that was cut into a tangled, frizzy blonde hair. Crows feet underlined her almond-shaped, emerald green eyes, and wrinkles were building up around her lips. Sepia colored liquid filled the glass in her hand, and she leaned back in her old rocking chair wearing an old, frumpy robe.

"No one's getting pregnant, Ma." I didn't feel like getting into it with her tonight. She wouldn't remember it tomorrow, anyways.

"When your father comes back, you know he isn't going to allow this kind of behavior to happen in his house." Anger flashed through me at her calling it *his house*. He'd never paid one damn bill for this place. It was my mom and I working to keep a roof over our heads and food in our mouths. When the cold winters came and our heat bill doubled, I picked up extra shifts delivering pizzas to pay it. Not him. He didn't do anything but selfishly take.

My head dropped back, and I inhaled a deep breath. "We both know he's never coming back."

I didn't even flinch at the sound of glass shattering against the wall beside me. She hated hearing the truth. "Don't you dare say that," she demanded, pointing her bony finger at me. "You're a goddamned liar. He'll be back, and you'll respect him. Otherwise, you'll be out of here."

I shook my head. "Goodnight. You need to get to bed and sober yourself up. You have to work in the morning. She worked in a factory in town and couldn't be hung over while operating machinery or she'd lose her job. That was the last thing we needed or could afford. I turned around and walked down the short hall to my bedroom. It was useless trying to talk sense into her, especially when it was a conversation about him.

I shut my door carefully, hearing the lock click as I threw my keys down onto the wooden desk at the corner of my room next to my computer. I opened a drawer and grabbed a pill from the bottle. Pulling my t-shirt over my head, I flipped the light off and collapsed onto my mattress. My doctor prescribed me Ambien because I was having trouble sleeping. It's hard to do when you have nightmares of shots tearing through your best friend's chest.

I was happy I'd forgotten to take them earlier tonight, or I would've been too knocked out to hear Tessa's call, and who knows where the hell she'd be. I shut my eyes, and my mind ran back to one of my many Tessa incidents as I drifted to sleep.

"I just don't get what you see in her," Tessa said, stretching out next to me on the couch in her living room me. It was the night, or early morning, of their annual pool party. Every year, their parents went out of town to visit their aunt, and we'd throw a badass pool party. The party had ended, and we'd kicked everyone out, leaving just the four of us. Daisy and Tanner had escaped to his bedroom, and Tessa and I were hanging out eating leftover chips.

Her hair was pulled back into a wet ponytail showing off her flawless face. She hadn't changed out of her skimpy as hell bikini covered with black stars against the white fabric. My fingertips throbbed, longing to trace the outline of each star. My gaze fell and admired her breasts pushed up by the strings tied around her back and neck. I licked my lips and moved my eyes down to her toned, tan stomach and smooth legs. I shut my eyes, envisioning what she'd looked like if I carefully untied each string and revealed every inch of her.

"Dawson," she shouted, snapping her fingers in front of my face and breaking me away from my dirty thoughts.

"Huh?" I asked.

"Kassidy," she answered, and I slumped deeper into the couch. Not this shit again.

"What about her?" I hated when she brought up other chicks.

"What do you see in her?"

I also hated it when she got jealous. Kassidy Belcher didn't mean shit to me. But I couldn't tell her that. I should've, but I couldn't. I ran my hands through my hair before grabbing my water bottle and taking a giant gulp to bide me some time before answering her.

"She's cool to hang out with, I guess." I shrugged my

shoulders. "It's not like I'm going to marry the chick or anything. We just chill."

She scoffed, kicking her bare feet up on the table. "You just chill? That's what you say about all of them, but you forget to mention the fact that you chill naked while you're inside of her." I choked on my water. *Tessa always got brave and outspoken when she drank.* "Are you trying to conquer the entire female student body before we graduate?"

I laughed, trying to make light of the situation. "I wouldn't say the entire student body per se." *She gave me a serious look, letting me know she wasn't in the mood for jokes.* "I don't want to conquer you."

Wrong damn thing to say.

I watched her face go from serious to seriously pissed off. "Wow, Dawson," she snarled. "I apologize for being so unattractive and inexperienced that I'm not up to your standards to conquer, but girls like Kassidy are okay. What? Do you not want your girls to be smarter than you because you suck in bed?"

I ran my hands over my face in frustration. The girl knew how to push my buttons. Every. Single. One. Of. Them. When she drank, she always ended up pissed off at me. Then she'd say some stupid shit, and I'd get pissed at her. She only brought up her feelings for me when she had alcohol in her system. Then the next day, she'd act like it never happened. It was a game to us, only more emotional, and not very entertaining.

"You know that's not what I meant," I replied, trying to backtrack my words.

She rolled her eyes and tucked her feet under her ass. "Whatever."

"You want to be conquered?"

Her light blue eyes narrowed my way. "No, I don't want you to conquer me, jackass. I'll never be one of your three-day flings."

"Then why are you so pissed?"

I scooted in closer and didn't miss the sudden heightening in her breathing. Her glossy eyes stared straight into mine. "It doesn't matter," she said, pushing a hand against my chest to shove me away from her. She began to get up, but I reached forward and grabbed her arm to stop her. Wrapping my hand around her face, I used a finger to outline her full, rounded lips and remembered what they tasted like.

I'd felt her lips on mine. I'd felt her tongue against mine. We'd get caught in the moment sometimes and do shit that wasn't supposed to happen. I'd pull away before we'd get too far, telling her we had to stop. That it wasn't allowed to happen. And she'd get pissed at me, run away, and not talk to me for days.

She trembled at my touch. "You deserve more than being someone's conquest, baby. You deserve someone who can give you the world. You deserve someone who can make you his girl and fight to never lose you. You deserve more than anyone in this town can give you, especially me." She was going places, and I wasn't. I didn't have money to get some fancy degree from an Ivy League school. I was little league, and I wasn't going to keep her in my field.

She recoiled at my touch and pulled away. "Spare me the bullshit excuses because I don't give a fuck anymore." Turning away, she stomped up the stairs and slammed her bedroom door.

"Fuck my life," I muttered, rubbing my forehead and falling back on the couch.

"Damnit, Tanner," I whispered to the ceiling. "You should've never made me promise. You knew if anything happened to you, I'd be the only person to save her. And now, it's too fucking late."

CHAPTER 5

TESSA

"Is cereal okay this morning?" I asked, blocking my eyes with my hand and wincing at the sunlight streaming through the kitchen window.

My head throbbed like a million bricks had busted through my skull and a mac-truck rolled over my brain to complete the job. The what-ever-meister I'd drunk had killed at least two organs in my body. I was sure of it.

"That's fine," Derrick answered, sliding books into his backpack and falling heavily into a chair at the kitchen table. "As long as it's the peanut butter kind."

"Of course." I forced myself to act like everything was okay around him. He needed to be happy, even if I couldn't. He needed a normal life. Our parents were practically catatonic – so I made it my responsibility to take care of him while trying to not have a breakdown at the same time.

I opened the fridge for the milk. I did all of the grocery shopping in the house now, the cleaning, and paid the bills. My mom walked into my bedroom two months ago, threw her checkbook and a pile of delinquent bills onto my bed, and instructed me to take care of them. And I did because I knew if I refused, they wouldn't get done, and we'd be out on the streets.

I poured his cereal and then grabbed a bottle of water for myself before setting the bowl in front of him.

"You're not eating?" he asked, shoving a spoonful of cereal into his mouth as milk dripped from the sides.

"I don't feel so hot today." My stomach was churning with queasiness just watching him eat. I didn't want to find out what would happen if I actually tried to consume anything. I swallowed hard, the taste of the alcohol and my vomit still lingering on my tongue, even after I'd brushed my teeth nine times.

"Don't forget you have to pick me up from school today. Sammy has a doctor's appointment so his mom can't bring me home."

Derrick was a mini-version of Tanner. That was one of the main reasons I think my parents couldn't stand to be around us. We were all strikingly similar to each other and a constant reminder of what they'd lost. When they looked at us, they only saw their dead son.

"I'll be there."

He smacked his palm into his forehead. "Shit, I forgot to tell you ... Dawson said to call him last night."

"Language," I said, giving him a stern look. "And I talked to Dawson. He's taking us to school this morning."

He looked up at me with the spoon still in his mouth. "Is there something wrong with your car?"

I bit my bottom lip and took a drink. There was no way I was telling my teenage brother I got wasted at a party and couldn't drive myself home. I was supposed to be the good influence in his life. He saw enough drinking and bullshit from our parents.

"Nope, just needed an oil change. It's in the shop, but we'll pick it up after school so I can come get you."

"Oh okay, I like that. I miss having Dawson around here. Can you ask him to go with you when you pick me up? Maybe we call all get ice cream and hang out."

I got up from my chair and grabbed his empty bowl. "I'll talk to him," I lied, ruffling a hand through his thick hair.

The doorbell rang, and Derrick jumped up from his chair to answer it. "Dawson's here!" he yelled, coming back into the kitchen with Dawson trailing behind him. "He said he's cool with hanging out after school."

Shit! I wasn't planning on actually asking him. I was going to tell Derrick he already had plans and couldn't make it. I raised an eyebrow and glared at Dawson. He shrugged and shot me a sarcastic smile. He knew exactly what he was doing.

The three of us hopped into his truck with Derrick sitting in the middle. The ride was quiet while Derrick flipped through the radio stations. He'd ask Dawson if he liked a song before leaving it on a station. I knew he missed having Tanner around, and Dawson could fill that void. I slid out of the truck when we reached the middle school and let him out as he waved goodbye.

The drive to the high school was longer since they'd moved us to a different county while they shut down ours as a crime scene. The town council couldn't decide what they wanted to do with the school. People wanted it torn down and a new one built. They didn't want something so tainted around them, or their children attending a school where such a gruesome murder had been committed. The problem was our small town didn't have the money to tear it down and rebuild. So it was left vacant until they could come up with a final decision.

"Tessa," Dawson said, parking his truck. "We need to talk about last night."

"No, we don't." I shook my head and pushed my sunglasses farther up my nose. My eyes wanted to shrink themselves into my skull to stop the sensitivity.

"Yes, we do. We need to talk about everything."

"No, we don't," I repeated. I would've rather jumped into a piranha-filled lake than have this conversation with him.

"I swear to God, you're starting to piss me off. Just fucking talk to me, *please*."

"I drank at a party. We've all done it. You have. My parents have. And I'm sure half of the people in this school have."

He rubbed his fingers against his forehead. "You were beyond drunk."

I tilted my head back against the headrest. "I promise I won't drink that much again, okay? It was a one-time thing. I wasn't thinking clearly."

"Damn straight you won't. Every party you go to, I'm coming with."

The hell he was. "I don't need a babysitter," I snarled, growing irritated.

He eyed me from his seat, and I noticed his tongue poke into his cheek as he inhaled a long breath. "Sure looks like you do. What would've happened if I didn't answer your call last night? Huh? What would you have done?"

I shrugged, averting my eyes from him and playing with the sleeves of my shirt. "I would've figured it out," I muttered.

He scoffed. "By what? Sleeping outside in a puddle of your vomit? Or being taken advantage of by some creep?"

"I get it. I promise to be more careful next time," I said, exasperated. "So please, quit. My head is killing me."

His voice softened. "I'm not trying to be an asshole. I'm trying to protect you."

I understood. He felt like he needed to do that for my brother. "I'll meet you here after school," I replied, getting out of his truck and heading inside. He didn't say another word or get out. He stayed in his truck, his body still as he kept his eyes on me walking into the building.

❦

"HEY LOVE, WHERE DID YOU RUN OFF TO LAST NIGHT?" Reese asked, leaning against the locker next to mine. "I went looking for you." He couldn't have been looking that far because I was just out the front door and the house was small.

He looked like he'd just rolled out of bed. His hair was a mess with curls poking out in every direction. His eyes were restless and still bloodshot from the night before ... or from something else he'd taken that morning. I wasn't sure.

"I had curfew," I lied. My parents didn't care where I went, what time I came home, or what I did anymore. I could be missing for days, and they probably wouldn't notice.

"Curfew?" He raised a brow. "That sucks. You could've at least told me goodbye. You went to the bathroom and then disappeared. I missed you."

"Sorry, I was exhausted and didn't see you anywhere." My brain throbbed as students began slamming their lockers shut and shouting down the hallway. Jesus, didn't they know people were hung over around here?

"Or you left with another guy?" he questioned, gazing at me with focus and catching me off guard. "Because that's what I heard."

My mouth flew open as I struggled for words. "My brother's best friend picked me up," I answered defensively, regaining my thoughts. "I didn't feel comfortable driving." And I was on the verge of having a nervous breakdown, but I wasn't about to explain myself to him.

He let out a sharp breath. "You could've asked me, love. I would've given you a ride."

"You had more to drink than I did."

"True. But I have a tolerance level of an Irish man," he said, pointing a finger at himself. "I've been drinking with my dad since I was nine." I wasn't sure if that was something to be proud of. "So what are you doing this weekend?"

I grabbed a book from my locker. "Nothing."

"Hang out with me?" He held his hands together in a pleading gesture.

"I'm busy this weekend." By busy, I meant I'd be sitting in my room or watching a movie with Derrick. Hanging out with Reese was a bad idea, especially since Dawson had suddenly decided he was going to play chaperone everywhere I went.

He pinched the bridge of his nose. "Bullshit, you're not going to be hiding out in your room all weekend on my watch, love." His finger tapped the tip of my nose. "I want to turn that frown upside down. Let me take you out this weekend. I promise it'll be something enjoyable."

"I'll think about it," I replied, already racking my brain for an excuse. He moved around me and snatched my phone from the top shelf of the locker. "What are you doing?" I hissed, making a grab for my phone as he took a step back.

He hit a few buttons, and I reminded myself to put a password lock on that thing. "I just called myself, so I know what number to look for tonight. If you're bored and want to talk, just hit this number right here." He held out my phone and pointed to his name on my screen. "And think about this weekend. I'll make it a good one." He handed me my phone and shot down the hallway while giving high fives to people as he walked by.

I stumbled back in surprise when I noticed Daisy sitting in the cafeteria by herself concentrating on a book in front of her.

"Hey," I said, dropping down into the seat next to her. "I looked for you yesterday and tried to call a few times."

Her brown eyes squinted over at me when she noticed I was there. It had been weeks since I'd seen her, and she looked in worse shape than me. Her raven black hair that looked like it hadn't been washed in days was pulled into a ratty bun at the top of her head. She was wearing one of Tanner's old football sweatshirts that smelled like it hadn't been washed in even longer.

"I had a therapist appointment and then ditched the rest of the day." She snorted and rolled her eyes. "Those things are like freaking torture. There's no way I can go through that and then come here, too." She threw her arm out and gestured to the crowded room. "I told my parents it's either therapy or school." I was jealous. Her parents were there for her. They were forcing her to get help. I envied that. "Everyone here looks at me like I'm a total nut job," she added, looking down at the table.

"No, they don't," I said, patting her arm. This conversation was more than we'd talked in months. We'd once told each other everything. We spent more nights together than we did alone. We'd planned on having a double wedding, having kids at the same time, and then buying houses right next to each other.

"Uh, yes they do. What would you think about a girl who breaks down and has an anxiety attack in the middle of class." She covered her face with her hands and groaned out in agony. My brain scrambled, thinking back to last night when I'd had my own attack. Should I tell her? The old Tessa would've opened up about it, but now it just seemed weird.

I felt like I was talking to a stranger. On the day of Tanner's funeral, I'd been strong for her. I'd taken her hand, led her into the room, and held it throughout the entire service. I'd called her every day after his death until eventually she stopped picking up. She was my one true friend, the person I could talk about things I couldn't with Tanner, and she acted like I was nothing to her now. It was like she'd hit a button and all of her memories of us had been erased. I missed her as much as I missed Tanner.

"What the hell is wrong with me?" she asked, staring back at me in horror.

I grabbed her hand and pretended not to notice her flinch at my touch. If Dawson hadn't been there for me last night, who knows where I would've been. I was humiliated with just him. I couldn't imagine going through it with a room full of teenage strangers.

"There's nothing wrong with you. We've all been going through it," I said, squeezing her hand. "It will get better." She nodded, gradually pulling her hand out of mine without trying to make it obvious. "How about you come over tonight, and we can talk about things? We haven't done that in forever, and I think we're due for a girls' night."

Her chapped lips formed a weak smile. "Sure, I'll call you after school." She hauled up from her chair. "I've gotta go."

"But lunch isn't over yet," I said quickly.

"I know, but I've got to run to the nurse's office. I feel like total crap and am going to try to convince her to send me home."

I threw my utensils down onto my tray and started to get up. "I'll come with you."

She shook her head and held her arms out to stop me. "No, it's okay. I'll call you after school."

A hot lump wedged itself in the center of my throat. "Please don't forget to call me," I pleaded.

She nodded without turning around to say anything else. I

watched her walk out of the lunchroom and race towards the nurse's office.

ᘓᔦᘒ

I THREW MY BAG ONTO THE SEAT BEFORE JUMPING INTO Dawson's truck and slamming the door shut. Grabbing it again, I shuffled through the compartments, pulled out my sunglasses, and shoved them up my nose.

"We should probably pick up your car first, drop my truck off at your house, and then pick up Derrick. Otherwise, he'll know you were up to no good last night."

I put my hand on the window knob and cranked it until it the window went all the way down while fanning myself with my free hand. "Up to no good? What are you? My dad?"

"Not trying to be your dad, Tessa," he replied, waiting on a few people to cross before pulling out of the parking lot. "But I am responsible for your well-being since Tanner is gone."

I groaned. "For the millionth time, I don't need a babysitter." I lifted the hair off the nape of my neck, pulled it into a ponytail, and pulled the elastic from around my wrist to hold it in place. "And are you ever going to get this damn air conditioning fixed? It's like an oven in here."

"Probably not," he replied, and I continued to fan myself. "And you do need a babysitter, considering you were the drunk girl who couldn't walk and had no idea where she was. You know what happens to girls like that? They end up slaughtered somewhere in a ditch."

I rolled my eyes and stuck my head closer to the open window. "Spare me the Lifetime movie crap. It was a one-time thing. I was drinking wager-bombs and didn't know those things were so brutal."

He scratched his cheek and looked at me. "I'm sorry, what were you drinking?"

"A wager-bomb," I confirmed. I glared at him as he burst in laughter. "What the hell is so funny?"

"Do you mean Jagerbomb, babe?" he asked, through his laughs.

I paused for a moment and sighed. "Whatever it's called. Jagerbomb, wager-bomb, same difference."

"Who the hell even gave you that shit? It tastes like turpentine."

I threw my hands up in the air. "Thank you! That's exactly what I thought."

"You think something tastes like a harsh chemical, yet you still drink it?"

"Nope, then I started taking shots."

His face went hard. "And that's exactly why you're not going to anymore parties unsupervised. You get me? You're naïve, Tessa."

"I'm not naïve." I was taking on a lot more responsibilities than most kids my age.

"I'm not trying to be an asshole." I gave him a look. "I swear, I'm not, but you grew up with a sheltered life. We always looked out for you. You never saw any of the bad shit that can happen to girls who go out to parties and drink too much. You can't go into unknown places or situations, drink shit you can't even pronounce given to you someone you hardly know, and not expect something bad to happen."

"Something bad?"

"You could've been drugged. Or raped. Or any of that shit."

He had a point. I was grateful he picked me up last night.

We pulled up to the house from last night. "Especially in a place like this," he said, nodding toward the old, rickety house. This time, there was no loud music, no people stumbling around the yard or drinking. There wasn't a soul in sight. I grabbed my keys from my bag and jumped out of his truck.

"I'll meet you at your house," Dawson yelled, waiting for me to get into my car and pull out so he could follow me. I immediately turned my AC on high and faced all the fans toward my face before pulling away.

I parked in my driveway at the same time Dawson pulled up in front of the house. He jumped from his truck and opened up my car door.

"I'm driving," he ordered.

"Alrighty," I said, not in the mood to argue. I slid into the passenger seat. "Since when did you get so bossy?"

"Since you started making dumbass decisions." He needed to let this go. He was beating a dead horse. "You're hanging out with that Reese guy? Really Tessa? You know he's a loser, right?"

"You don't even know him." Reese didn't make me do anything I didn't want to do. I drove myself to that party. I drank the alcohol he gave me. I took the shots. He might've encouraged it, but I was a big girl.

"True, but I know *of* him. I've seen him around other parties and heard plenty of rumors. He's bad news. Plus, he's not even your type."

I fidgeted in my seat. "I thought I'd try a new type." A growl came from the other side of the car, and he whipped around a turn quickly. "I mean, what I thought was my type didn't want me, so it might be time to try something new." My voice was playful, but he didn't miss my insult and the point I was seeking trying to make.

We pulled into Derrick's school. "Don't start this shit," he spat out angrily.

The back door opened, and Derrick jumped into the backseat before either one of us had a chance to say anything else.

"Ice cream, here we come!" he yelled, throwing his fist up in the air and tossing his book bag to the other side of the seat. "I've been craving this all day."

Dawson and I laughed. "You've been craving this all day?" I asked, looking back at him.

"Yep, and it's good to have a guys day, too." He leaned forward and patted Dawson's shoulder.

"What am I?" I asked. "Chopped liver?"

Derrick laughed. "No, you're allowed to come too, sis."

"Glad I'm so wanted." I looked over at Dawson. "Did you get this excited about ice cream and guys day when you were fourteen?"

He smiled mischievously. "You don't want to know what I was excited about at that age, but it sure as hell wasn't ice cream and hanging out with guys."

I smacked his arm as we headed to the small diner in town. The three of us hopped out of the car, went inside, and slid into an open booth. I sat beside Derrick, and Dawson squeezed in across from us.

"Do you know what you want?" I asked Derrick.

"Hot fudge sundae and a chili dog, please," he answered. I nodded and grabbed my wallet from my purse.

Dawson snatched it from my hand and tossed it back into my bag. "I got it."

I shook my head. "Nu uh, this is on me." Money was tight with Dawson and his mom.

He got up from his seat. "I got it."

I got up. "No, you bought Derrick's food last night."

He grabbed my shoulders and pushed me back down into the booth. "I said I got it." He whipped around on his heels and walked up to order.

I sighed, shrinking back against my seat, and Derrick grabbed his phone to play a game with flying pigs.

"All right guys, here you go," he said, returning with a full tray of food in his hands. "A hot dog and a sundae for the man." He set the food in front of Derrick who then let out a *"whoo!"* before thanking him. "And a chicken sandwich, a cherry coke, and banana split for you." He set the same food I ordered every time I was here in front of me.

"Thanks," I said, grabbing a straw and poking it through the lid of my cup.

"How was school today, buddy?" Dawson asked Derrick, snagging a few french-fries and tossing them into his mouth.

Derrick shrugged and swallowed his food. "It was okay. People are always asking me about Tanner. It gets annoying." I knew he was getting the same pity stares as me. His was probably worse since he went to school with everyone in our town. "I miss him, a lot."

"We all miss him," Dawson said. "And I know he misses you, too."

"What about mom and dad?" he asked, looking up at us. "Do they miss him? Mom cries all the time and screams at me every time I bring him up."

I nudged his side with my elbow playfully. "She's just having a hard time right now. It'll get better, just give them time."

His shoulders drooped down. "But what about me? Don't they miss me? Miss us? Dad doesn't play football with me anymore, and mom complains if I ask to have friends over."

I knew I wasn't that great in helping out in the boy department like my dad and Tanner had been, but I was trying. I'd attempted to help him with his sports, but I couldn't throw a football more than six inches before it fell to the ground.

"How about every Saturday, we'll go toss some balls or do something fun?" Dawson asked him.

Derrick perked up and smiled. "That would be awesome!"

"You still have my number?"

"Sure do." He grabbed his phone and showed Dawson his name.

"Good, give me a call anytime."

Dawson and Derrick talked about sports as we finished our meal and then headed home.

"Call me if you need anything," Dawson said, after Derrick got out of the car and went inside.

"I will." I started to get out of the car, but he grabbed my shoulder and turned me around. His eyes searched mine, and he leaned in closer. "Promise me, Tessa."

"I promise. Thank you for offering to take Derrick out, but you don't have to if you're too busy. I'll take him to watch a movie or something. He'll be fine."

"I'm not bailing on him. Your family is my family, Tess. I spent almost every single day with you guys. Do you think I'm just going to forget the rest of you because Tanner's no longer here? Not happening. Derrick has always been like a little brother to me, and with Tanner gone, he needs someone now more than ever. So if you don't want to be around me, so be it, but don't hold him back. That's selfish."

He was right. "I won't."

He seemed satisfied with my answer and got out of the car "Have a good night," He called out, circling the car and smacking the hood before getting back into his truck to leave.

I took a deep breath and stayed in my seat for a few minutes to get my head together before going inside.

⚜

I KICKED A T-SHIRT LYING ON MY BEDROOM FLOOR AND collapsed into my bed.

I'd tried calling Daisy five times, but it kept going straight to voicemail. She'd turned her phone off to deflect having to talk to me. Her promise was nothing but a lie. She'd never planned on coming over. I grabbed my phone from my nightstand and played with it in my hands before hitting the button to my call history. I waited a moment, going back and forth on whether or not it was a good idea. It probably wasn't, but I took a deep breath and hit the name.

"You called," the surprised voice greeted from the other end. Loud music blared in the background.

"Is this a bad time?" I asked, nervously. Maybe this was a sign that I shouldn't be calling him.

"No, hold on a sec," he shouted over the music. "Let me just go somewhere quiet." I heard shuffling, and the chaos faded away a few seconds later. "Sorry 'bout that, my boy's band is playing at this gig tonight. You should come out."

I glanced over at my alarm clock. "It's a little late." I was still recovering from last night. There was no way I could put my body through that hell again so soon.

"Curfew again?" he joked.

"Yeah."

"But no other boys this time?"

I wasn't sure why, but I smiled widely at his question. "No other boys."

He whistled loudly. "Good, I wouldn't want to have to fight anyone off my girl." That smile grew wider. "I wish I could see that pretty face right now. What are you doing?"

I settled back into my bed and moved around until I was situated comfortably under my blankets. "Laying in bed."

"And what are you wearing in bed?"

Tingles spread through my body, and I fidgeted with the sleeves of my sweatshirt. "We are so not going there."

He laughed, and it sounded like he'd taken a hit from a cigarette. "Come on, babe, let's have some fun. I know you're bored over there."

I yawned. "Not happening." I hadn't even had sex yet, how in the world would I manage to do something over the phone that I'd never done in real life?

He laughed again. "Fine, have it your way. I'll let it slide this time, but tomorrow night you're letting me take you out."

"Like out on a date?" There was no way I was going out with him.

"Yes, like out on a date."

"I'll think about it." I needed some extra time to create a good excuse. I knew Reese wouldn't go for the whole I have to wash my hair sixteen times.

"If you stand me up, I'll be calling you, and you'll have to describe piece by piece what you're wearing. Are you wearing pajamas? Or panties and a tank top? Or are you naked?" Warm sensations flooded my body. "Just answer me, baby."

"Goodnight, Reese," I drew out slowly, fighting a smile.

"Goodnight, beautiful. Have sweet and naughty dreams about me."

I could hear him laughing when I hit the end button and shook my head. I pulled out a drawer, snagged one of my sleeping pills, and swallowed it. I took one every night, but it would still take hours to kick in before letting me drift to sleep.

CHAPTER 6

TESSA

"Damn babe, you clean up nice."

I walked out my front door to find Reese leaning against an old, rusted, burnt-orange, sedan. He tossed a cigarette on the ground before making his way up to me. A pair of cargo shorts hung low on his hips, and his hair was swept back in another ball cap.

"Thanks," I muttered, I'd managed to run a straightener through my hair and swiped some mascara on my eyelashes.

He bit his lower lip, clasping his lip ring between his teeth. "You ready for a good ass night?" he asked, wrapping his arms around my waist and pulling me into his chest. His lips smacked into the top of my head before grabbing the handle of the passenger door as it squeaked open. The stench of stale cigarettes and old socks hit me when I got in, and I held my breath while rolling down the window.

"I was thinking we could get some grub first?" he asked, getting into the car and looking over at me.

"Sounds good." I was curious what he had planned for us. I didn't see Reese as the romantic date night guy, but hey, I never thought I'd be out getting wasted alone, either.

"Is pizza cool with you? I know this killer pizza joint." I nodded, and the car's engine slowly stirred to life after a few turns. "Damn babe, you're easy to please." He laughed while grabbing a pack of cigarettes from the cup holder. He brought the entire package to his mouth and slid one out with his teeth. "You mind if I smoke?"

I'd always hated the smell of smoke. I'd been lucky enough that neither of my parents smoked, and I'd never picked up the habit. Tony Higgins dared me to try one during a game of truth-or-dare freshman year. I'd stuck the cigarette in my mouth, inhaled gently, and nearly choked while everyone cracked up in laughter around me. It wasn't a good experience, and I'd always liked Tony for that.

"Go ahead," I grumbled, rolling down the window further and wishing I'd backed out. Why was he so persistent for me to go out with him? I'd noticed the girls he hung out with at school. They were nothing like me. "But you know that stuff will kill you, right?"

"We all have our vices, sweetheart," he said, a flicking his lighter open. The tip of the cigarette burned orange. "We all have our vices." His words hit close to home. Yes, we did. "I've got some kick ass jams in here." He hit the volume button on the radio, and rock music came through the speakers. "This is my friend's band."

I nodded, wincing at the loud screaming, and I knew I'd have a headache by the time we got to dinner. Reese either didn't seem to notice or care, because he kept his eyes on the road, and he bobbed his head to the beat.

He pulled into the parking lot of a building with a giant pizza sign at the entrance. I hopped out, adjusted the bottom of my shorts, and shut the door. "I've never been here before," I commented. He grabbed my hand and led me through the entrance.

"They have the most bomb pizza in town," he said, opening the door for me, and we walked into the busy restaurant. Tables were spread throughout the middle of the room, and large booths lined the windows. Red and white checkered tablecloths covered each table with containers of Parmesan cheese and spices stacked in the corners. I followed him down the middle aisle, passing full tables, as we tried to find an empty one. I spotted a few waitresses, all of them wearing tall, white chef hats with checkered aprons as they scurried around with drinks and pizzas in their hands.

"Found one," Reese called, pulling my hand, and I stumbled forward when he charged across the room and sat down into the hard booth. He dropped my hand, and I sat across from him. "What kind of pizza do you like?"

I shrugged. "Whatever is fine," I answered, scanning the menu and the variety of choices. The only topping I preferred on my pizza was chicken, but I didn't have an appetite, so I wouldn't be eating much anyways.

"Babe," he said slowly, and I looked up from the menu to him. "Tell me what you want. Don't be shy. This is our date. I want us to get to know each other, and I think knowing what kind of topping you like on your pizza is very important."

"Can we do chicken?"

He clapped his hands together, grabbed my menu, and placed it at the edge of the table on top of his. "Chicken it is."

The waitress waiting to the side sauntered over to us when he waved her over. "Hey Reese," she greeted with a sweet voice. She smiled at him with bright pink lips while pulling a pad from her apron.

"What's going on, Molly," he replied, looking at her briefly before putting his attention back on me. "What do you want to drink, babe?"

"I'll have water, no lemon," I answered, and she scribbled it down without looking at me.

"I'll have what my girl is having," Reese said.

"Right," she drew, tapping her pen against the edge of the pad. "Are you ready to order for you and *your* girl?"

Reese grabbed our menus and handed them to Molly. "Large chicken, extra cheese, and a small order of breadsticks."

"I'll get that in for you," she said, jotting our order down and walking away.

"I'm glad came out with me," he said. "I thought you were going to bail on my ass." Molly returned with our drinks and set them down without saying a word.

I played with the straw in my water. "I was sure I was going to bail."

He laughed, playing with his piercing, and grinned widely. I eyed him, wondering what it would feel like to kiss him. I'd never been with anyone sporting mouth metal.

"You didn't, and that's what's important. I think you're starting to warm up to me. Sooner or later, you'll be completely comfortable, telling me everything."

"Oh really?" I asked, forcing a small smile. Nobody would ever know my secret.

I picked at my pizza while Reese told me about going to his friend's show the other night. "You have to come with me next time. They're so kickass. I know they'll make it big time, and I'm planning on being a roadie for them. Maybe they'll let me drive their bus or something," he told me. I didn't say much while listening to him ramble about his partying lifestyle and friends.

Molly came over to bring us our bill, and Reese picked it up.

"Here, let me get mine," I said, unzipping my purse.

"Cool. It's twenty-five bucks. How about you give me a twenty, and I'll leave a tip."

My head jerked up in disbelief. I always offered to pay my half on the few dates I'd been on, but the guys always fought it, insisting dinner or the movie was on them. But not Reese. He was siting there holding out his hand waiting for me to pay for the both of us. I grabbed the money from my wallet and handed them over.

"Thanks, babe." He pulled out a five from his pocket and shoved it on top of my money.

"You're going to have fun tonight," Reese said, getting back into his car. "Even if I have to force it out of you."

I pulled the seatbelt across my body, and the music shot to full blast again. I didn't ask him where we were going. I only kept my eyes on the road and hoped we'd get there soon before I had to start plugging my ears. The band wasn't terrible, but they weren't going to be hitting the big time in my opinion. We turned down a dirt road that led into an open field lined with cars and trucks. I squinted and made out bright flames in the distance as a few people walked across the lot towards it.

Great ... so much for him not taking me to another party. Some date.

I enjoyed bonfires – don't get me wrong. They were popular in our town. We didn't have fancy hangouts, bars, or clubs here. The problem was I had expected something else. I had expected him to actually *try*. I wanted proof he was a decent guy. I looked down at the grimy floorboard covered in bags of Cheetos in disappointment.

He got out of the car and pulled a lever underneath his seat. I watched from the side mirrors as he opened up the trunk to pull out a case of beer and set it onto the ground.

"Yo babe, a little help here!" he shouted. I secured my purse across my chest and got out. He could've at least given me a heads up. I was wearing flip-flops. He handed me a few bottles of alcohol and grabbed the case of beer. I held a green bottle out, reading the label, and my stomach twisted.

He looked over at me and laughed. "That's your best friend, babe. I got that just for you."

"I don't think my stomach can handle that again," I said, holding out the bottle and examining it. He continued to laugh while pulling out a flash from his pocket and filling it up with a dark liquid. "How did you even get all of this?"

"My dad. I also stole some from my older brother."

"Oh." He rested his hand on the small of my back and led me toward the flames.

CHAPTER 7

DAWSON

"Thanks for coming with me, man," Cody said, hopping into my cab and slapping me on the back. He slammed the door shut as I reversed down his driveway.

"No problem," I replied. He'd asked me to be his wingman tonight to make sure his ass didn't get into any more trouble. He'd been arrested twice since the shootings. "You sure you're cool to do this? If you get busted, they're going to put you back in the slammer."

He rolled down the window. "My probation officer is cool. She doesn't give a shit what I do as long as I pass my drug tests, and we both near I ain't going anywhere near that stuff." Cody's dad had died of a drug overdose, so he'd never messed with that shit. Alcohol, yes. Drugs, hell no.

"Or hit someone," I added.

He laughed while rubbing two fingers in-between his

eyebrows. "Yeah, that too. That's the sucky part about being on probation. I can't punch assholes."

All of us changed after shooting that took so many of our friends. Not one of us was the same. Cody's coping mechanism was beating the shit out of anyone who said the wrong thing to him. Our friend, Ollie, had resorted to drinking and having sex with any female that looked his way. Daisy became a recluse, refusing to leave her house, or talk to anyone – unless you count the ghost of Tanner. As far as Tessa, I wasn't sure about her yet, but I was trying to figure it out. Me? I was the one trying to pick up everyone's broken pieces and get us to come together again. We were all stronger together.

I pulled into the trailer park next and honked the horn in front of Ollie's place. He rushed out, his mom trailing behind him in a robe and slipper with a cigarette hanging out of her mouth.

"You keep an eye on my boy, Dawson," she shouted, taking the cigarette out and pointing it to me when squeezed into my truck.

"You know I always do, Laura," I yelled, waving to her before pulling away. Ollie's mom was a bit overbearing, but he was the only person she had in her life.

"Boys, we haven't been to a party together in months," Ollie shouted, slamming his palms up on the headliner of my truck. "Let's make this shit count for Tanner."

"For Tanner," Cody shouted, and we all repeated him as I turned out of the trailer park. He guided the way and finally pointed to a hidden drive. "It's right here."

I drove through an old iron gate and headed into an open field packed with cars parked in every direction. I inhaled the scent of fresh wood burning through my open window and watched the bright lights flicker from afar as the gravel crunched my tires. I kept driving until we hit the back that led to another dirt road. I parked there in case the party got busted, and we needed a clean way out. Ollie pulled some beers from his backpack and tossed a couple to Cody and me.

"I'm good," I replied, throwing him back the beer.

"Come on, man," Ollie said, taking his cap off and running his hand through his brown hair.

"I'm the DD. I have to make sure you crazy fucks stay out of trouble. Have your fun tonight, and next time, one of you will be taking my place."

"One beer won't hurt you," he replied, pushing the beer back my way, but I shook my head. He shrugged and opened his drink. "More for us then. Let me know if you change your mind."

We got out and started pulling lawn chairs from the bed of my truck. The party was in full swing when arrived. I recognized a few people – both from our new and old schools, and there were others I'd never seen before. It wasn't unusual though. The counties and school districts were small around here, so we'd sometimes end up in one place.

We set down our chairs and got comfortable a few feet away from the fire. "Damn, what's Tessa doing here?" Ollie asked, pointing his beer towards the two moving figures walking towards the fire. I blinked a few times and prayed we were imagining her with that douchebag. A case of beer was gripped in his hand. The other was wrapped around her waist. I ground my teeth together when I saw the two bottles of alcohol in her hands.

Fuck, he was treating her like his damn mule.

"You've got to be shitting me," I growled.

Cody whistled. "That dude is bad news. We have the same PO, and he's always on her shit list. We were locked up together for a minute, too." He shook his head and took a drink. "And I'm sure it won't be his last trip there, either."

I kicked an empty can on the ground and lifted myself up from my chair.

"You need us?" Ollie called, and I shook my head. This shit

wasn't happening on my watch.

Reese still had his hold on her when he set the alcohol down on the ground and fist bumped a few guys. Most of them greeted Tessa by her name, which surprised me, and I watched her wave to them. How the hell did she know these people? My eyes fastened in on them, looking at her lean into him, and he tightened his hold on her. I stayed to the side, crossing my arms, and waited for the best time to confront him.

I noticed the second she turned around and saw me. Every muscle in her body locked up, and she stood on her tiptoes to whisper something into Reese's ear. He nodded, and my pulse pounded when I saw him lean down and kiss her on the lips. She smiled, pulling away from him, and walked towards a girl with red and blue hair.

He didn't deserve to kiss her. His tainted lips that overflowed with lies and deception never should've been given the opportunity to touch hers. She deserved truthful lips that whispered honesty and love. He was poison, and each time those lips touched her, the corruption would sink in deeper.

"We're going to the restroom!" the girl announced to everyone and signaled to Tessa and herself. Reese saluted them and turned his attention back to the group of guys.

This was my opportunity. I stalked closer to the fire pit and stood behind them. "Hey," I said. The group turned around to look at me. I pointed at Reese and jerked my head to the side. "We need to have a chat."

His groupies started to zero in on me like they were his damn bodyguards. "What's up dude?" he asked, taking a long swig from his flask.

"We nee to have a chat *alone*," I told him, my upper lip snarling as he let out a bellowed laugh. He must've been confused because this wasn't a fucking joke.

"Give us a minute," he instructed, calling off his reject

cronies, and they all mumbled some shit to him before walking away. He took a few steps away from the fire before saying anything. "Do I know you?"

"What the hell are you doing with her?" I growled, getting straight to the point. I didn't want to shoot the shit with this guy. I wanted answers. I wanted to stop the game he was playing with her.

He smiled at me wickedly. "I take it you're a friend of Tessa's?"

"I'm more than a friend," I spat.

An eyebrow shot up. "You an ex?"

"Doesn't matter, you just need to stay the hell away from her."

He grabbed a cigarette tucked under his ear, stuck it in his mouth, and lit it. "Ain't happening." He took a long drag and blew out a cloud of smoke.

I kicked the ground with the tip of my shoe. "She's not even your type."

He laughed. "You don't know what my type is."

I pointed to a group of half-dressed girls grinding against each other around the fire. "Really?"

He shrugged. "That's why I like her."

"That's a pretty shitty reason."

"And yet, that's why you like her." I opened my mouth, fully prepared to tell him he didn't know shit about her, or me, but he kept talking. "She isn't like all those girls here running around, begging for the attention of every guy. She doesn't take twenty damn minutes trying to squeeze her ass into a pair of jeans that are two sizes too small. She's chill, and I don't have to worry about every asshole here hitting on her the second I turn my back because they know she'll cave in. The girl is gorgeous, man, but she doesn't have to flaunt it. But you're well aware of that, or we wouldn't be having this conversation." He took another hit.

"She's going through shit. She's breaking, close to the point of losing it, and someone needs to be there to pick her up. I guess I nominated myself to be that guy."

He nominated himself? This guy was a joke. "You aren't going to be there to catch her. When shit gets tough, you'll bail and only make it worse."

I knew how these guys operated. They loved the chase, and Tessa was the perfect prey. She was the girl who'd never give him the time of day until she was in a low moment in her life. She needed a hero. Enter Reese. He'd say all the right shit, make her feel like she needed him to breath or she'd lose her breath, and then drop her like a bad habit when she was hooked. He'd destroy her and move on without a scratch while she was bleeding out.

"You don't know me, pretty boy. Don't be pissed at me for your own mistakes," he fired back.

"My mistakes?"

"You couldn't man up and grow a dick to tell her how you feel. You're pissed that you're a goddamn pussy, and I'm not. You hate me because I have the balls to do what you can't."

"You're right." He looked shocked at my admission. He was waiting for me to deny it. "I didn't have the balls to tell her how I feel, but I will make you one promise."

He raised a brow. "What's that?"

"You hurt her, I promise and swear on everything, I'll have the balls to beat your ass, and you'll regret you even talked to her."

He chuckled, flicking his cigarette onto the ground, and twisting it with the front of his boot. "Try your best, pretty boy." He smacked me on the back and walked back to the party.

I took in a deep breath and repeatedly began to talk myself out of tackling him into the burning flames.

"About time you admit it," Ollie said, walking up to me with Cody.

"Admit what?" I asked.

He pointed to me. "That you." His finger, along with my attention, went to Tessa who was standing by Reese again. "Want her."

Reese's arm was back on her waist, his hand on her ass, while he kissed her neck. The motherfucker was taunting me. He grabbed a blanket from a bag, bundled her up, and sat down before dragging her down onto his lap.

"I think you've had too much," I said, reaching for Cody's beer, but he took a step back.

"Nu uh, don't try to change the subject." He laughed, chugging the rest of his beer. "Don't let her get wrapped up in him, man. Go get her. That girl used to look at you like you created the damn sky, now go name a star after her and fall in love before some asteroid hits you guys, and it's too late."

Ollie laughed at Cody's words, and I rolled my eyes. "This discussion is over, assholes," I demanded, stepping around them and heading back to our chairs. I grabbed a beer from Cody's bag, popped the top open, and took a drink.

I needed it or I was going to snap.

"You know Tanner would've been okay with it," Ollie said, sitting down beside me. "If it were anyone else, he would've killed them, but you, he would've been okay with."

I dropped my head down to look at the ground. "Shut the fuck up, man. He's dead, how the hell can you say whether or not he'd be mad at me? You guys don't know shit," I snarled.

"Don't get shitty because we're speaking the truth. If you don't want to date her, don't get pissed when she finds someone else. That's all I'm saying."

"You okay, dude?" Cody asked, patting me on the shoulder. I was making myself look like a dumbass, and I was supposed to be the rational one. But I couldn't stand seeing her with someone else.

"Yeah, I'm cool. *Fuck.* I didn't mean to put a damper on the night."

"No worries, I won't say anything else about it. We only want to see you and her happy." I grabbed the beer on the ground and handed it over to Cody. He took it and chugged it quickly before I changed my mind.

"Seriously?" I asked. "You're supposed to be staying out of trouble."

"Can't waste beer. That's a party foul. And a crime."

I shook my head at him. "I think you've committed enough of those already."

The three of us laughed, leaned back in our chairs, and watched the party grow louder and crazier as the night went on.

I was a people watcher. I noticed shit others didn't see. I didn't always say something about it, but I saw it. And tonight, I focused my all of my attention on Reese. I counted the endless drinks he went through, mixing them with a combination of cigarettes, weed, and whatever else he was popping. Then I'd look at Tessa, watching her drink anything he handed her, while she talked to him and his friends.

Who was this girl? She looked like the Tessa I knew, but she was different. Her smile wasn't genuine anymore. It was fake. So was her laugh. She wasn't entirely comfortable with Reese and his friends, but she was trying her hardest to adjust to it by drinking their alcohol and laughing at their jokes. I silently prayed she'd come over to us, plop down onto the grass, and hang out like she used to.

"You sure you don't want to save her from that shit?" Ollie asked. I looked away from her to see Reese stumbling around, high-fiving guys, and dancing with girls that weren't Tessa. He smacked a few asses, rambled, and staggered back to her when he was done harassing people.

If Tessa noticed what was going on, she didn't let it look like it affected her. She stayed in her chair with her arms wrapped around her body and snuggled into the blanket. Her eyes watched the fire like she was waiting for it to give her all the answers she was looking for.

That was enough for me. I had hit my breaking point. I jumped up from my chair, and the guys immediately were at my back, ready to fight with me. Ollie grabbed our chairs, and we stood around Tessa when we reached her. I stared down at her and held out my hand. Her eyes flickered from the fire over to me, and she gaped when she noticed us.

She was fucking lit.

"Tell your little boyfriend you're leaving," I demanded.

"What?" she stuttered out.

A hard weight suddenly smashed into my back, and Reese practically fell on top of Tessa in her chair. He squeezed himself in-between Cody and me.

"You ready to go or something?" he asked Tessa, the words sounding like one.

She looked at him, then to me, and back to him. "I, uh, don't."

"There's no way in hell you're driving her home," I said, answering for her. I didn't care if Tessa would be mad at me for the rest of her life. I wasn't letting her get into a car with that drunken maniac.

"And why not?" he asked, gripping his hold on the cup in his hand.

"You're wasted off your ass, dude," Cody told him, pulling Tessa up from the chair and tucking her into his side. She fell into him like a rag doll, letting us move her around as we pleased. If I hadn't been watching him all night, I would've been positive he'd drugged her.

"How about we ask Tessa what she wants," Reese yelled, shoving through us to face her and grab her arm. "What do you want, love?" He leaned forward and ran his hand against her cheek. Watching him touch her so intimately sent chills up my spine. Her eyes slowly closed as she took a deep breath.

"Tessa, girl, he's fucked up," Cody said, bringing her closer to him and farther from Reese. "Dawson is sober. He's our DD. Let us take you home, and you can talk to this guy tomorrow. We only want you to keep you safe."

"Look at all of you preppy boys," Reese cackled, getting into my face. "You're trying to come up here like knights in fucking shining armor. You guys are nothing but losers." He whipped around, getting closer to Tessa's face. "And you, I thought you were different."

"Tessa, say something, dammit!" I yelled, keeping my focus on him. His friends started to move in our direction. A fight was coming if we didn't get the hell out of there, and we were way outnumbered. "Tell him you want to leave with us." She sat there silently. "God, you're fucking wasted." I pushed her away from him to haul her over my shoulder. She'd get over it.

Cody jumped to my side, instantly ready to back me up. Reese started to follow us, but Cody pushed him away, harder than necessary. "She'll call you tomorrow, bro," he told him. Reese was a big guy, but Cody had played defensive line on our football team. He was bigger, muscular, and had a brain that functioned properly.

"This is fucking bullshit," Reese snarled, clenching his fists.

"I don't feel good," Tessa whined. She looked up to look at Reese. "I promise I'll call you tomorrow. I just want to go home."

His face twisted with what looked like regret and fury. "You know what? Don't even bother. Have fun hanging out with your lame, pussy ass boys," he spat. He stumbled over a chick in the crowd, grabbed her ass, and pulled her against him. If I didn't have Tessa hanging over my shoulder, I would've punched him in his arrogant face. "I'll be having plenty of fun without you."

"Fucking douchebag," Cody said, and then looked over me. "You want me to hit him?"

"Nah, don't worry about it. He's not worth you getting in trouble," I replied. He nodded and started to follow Ollie and me back to the truck while Tessa was still hanging over my shoulder.

"But Tessa girl, you've got to kick that asshole to the curb," Ollie said.

"Like I've told Dawson a hundred times," she yelled, slapping my back and hiccupping. " I don't need a babysitter." She struggled against me.

"Cut it out, Tessa," I demanded.

She smacked my back again. "Then let me down!"

"No!"

"I swear to God, you let me down, or you'll regret it!"

We were only a few feet away from my truck when I felt something wet against my back. She gagged, and I felt it again. Jesus Christ, this wasn't happening.

"Oh shit," Ollie said, trying his best to hold back his laughter but failing.

I halted in my step. "Please tell me you didn't just barf down my back," I grumbled and flipped off the guys rolling with laughter.

"Sorry," she replied innocently. "But you can't say I didn't warn you."

"Not once did I hear you tell me you were about to go all Exorcist on me."

I set her down in the seat when we reached my truck. Pulling my shirt over my head, I tossed it onto the ground and jumped into my cab at the same time the others did. The seat was small, so everyone was scrunched in, elbows hitting elbows, and bodies smashed into bodies. Tessa was in the middle between Cody and Ollie, who was pushed up against the passenger door.

I pointed down to the floorboard. "There's a water bottle under there somewhere. Get it for her."

Ollie bent forward, his head and hand disappearing before jerking back up. "Here," he said, unscrewing the cap and giving it to her.

"Thank you," she breathed out, bringing it to her lips and taking a large gulp. She leaned across his lap and grabbed some napkins from the glove compartment.

"We got you, girl," Cody said, wrapping his arm around her shoulders and pulling her into his side. If it were anyone else doing that, I wouldn't like it. But these were my best friends, and they knew Tessa was off-limits. "You know we always got your back. You let us know if you need anything." Tessa nodded, and he gave her a squeeze. "One thing I have to say is that you've never been like this before, though." I was surprised he was bringing up the touchy subject. "I'm well aware you're going through some shit, but trust me, doing this isn't going to help."

Tessa wiped her mouth with a napkin. "I'm not doing anything wrong, you guys. I got drunk at one party."

I opened my mouth to call her out on her lie but decided against it.

"Yeah, but one turns into two, and then you're doing it everyday," Cody argued.

"I'm not doing drugs. I'm drinking," she said. "And you better shut it before I puke on you next."

Cody held his hands up in surrender. "You don't have to tell me twice," he nudged her side, and she shot him a small smile.

I dropped the guys off at their houses and headed towards hers. As badly as I wanted to rip her a new asshole for being so damn irresponsible, I held it in. She didn't need that right now, and we didn't need another argument.

"Can you get out drunky, or do I need to carry you?" I asked, pulling next to the curb in front of her house.

"Funny," she grumbled, sliding to the edge of the seat and throwing the door open. This time, though, she was smart enough not to jump. I went to her side before she changed her mind and face planted into the ground again. She wasn't a very coordinated drunk.

"Your parents home?" I asked her, stabilizing her, surprised at how well she was walking.

"Yes, but they've probably taken enough sleeping pills to knock out a horse." She shuffled through her purse and handed me her keys. Her answer hurt. I hated seeing people I'd looked up to so much going down that road.

"Do feel like you need to get sick before we go in?" I asked. Her puking out here would've prevented me from having to clean up a mess in there or anyone hearing her.

She shook her head. "No, I feel better now that it's all out of my system."

"And onto my back," I joked, following her up the stairs, my hand resting on the small of her back to be sure she wouldn't fall.

"Again, I forewarned you."

I opened up her bedroom door, and her purple walls came into view when I flipped on the light. I'd been in her room hundreds of times. I'd been on her bed that was covered with a white, lace comforter and a ridiculous amount of pillows. We used to watch movies together when Daisy and Tanner ventured off to his bedroom to screw.

The room was still the same. Not one thing had changed. The same pictures covered the walls and her desk.

"You kept them all," I whispered.

She was down on her knees and sorting through her dresser drawer while giving me an incredible view of her perfect, rounded ass. I stumbled back, my mouth growing dry. There was no way my eyes would leave her body. I couldn't stop myself.

She looked over her shoulder at me. "Kept what?"

"The pictures. You didn't take them down."

She shrugged. "What can I say? I'm a sucker for nostalgia." She found what she was looking for and shut the drawer. "I'm going to change real quick." She got up and balanced herself with her dresser before heading to the bathroom.

"How about you get dressed in here and let me jump in the shower." She raised a brow. I pointed my thumb behind me. "Vomit on my back."

"Oh yeah," she drew out. "Towels are in the closet, and I hate to break it to you, but you're going to smell like passion fruit."

"It's better than your regurgitated food."

I walked into her bathroom and got into the shower. She wasn't lying. Everything was either flower or fruit scented. Where the hell did they come up with all this shit? Passion Fruit. Love Spell. Lavender Daisy. I opened up her bottle of body wash and got a whiff of something that smelled like air freshener.

I stepped out of the shower, toweled off, and looked down at my dirty clothes on the floor. I either had to put my dirty clothes back on or get something of Tanner's.

"Not happening," I whispered to myself. There was no way in hell I was going there. I snagged my boxer briefs and quickly put them back on before walking into her bedroom.

"You're only wearing those?" Tessa asked, her eyes nearly bulging out of her head, as she situated herself against her pillows. Her gaze swept down from my bare chest to the thin fabric of my boxers.

I pulled down the blankets on the other side of the bed. "Yes, I'm not about to put on shorts that have vomit on them, and we know what happened to my shirt. Just think of it like I'm wearing shorts."

"Shorts that show me *everything* you have to offer."

"Everything I have to offer? Are you trying to ask me something?"

"Nope," she clipped. "I'm just saying what you've offered to other girls." She turned around to look at me with half of her face smashed against the pillow. Her lips were parted and moist. "Have you ever thought about it?"

"Thought about what?"

"What it would be like being with me?"

Her question caught me off-guard. "I don't think we should be having this discussion right now when we're laying in bed half-naked. Plus, you've been drinking." Again, Tessa always wanted to bring this up when she was intoxicated.

"Just answer the damn question, why do you always have to be so complicated?"

I laughed and pointed to myself. "Me complicated? You've got to be joking." I reached out and ran my hand over her face. "You, my dear, are the most complicated person I've ever met."

"That's not true. You've always known what I wanted. I've laid it out for you countless times. But you, you never tell me. You'll give me a little and then pull away, telling me it's wrong. I don't see what was so wrong about us being together."

I grabbed my pillow and smacked it a few times before making myself comfortable. "You need to get to sleep."

She rolled her eyes, muttered some smartass remark, and turned her back to me.

I shut off the light, and the darkness gave me courage. "Yes," I said, suddenly.

I couldn't see her, but I made out the shadow of her turning around and looking at me. "Yes?"

"The answer is yes. I've thought about us being together."

Her voice perked up. "A lot?"

"Too many times to count. All the time. Every single day."

"Then why have you never acted on it?"

"It's too complicated."

"Why can't you make it uncomplicated?"

I paused, wondering if I should tell her about the promise I made Tanner. "I just can't."

"And then here we are – having the same lame ass conversation for the hundredth time where I ask you to give us a chance and you shoot me down. Do you know how hard it is for a girl to keep getting turned down?"

"I'm sorry. I'm truly so fucking sorry. If the circumstances were different there's no way I'd ever be able to turn you down." I loved her. She loved me. It wasn't that simple, though. "You're smart. You're beautiful. You're the most amazing person I've ever had the pleasure of knowing."

"But still not good enough," she huffed, turning back around. "Goodnight, Dawson."

"Don't be mad."

"I'm not mad. I'm used to it now. I've got myself, and that's it."

"Just because we're not screwing doesn't mean I'm not here for you. You were one of my best friends too. It kills me to see you doing this to yourself. I want you to be happy and with a guy who treats you right."

"But you keep fighting them away from me."

"I'm fighting away the ones who don't deserve you, and please don't say that asshole does."

"Goodnight, Dawson," she muttered, closing the conversation.

"Goodnight." I moved closer to her, making a bold move, and wrapped my arms around her waist. "I'm never going to stop keeping you safe," I whispered into her ear, pulling her close.

She snuggled in closer and stayed quiet as she tucked her body into mine. Hours passed before I could fall asleep. I finally had the girl I loved in my arms. She was finally letting me in to keep her safe, but how was I supposed to protect her without loving her?

CHAPTER 8

DAWSON

I woke up with my arm clasped around Tessa and her ass pressed against my fully alert cock that was ready for an early morning romp.

Fuck.

I tried to gently push her forward without waking her, but she muttered something and pressed into me harder. Taking in a deep breath, I did a lame-ass tuck and roll off the bed. I silently cursed at the loud *thud* coming from the floor when my body hit it.

Tessa rolled over and looked at me while rubbing her eyes and yawning. "Did you just fall out of bed?"

"Sure did," I answered. "Your bed is a little small for the both of us. You practically pushed me off."

"It's a full-size bed. I've never had any problems."

"You've also never had a guy in your bed." I paused, waiting to see if she'd tell me any differently, but she only stared. "I have to head out." I walked sideways over to the bathroom so she wouldn't notice my hard-on and grabbed my shorts from the bathroom. I slipped them on and peeked my head out of the doorframe to look at her. I was sure it would be a sight of someone saw me leaving her house this morning shirtless and with a serious case of bed head.

"Thank you," she said as I made my way out.

"You don't have to thank me for watching out for you," I replied.

Tessa in the morning was my favorite view. A glimpse of light peeked through the blinds and hit her fair skin as she peeked up at me with sleepy eyes. Memories shot through me of when I used to spend the night here. I'd always make sure I was awake when she came downstairs to start making breakfast for everyone. She'd throw on an old t-shirt, usually one of mine, and wear tiny ass pajama shorts while dancing around the kitchen fixing pancakes.

"I'll always be here. Remember that," I went on. I walked to her to press a kiss on the top of her head and tucked the blankets tighter around her body. "Now go back to sleep. It's early. I'll call you later to check up on you."

She nodded as I left the room. I held my breath as I passed her parent's bedroom on my way to the stairs.

"Late night?"

I jumped at the sound of the voice when I hit the bottom stair and looked up to see Derrick looking at me from the couch.

Well, fuck. I didn't know what was worse – Derrick or his parents catching me.

"It's not what it looks like," I rushed out. What the hell was this twit even doing up this early? Weren't middle school kids supposed to sleep in?

"Right," he drew out, a smile spreading across his face. "It's cool. I'd rather she hook up with you than anyone else. You pass the brother stamp of approval." At least I got one that from one brother.

"We weren't ... and aren't hooking up," I clarified. The last thing I needed was for him to say that to Tessa.

He shook his head, laughing. "If you say so."

"Do me a favor and don't say anything to anyone about you seeing me, even your sister, okay?"

He saluted me. "I got your back. Are we still hanging out today?"

"You know it." I was

"You know it." I was exhausted as hell, but there was no way I could bail on him. "I'll be here around noon. Think about what you want to do."

I waved goodbye, and he turned his attention back to the TV. I ducked behind the bushes when I made it outside and noticed a few neighbors. I waited until they left before sprinting over to my truck and getting in.

૭❦ଓ

"YOUR FATHER WANTS TO SEE YOU," MY MOM SAID WHEN I walked through the back door and into the kitchen.

She was sitting at the table with a coffee cup in her hand and an open letter in front of her. She didn't ask where I'd been this time. She was sober, so she didn't give two shits. She only cared when she was drunk. Man, why did people always show their true emotions when there was alcohol streaming through their veins.

She shook her head as I moved farther into the kitchen. "And I'm not even going to ask where your shirt is," she went on.

I yawned and poured myself a glass of orange juice before

sitting down. "Too bad I don't want to see him. I'm not visiting him, Ma."

The grip on her coffee cup tightened. "This is important."

"It's always important. He should've thought about his family before he did what he did. I have no sympathy for him, and I never will."

"He's your father."

"Sometimes morals are thicker than blood."

"You don't have to agree with what he did, but he's your father. You have to support him. Seeing him isn't a request, Dawson. It's a demand. You live under my roof, and you'll obey my rules. You will go see him."

I slammed my hand down on the table. "The hell I will."

"Be there at ten tomorrow morning. Don't be late, or I'll have your bags packed, and you can stay somewhere else."

"You need to get over that prick."

I left the kitchen and kicked my bedroom door shut. I punched the back of it and stuck my fist into my mouth to stop myself from yelling what I really wanted to say. He was a fucking loser, why did she give a shit about him? If I went, I couldn't fake caring about him. There was no way I could play nice to him, and that's what she expected me to do.

⚜

"CALL OF DUTY?" DERRICK ASKED, JUMPING ON THE COUCH and grabbing a controller.

We'd gone to the batting cages when I picked him up and then got pizza.

"Maybe later. I'm going to talk to Tessa for a second," I answered, heading up the stairs with a to-go box in my hand.

He laughed. "Okay, you can go *talk* to her."

I snapped my fingers and pointed at him. "Not funny."

"Hey man, I'm not stupid. I know what you people do in high school."

"You have no idea," I muttered.

She yelled for me to come in when I knocked on her bedroom door, and I found her lying down on her bed with her feet facing the headboard and her head at the end so she could watch the TV on her dresser.

"Brought you some pizza," I said, holding up the box.

"Thank you," she moaned, reaching for the box. She took a giant bite as soon as she opened it. "I'm freaking starving."

I sat down on the edge of her bed. "So have you talked to douchebag?"

She wiped cheese from the side of her face. "And by douchebag you mean?"

"Don't play with me. You know exactly who I'm talking about."

She focused on chewing. "He called me earlier."

"And you answered?"

"Yes."

"Why? Were you too drunk to remember what he did last night?" There was no way she could forgive him for how he acted and talked to her. He drank himself into oblivion and grabbed other girls' asses to taunt her.

"He was drinking, and he only said that stuff because it hurt his feelings when I left with you. He told me you threatened to beat his ass if he keeps talking to me." She set the box on the floor and brought herself up, tucking her knees underneath her ass. "You can't do that shit, Dawson. You have to understand how me leaving like that would hurt his feelings. I'd get mad if he did something like that to me."

Was this really happening?

Was she actually feeling sorry for this asshole and understanding his bullshit excuses?

I scoffed. "I think him grabbing asses and dry humping chicks in front of you is worse than you leaving with a goddamned sober driver. I also didn't threaten him to stay away from you. I told him I'd kick his ass if he hurt you. Don't you dare let him use that excuse to feel sorry for him."

"I don't want to argue with you about this, okay? Please just stay out of it."

"You're making a mistake," I insisted. "You're not thinking clearly."

She groaned and tilted her head back. "I'm so sick of you trying to tell me what the hell to do. Why don't you let me make my own decisions for once?"

"What the hell does that mean?"

"Nothing," she said, looking straight at me. "I haven't forgiven him. So let's just stop talking about it."

"Fine, have it your way," I muttered, pushing myself up from her bed. "But don't think I won't say I told you so when this shit happens again."

Her voice lowered. "Maybe I need to see for myself. I need someone who wants to help me with my problems – who wants to help *me*."

I smacked my chest. "And why the hell can't that be me? We're friends, Tessa. I'm here for you, and you're running away from me and into *his* arms!"

"You can't help me because you are the one who made me this way!"

I stumbled back. "What?"

Her lower lip began to quiver. "If you would've just let me do what I wanted that day, I wouldn't be going through this."

"What are you trying to say?" I drew out. "Please tell me you're not pissed at me because I wouldn't let you go out and get yourself killed. You think I would let you walk into a death trap?"

She shrugged. "I think you should've let me decide what I wanted."

I ran my hands over my face in frustration. "You want to be dead? Is that what you're telling me?"

"Most of the time, yeah. I wish I were with him."

What the fuck? I walked the few steps to her and leaned down so we were face to face. "If you're feeling like that, you need to talk to someone. Drinking and partying with Reese isn't going to help. You need to talk to your parents and see a therapist."

Her light blues eyes narrowed my way. "Just because I say I feel that way doesn't mean I'm going to do anything about it." I moved to sit back down beside her, but she stopped me. "I'm not in the mood. I'm rambling because I don't feel good. I think it's normal to feel like this when you're going through loss."

"Babe," I said softly, slowly rubbing my hand over her arm, but she pulled back.

Her eyes slammed shut. "Please, just go. I'm not in the mood, and you promised Derrick you'd hang out with him."

I wanted to stay with her. I wanted her to confide in me. She didn't want that unless she had all of me, and I couldn't give her that.

"Okay," I said. "If you need me, call."

She looked away from me, and it felt like I'd been punched in the gut.

She was no longer my Tessa, and I wasn't sure who the new one was, or what the stranger turning her back on me was thinking.

CHAPTER 9

DAWSON

WE MOVED TO INDIANA TO BE CLOSER TO MY FATHER, BUT IT was still a forty-five-minute drive to get to him. He was in the middle of nowhere, and my mom had to be able to get back and forth to her job without paying a fortune in gas. I'd only visited him three times in the five years he'd been there, and my mom had forced each miserable one.

I drove across railroad tracks, and the large, brooding building came into view. Two tall guard towers were in the middle of a barbwire-fenced yard that led away from the long, brick building. "I hate this damn place," I muttered to myself as I pulled into the eerie parking lot.

I slid my phone into my pocket, got out of my truck, and headed towards the entrance. My mom had threatened to kick me out over him before, but I wasn't sure if she'd actually go through with it. Deep down, I was scared to find out. The thought of her doing it made me physically ill, not because I'd be homeless, but because that meant she chose him over me. That would hurt more than anything.

I walked through the front entrance, landing in a frigid room, and noticed the place was empty with the exception of the two guards standing to the side, and a correctional officer sitting behind a desk. I stalked to the front counter, and the woman looked up at me.

"Driver's license," she said quickly. I pulled it out from my wallet and handed it over to her before signing in. "You're here early." She punched in some information into the computer.

"I don't like to wait," I answered. I always came in early to avoid waiting on rotations. The earlier you got in, the quicker you got out.

She slid my license back to me. "We'll call for you when we're ready."

"Thanks."

A row of lockers was perched against the wall. I opened one and tossed my phone and keys into it before slipping two quarters in so I could lock it. I sat down in a plastic chair and shut my eyes, taking in a deep breath. I stared straight ahead and read the poster of approved items while people began to trickle in.

He wanted something. I was sure of it. I was only summoned when he needed something from me. I hated doing anything for this selfish asshole. I stared straight ahead

"Thomas," an officer called out, and I lifted myself out of the chair. I walked up to him and stopped at a taped line while he read more names from the list. I grabbed a container and slid my belt from my jeans off and tossed it inside. Next to come off were my shoes, and I set them in. The container streamlined through the conveyor belt to go through the x-ray machine. I moved my sock-covered feet through the metal detector, and a guard started to pat me down.

"Good to go," he said.

I grabbed my belt and shoes and was led into a smaller room as the people behind me began to crowd in. The automatic doors shut and the guard gave another *"all clear."* The door on the opposite side opened, and I walked into a large room packed with inmates sitting at small tables, waiting anxiously. I led the line, walking to a counter in the front of the room, and told them my name. A woman scanned the sheet in front of her and pointed to him.

I turned around and my muscles tightened when he had the nerve to smile and wave.

Fluorescent lights hummed and flickered above me while I made my way to him. I took in the pungent smell of bleach and what smelled like sewer water as I took each dreaded step. I watched people greet their loved ones, giving them hugs, and some tears were shed. I didn't want anything like that with him.

"Nice of you to finally visit your old man," he greeted, standing up and slapping me on the back in a half-way-hug kind of way. I didn't hug him back. I just took a step back and pulled out a chair to sat down.

"I've been busy," I said.

It had been a year since I'd seen him, and his age was beginning to take a toll on him. He'd cut off his long beard – now only having a goatee. His blonde hair was shorter, beginning to recede, and was pulled into a small ponytail. Wrinkles crisscrossed each other like cracks along his face.

He rubbed his calloused hands across his goatee. "Your mom said you've been going through some shit. I wanted to make sure you're okay."

"I've been going through it for four months," I bit out. I wasn't buying the sympathy bullshit.

"I understand. I've tried getting you to come see me, but your mom tells me you're busy. I'm glad you finally came."

"It hasn't been easy." I looked down at the table and played with my hands in front of me. This wasn't supposed to be some father-son bonding time. I wanted to get to the reason why he wanted me here so I could leave.

"As you get older, it gets easier."

I looked up at him. "What does?"

"Losing people. This is the first time someone close to you has died. It's hard, but it won't be your last. I can promise you that. As the years go by, it'll happen again and again."

I shivered, not wanting to think about anyone else I cared about dying. I couldn't lose anyone else. "Your world is different than mine." My friends weren't in prison or out committing federal crimes.

He gave me a cruel, condescending laugh. "Only one world and we're all livin' in it. Ain't nothing different, only different perspectives, but we're all on the same planet. I bet you didn't think your friend with the loaded parents would die so young, given that he was squeaky clean and stayed out of trouble, but it happened. There aren't separate worlds for good and bad people. We don't live in a place where Heaven and Hell is separated. That's only when we die. Until then, we're all stuck in this shit hole together; the good, the bad, the ugly, and the evil."

He had a point. His bad decisions affected the good, the bad, and the innocent. He'd killed a man, took him away from his wife and kids, because he was a coward. He took a life because he was too lazy to go out and find a job. He wanted the easy way out, and now he was sitting in prison for it.

"What do you want?" I asked. I knew he didn't want me here to talk about my loss. The man didn't have one empathetic bone in his body.

"I have a parole hearing coming up."

I threw my hands up. "And there it is. You could've saved

both of our time by being upfront with me and giving me a phone call."

He leaned forward to lace his hands together and set them on the table. "I need you to speak on my behalf. Vouch for me."

"Vouch for you?" There was nothing to vouch for him for. What he'd done was black and white. The evidence was so strong he took the plea, or he knew he would've been facing a lot more time than eight years. He'd ruined a family. He didn't deserve to walk free after only serving five.

"I need you to tell them how much you need your dad right now. You're a survivor from a tragic school shooting, and you're taking it hard. You need your old man by your side to help you get through it. I've been on good behavior, and with you and your mom's statement, I could be out of this shithole soon."

He was using my loss to his advantage. He'd never change. "So you want me to lie?" If he got out, he wouldn't stay around long. He'd use my mom until we were broke and run off to do more stupid shit.

He grimaced. "I've done my time. I've paid my dues."

"You paid your dues? How do you pay your dues for what you did?" I asked, my voice getting louder and harsher, causing a few people to look our way. "You can't bring someone back to life."

"You know that was an accident."

I scoffed. "What? You tripped, fell, and the trigger pulled while you were in the middle of robbing a bank?"

"The cameras showed it was an accident. That's why I got manslaughter. I didn't go in there with the intention of killing anyone. He was fighting me for my gun, and it fired."

"Maybe you shouldn't have been robbing a bank in the first place, and none of this would've happened."

"I was trying to provide for our family."

"Oh, spare me the bullshit lies. You didn't provide shit for us.

Mom did. Everything you did, you did for yourself. We never got a dime from you."

He shuffled his hands through his hair in frustration. "You're a good boy. I can see it just by looking at you and from what your mom says. Not sure how you turned out that way 'cause of the way I am, but I like that you are."

I was his perfect pawn. "I stay out of trouble because I have to take care of us, you know ... the family you bailed on."

"You can hate me all you want, but I'm still your father, your blood. You need to respect and look out for your family. The hearing is in a few months. I'll keep you updated."

I felt my veins straining against my skin. "We finished here?"

"Your mom said you haven't opened any of my letters."

"You've sent me two. Two in five years."

He winced at the truth. "Read them."

"Kiss my ass. I've gotta go."

I started to get up, but his hand shot out to stop me. "We still have thirty minutes," he said, turning around to look at the clock on the wall.

"I've got homework."

He nodded, fully aware I was blowing him off, but chose not to say anything. "All right. I love you. Come visit me, again."

"Yeah sure," I grumbled, and turned around to walk away.

CHAPTER 10

TESSA

"BABE," REESE SAID, LOOKING DOWN AT ME AND STROKING my chin. "You've been quiet as hell all day. What's going on in that head of yours?"

The couch cushion caved in when he sat down next to me. He stretched his arm out and pulled the small coffee table across a thin, washed-out blue rug. I couldn't quite distinguish the exact color because multiple stains covered the fabric. He stopped when it was close enough, stretched his legs out, and propped his feet up on the table.

I wasn't sure how to describe my relationship with Reese. Things were growing. We were spending all of our free time together, and he sat with me at lunch every day. He called me every night we weren't hanging out to tell me sweet dreams. He'd also apologized about the bonfire disaster, telling me he only acted that way because he was drunk and pissed off that I was leaving with Dawson.

He'd felt like I was cheating on him. I'd fired back with what he'd said about hooking up with other girls, but he insisted that he was lying because he was pissed. He swore he went home alone after I left. I believed him. Or at least I forced myself to. But deep down, I wasn't sure if I could trust him.

He'd fulfilled his promise of making me immune to the pain beating through me. He led me to the world of using drinking and other things to make it all fade away. My pain and unhappiness had dried up. Every ounce of torment I'd been living had drifted away from my body.

And I liked that. It helped. That was, until the high ran off and the feeling resurfaced, and I had to go back to Reese for another hit. I was latching onto him. I knew what I was doing was only a temporary fix, a Band-Aid covering my wound that was giving me momentary relief to my agony. It wouldn't last forever. I knew eventually those bandages would strip away, and my lesions would bare again, but I didn't want to think about that day.

"My friend left," I replied, eyeing the clear, plastic baggie he pulled from his pocket.

"What friend?" He set the baggie down on top of a tattered magazine on the table.

"Daisy."

He nodded in recognition. "Ah, the weird mute one."

He'd met Daisy a few times. She'd sit with me silently for a few minutes at lunch sometimes before saying she had to go and ditched me again. Reese said 'hi' to her every single time. She'd grimace, and not say anything back like he was carrying some contagious, life-threatening disease.

"She's not weird," I argued. I'd let him call her a mute

because that wasn't necessarily a lie, but I was the only one allowed to call her weird. No one else was allowed to insult her.

He shrugged and pulled out two, long white pills from the bag and began breaking them up. My mouth went dry when he fished out a membership card from his pocket and started to crush the pills with it on top of the magazine.

"I think she's scared of me," he said, shrugging his shoulders like the fact he was crushing up pills was normal.

"She acts like that towards everyone." I missed my best friend. She used to be so full of life, and now all of that energy had been sucked out of her.

"I'll be right back."

He got up and walked into the kitchen. I glanced back to see him shuffling through the drawers in the tiny space before turning my attention to the crushed up pills sitting across from me. I jumped when he sat back down with a straw in one hand and a bottle of vodka in the other.

"Where'd she go?" he asked, using the card to create a line with the crushed pills. He stuck the straw to the end of the line and snorted it.

I gulped and ran my hand over my own nose. That was one thing I'd refused to try with him. We drank. I'd smoked a few joints with him and popped some pills he'd given me. He'd offered me a line once, and I declined. He'd never brought it up again. At times, I wished he would've. I

"Atlanta, I guess. Her aunt lives there," I answered. Her mom had called me last night and told me her dad forced her to go.

He pulled at his nostrils when he finished the line and breathed in hard while shaking his head. The first time I saw him snort pills was a few weeks ago at a party at Bobby's. I was shocked, but the more he did it, the more I grew familiar with it. I glanced down and looked at the magazine, noticing the few grains he'd missed and wondered what it would feel like doing it. He acted like he was at the top of the world when he was high.

"She wasn't even the one who told me she left. Her mom did," I added, wanting him to ask me more. I wanted to talk about it. Daisy leaving without telling me was what hurt the most. I got nothing from her. No call, no text, nothing. It was like I didn't matter to her anymore.

He pulled a rolled up joint from his ear and lit it up before taking a large hit. The tip turned bright orange, and he let out a cloud of smoke.

"What a bitch. Atlanta sucks add, babe. She'll regret that shit. I went there for a buddy's show last year. Too many people. Too much traffic." He took another hit and bent his wrist my way.

I blinked at the smoking joint before snatching it up and sticking it to my lips. The first time I smoked with him, we were in a room full of people, and I was scared that I would look stupid. So I did it. Not everyone snorted shit at their parties, but everyone smoked, so I joined them. I didn't clarify it as a habit because I didn't have the urge to do it all the time. I only did it when I was with him.

I let the smoke slide down my throat and fill up my lungs. My entire body tingled as every ticking nerve relaxed. I took another hit and slowly all of my troubles began to fade away with the smoke. I had no inhibitions. My sweaty fingers gripped the joint, and I took another long draw. The buzz hit me hard this time, causing me to cough. I shut my eyes as Reese's laughter rang out, and he smacked my back.

"You gotta take it easy, love. You're just getting used to it." He gave me another pat on the back and grabbed the joint.

"Where are we?" I finally asked, taking a good look around the room.

He'd talked me into skipping school and hanging out with

him. We were in a small studio apartment. Movie and band posters held up by scotch tape and wrinkled at the corners hung on the walls. We were sitting on an old, tattered blue futon, and the only thing that didn't look like it was picked out of a trashcan was the big screen TV hanging on the wall across from us. In the opposite corner, a large mattress was lying on the floor without a bedframe, covered with sheets and un-made blankets.

"This is my bro's place," he answered, finishing the joint off and kicking his feet up on the table. "He doesn't care if I hang here sometimes."

"How old is he?"

We didn't share much about each other. He'd only mentioned his brother a few times. We didn't talk about our personal problems, dreams, or goals – most likely because we didn't have any. Our hanging out consisted of partying at his friend's houses. I'd invited him over to watch a movie once, and he spent the entire time sticking his hand up my shirt and slobbering all over my neck. That was the last time that happened. I needed alcohol before I was going to be able to handle that shit.

I was afraid for him to find out how inexperienced I was. Sure, I'd messed around with guys before, but I still had my v-card. It was hard for me to even get to third base with my brother and Dawson playing bodyguard to me. They'd let guys take me out and then threaten them the next day at school. Finally, guys quit asking. Boys, especially high school boys, didn't want to deal with threats. They only wanted to get laid.

"He's twenty-two and tight as fuck, so don't worry," he replied. "If he comes home, he'll be cool and won't kick us out or anything."

"Oh," I said.

"He won't be home for awhile. He usually goes to work and

then shoots darts at the pub around the corner." He grabbed the vodka bottle, moved the heel of his foot to the edge of the table, and slid it forward. He winked before taking a swig and handing it to me.

I grabbed it with both hands. "Chaser?"

"He doesn't have shit in his fridge unless you want water?"

I curled my upper lip. "That'd probably taste worse."

"Babe, it's just like taking a shot," he insisted. Instead of answering him, I nodded my head, took a gulp from the bottle, and swallowed it roughly. He laughed while grabbing it back and took another drink as I handled the after-effects of the harsh liquid rushing into my belly. "See ... I told you it wasn't so bad."

The bottle came back my way, and I took another drink ... and another ... and forgot how many I'd ingested. I gasped when I was suddenly shoved back onto the couch. My eyes shot wide open, and I tensed as Reese's weight hovered above me. I attempted to push myself forward, but my shoulders hit the arm of the couch at the same time he grabbed my hand and settled it down against his jean-covered bulge. I flinched, immediately reacting, and pulled my hand back, but he stopped me and kept it there.

"It's okay, love," he whispered, leaning down and pressing his hot lips against my neck. "I know you're inexperienced, and I fucking dig it."

I pushed on his chest and managed to yank my hand away from his crotch. He pulled away as I lifted myself up with my elbows and looked directly at him. "You do?" I asked, shocked.

There was no way he dug me not putting out. He'd been frustrated with me before when he was drunk a few times but never forced me to do anything. Deep down, I knew sooner or later, the day was going to come. He'd get tired of waiting. I knew what Reese liked, I'd overheard plenty of conversations, and it wasn't about his fondness for dating virgins. It was about him steering clear of girls who didn't spread their legs and entertaining those who did.

The weight of his fingers brushed against my arm. "Hell yeah, do you know how damn hot it is to have someone who hasn't fucked all of your friends?" I tilted my head up at him. Uh no? "How hot it is that you haven't been screwing every guy in my neighborhood?" His mouth got closer to mine, and I immediately got a whiff of the aroma of alcohol. "You're clean and pure, love."

But he wanted to change that. Day by day, he was changing me. I was no longer that pure girl. My lungs were filled with smoke, my stomach poison, and my heart was paralyzed.

My head spun as his mouth worked its way to my neck. I shut my eyes, and my body shivered when his hand began to slowly glide up my shirt to rub the bare skin. I was rushed into a whirlwind of emotions, losing myself. My bra was loosened and pulled down, and I gasped when he added his other hand to grope both of my breasts. A loud groan came from his throat as he massaged them in a circular motion.

I grew more lightheaded with every passing second. His body began moving in rhythm against mine while he whispered all of the things he liked about me in my ear. He told me I was sexy. He told me I was special. His words worked my brain, his hands worked my emotions, and he grinded his hard-on against my core. I suddenly awakened, the cloud of fog still there but growing clearer as excitement began to hit me. I lifted my arms up, and he pulled my shirt over my head.

"This cool?" he asked, his dark eyes staring down at my chest.

I nodded in response while trying to control my breathing. His hips pressed into me harder, and his groans grew more louder. My drunken mind took over, and warmth began to spread through me. I moaned, moving my hips faster against his, pelvis hitting pelvis, and his erection rubbed against my sensitive spot. I tilted my head back when his mouth latched onto a nipple, and a hand went to the button of my jeans, flicking it open.

That's when I immediately froze. I raised up but was immediately stopped by the sound of a door slamming shut.

CHAPTER 11

TESSA

I screamed and my smacked into Reese's, resulting in us both to cry out in pain.

"What the fuck?" Reese snarled, rubbing his forehead and glaring past me. I crossed my arms tightly across my bare chest, trying my hardest to cover up, and reached for my shirt at the same time. Reese's arm dropped down to hand me my bra. I hurriedly pulled my shirt over my head and tossed my bra into my open bag sitting on the floor.

My face heated as I slowly rotated my body around to see what was going on. I gasped loudly, and my hand flew up to my mouth. It was him. The guy from the party who'd sat with me and given me his flannel while I waited for Dawson to pick me up.

His eyes widened, and I knew he recognized me. His legs planted wide, those eyes now focused on me. His gaze moved to

Reese who was still halfway on top of me, to the bottle of alcohol, and then to the crushed up pill residue. I was sure he didn't miss the smell of weed wavering through the air, either.

"Take her the fuck home," he demanded, his voice rough as he pointed a thick finger at me.

"Bastion, what the fuck is your problem?" Reese fired back, pushing his weight up off me and sitting up. He leaned forward, his elbows hitting his knees, and eyed his brother harshly. I kept my arms around my body and pulled my bag into my lap. The more I could cover myself the better.

Bastion kept his eyes on me and ignored Reese. "I told you to stay away from his shit. If I would've known you were hanging out with him, I would've warned you even more."

"Huh?" Reese asked, his back going straight. He looked from me to his brother. "You two know each other? What the fuck?"

"Yeah we know each other," Bastion answered, and I opened my mouth to argue we'd only met once, but he didn't give me the chance. "I found her stumbling around Bobby's yard drunk and oblivious to where the hell she was." His eyes glared into Reese's. "She's not like us, and you fucking know it. Quit whatever bullshit you've got going on with her and take her home. And don't you dare bring her here again, or I will confiscate my key. I'm giving you five minutes. Get this shit," he pointed to the mess on the table, "cleaned the fuck up."

He stormed out of the room and slammed the door shut. I smacked my palm against my forehead and groaned. "That's your brother?" I buttoned my pants, and Reese adjusted his clothes.

"He's being a complete douchebag," Reese replied. "Why didn't you tell me you knew him?"

Did he not realize we were all just as shocked at the revelation? "I wouldn't say we know each other. He gave Dawson directions to come get me."

His head jerked sideways, and his eyes turned cold. A vein began to pulse in his neck.

Shit, wrong thing to say.

He grabbed the vodka bottle on the table, and I jumped when it shattered into a *Sports Illustrated* poster of a model in a bikini . "Of course, he fucking gave your pussy-ass boyfriend directions to come get you and take you away from me!" He seethed, jumping up from the couch, and started to pace in front of the table. He sniffled a few times, rubbing his nose in the process, wile he tried to control his anger. It didn't work. He kicked a few magazines lying on the floor and cursed under his breath rapidly.

"He's not my boyfriend. You know that," I said, nervously.

"Who knows who the fuck he is, Tessa. You barely talk about shit with me." It was the same with him, but I chose to not point that out. I just wanted to go home.

I grabbed my bag and fished for my keys when I realized I couldn't drive home. We were both drunk and high. There was no way either of us was getting behind the wheel.

"How am I going to get home?" I asked, changing the subject.

He stopped his pacing and gave me a penetrating stare. "Is your car here?"

"Uh yeah, I followed you." Did he really forget that?

He threw his hand out and motioned to the door. "Then go home."

I flinched at the cruel tone of his words. "I can't drive like this."

"Then I'll fucking follow you home in my car. You need to go see your other boyfriend or something?" He kicked the wall and yelled out to the ceiling.

"Please stop," I said quietly, my voice breaking.

He looked at me, something suddenly hitting him, and his face fell. "Fuck. I'm sorry. I just like you so much, and I don't know what's going on with you guys."

"Nothing, okay? Just let it go," I said, exasperated.

He shook his head and blew out a hard breath. "Let's just get out of here."

I nodded, knowing I had no other option. I could handle this. It wasn't a far drive. I'd drive slow and carefully. I rested my bag on my shoulder and followed him out the door.

His brother was leaning against the wall when we walked out of the door, startling me. His arms were crossed, one leg kicked back against the wall, and he eyed us suspiciously.

"I hope to God you're not planning to drive?" he asked me.

"I'm following her in my car. She'll be fine," Reese explained.

"You're not driving either, drunk ass," he told him.

"You just kicked us out, how the fuck do you think we're supposed to leave?"

"You stay here. I'll take her home."

"But my car is here," I said, finally joining the conversation.

"I'll drive your ride and have a friend pick me up from your place." He pointed at Reese. "You get your ass back in there and clean up my place before I beat your ass."

"She's not leaving with you," Reese argued. I clasped my hands in front of me, leaning against the wall as I suddenly grew dizzier, and watched their heated exchange as my stomach rumbled.

"Don't start this shit," Bastion said. "I don't fuck around with drunk girls. I'm better than that shit." Reese winced at his words, and my stomach grew more nauseous. What did that mean? He looked at me. "Give me your keys." I handed them over with shaky hands. "We'll be back." He didn't wait for Reese to say anything. Instead, he grabbed my hand to pull me down the hallway.

"But you have no problem fucking my leftovers," Reese yelled from behind us.

It happened so fast. One second Bastion had my hand, and

the next he had Reese pinned against the wall. "Reel the fucking attitude in and quit with that crap. You have no idea what you're talking about!" he yelled.

Reese pushed him away and walked to the side. "Whatever. Take her the fuck home. I don't give a shit." He walked back into the apartment and slammed the door behind him.

"Come on," Bastion said, gesturing to the door with his chin. He unlocked my car and hopped into the driver's side while I got into the passenger's. "Where we headed? I need to tell my buddy where to pick me up."

I gave him directions, and he typed them into his phone. The motor purred to life, and we took off down the street.

"What's your name?" he asked, beating his long fingers against my steering wheel to the low music coming from the speakers.

"Tessa," I answered, playing with my seatbelt.

"Tessa, why didn't you listen to me?"

"I don't even know you."

He looked over at me while steering with one hand. "So you don't take advice from strangers? Sometimes we're the best people to listen to. We're not afraid to hurt your feelings."

"What did he mean about you messing with his leftovers?"

"It's a long story."

"Shorten it then." There was more to the story, and I needed to know why Reese had looked so pissed at him. The altercation and chaos was pulling away my high, and I was falling back into reality.

He groaned. "He dated this girl for awhile."

"Alexa?"

"My shortening it means I'm not saying names. I'll tell you the story, but you aren't getting specifics."

"Fine, carry on."

"He treated her like shit, cheated on her all the time, and got into heavy drugs. Eventually, he ended up taking her down that road with him. He had her drinking, doing drugs, and whatever he wanted her to do. I came across her crying at a party one night. She was so messed up she could barely stand."

"Sounds familiar," I said quietly.

He nodded his head in agreement. "She was hysterical and crying about Reese hooking up with some other chick upstairs. I've known the girl since she was little, we'd all grown up together, and I wasn't leaving her alone like that. I didn't give a shit if she was my brother's girlfriend or not. I only cared about taking care of her. So I put her in my car and drove her to my place to crash. I slept on the futon and let her have the bed. Reese stumbled in the next morning, still wasted and high off his ass, and flew off the handle. He always thought she'd be there, no matter what terrible shit he did to her or to himself. But she finally grew tired of his shit. I want you to do the same thing."

"He probably needed an explanation," I said, trying to avert the attention away from me. "I'm sure it looked bad."

He shook his head. "Reese isn't as dumb as he leads people to believe. He put his hands on her. I interfered, and that's why he thinks something happened. He's so fucked up he believes that only a guy sleeping with a girl would protect her. Now he wants nothing to do with her and blames me for their break-up."

"Why does she still hang out him if he did all of that?"

"She's a strong girl. She acts like nothing bothers her. But deep down, she still feels love for him. He was her first boyfriend, her first love, and there's always something about the bad boy that wronged you. For some reason, you girls always love them."

I grabbed an old water bottle sitting in the cup holder and took a drink. "So you're not a bad boy?"

"I'm not a fan of labels, but I'm nothing like my brother. My dad isn't around to look out for him, so I try my best to help him."

"But you buy him alcohol?"

"I don't buy him shit. He has a fake."

"Why would he lie about that?"

"Probably because he didn't want you to know how often he frequents bars and gets wasted."

I avoided eye contact and looked out the window, watching dead leaves fall to the ground to their new home. What a simple way to go. You die along with everyone you're surrounded with, fall onto a beautiful setting, and then get blown away for a short ride.

"Oh," I said quietly. In a way, I felt sorry for Reese. Maybe that was in his past. Maybe he was trying to change.

"You realize now why you need to stay away? I know he's my brother, but like I said, you're a good girl, and you know it. You can tell just by looking at you you're dealing with some heavy shit. That's obvious, but he will break you, girl. He will make your problems ten times worse without you even realizing it until it's too damn late. He's fucking toxic. He will poison you."

"Maybe he's changed," I said hurriedly. "He says he hasn't met a girl like me before."

He snorted. "I hope you're smarter than that."

"I don't know what I am anymore," I grumbled.

We pulled up to my house, and he turned in his seat to look at me. "Look, take my advice, don't take my advice, it's up to you. If you feel like Reese can help you get away from whatever you're going through, then fine, whatever. Just be careful and don't tread so deep you drown." His phone beeped, and a black truck pulled up behind us. "That's my ride. Be careful, and I hope you find what you're looking for. I hope you find happiness before you let my brother ruin you." He swiftly jumped out of my car and got into the truck.

I sighed, tossing my head back against the headrest. I didn't understand anything anymore. Everyone was warning me away from Reese like he was some boogeyman creeping under my bed at night, but he made me feel so safe. It hurt me to think about what it would feel like losing him, losing the way he made me feel, and the attention he was giving me. A single tear fell down my cheek. I was different. That's what he said, and I believed him until it hit me when I was walking through my front door. And I felt like such an idiot when it did. Reese had his lips and hands everywhere on my body, but not once did he kiss me on the mouth.

૭৵৩

"GET UP!" A VOICE YELLED, STARTLING ME, AND I QUICKLY jumped up from my bed.

The room was dark, and I shook my head to be sure I wasn't dreaming. I winced when the light was suddenly turned on, and my eyes took a minute to adjust to the light. I saw my mom standing in my doorway and looked at my alarm before falling back down in bed.

"It's four in the morning," I said, raising my arm up to block the light from my eyes "Go back to bed." She had to be drunk. What a good combination we were. I was hung over, and she was drunk.

"Your father's in jail," she spat, and I moved my arm away to see if she was kidding.

"What?" I asked, still in shock from her words. My dad, the professional, well-respected lawyer was in jail? I moved my hand to look up at her. She was in her pajamas. Her hair was a mess on top of her head. I remembered the woman I'd once admired, the woman who helped me with my homework and with my hair before school dances. That woman was gone. She'd died alongside Tanner.

"Your dad got arrested. Now, get up."

"Dad's in jail? Are you sure?" She'd drunk too much. There was no way.

"Yes, your friend's piece of shit father arrested him for drunk driving. Years of friendship with those people, and he pulls this shit on us. After everything!"

This wasn't good. Daisy's dad was the town sheriff. My parents had been friends with Daisy's since they were in grade school. They'd all grown up together. My parents had been in their wedding and vice versa. We vacationed and celebrated birthdays together. Daisy and her family were in every great memory I had.

Her dad couldn't be blamed for his. It was mine who got behind the wheel drunk. Daisy's was only doing his job.

"I'll get dressed and go with you to bond him out," I said, wanting to diffuse the situation. She'd be the next one arrested if she stomped into the jail and screamed like a maniac.

Tears streamed down her face. "Thank you, sweetie. I don't know what I'd do without you," she said, softly. "I'll change and meet you downstairs."

I nodded and swallowed the large lump in my throat. Seeing my mom like this was heartbreaking. I jumped up from my bed, threw on some yoga pants, and raced down the stairs to find her waiting for me.

"You should probably let me drive," I suggested, holding my hand out for the keys dangling from her finger. The last thing I needed was for both of my parents to be in the drunk tank tonight. I'd slept my alcohol off, but I could still smell hers.

She set the keys in my palm and followed me into the garage. I got into the driver's side of her SUV, and she jumped into the passenger seat. I opened the garage door and geared the car into reverse.

"Do we need to go to a bail bondsman or the jail?" I asked. I'd heard stories about people getting DUIs before when I'd been at Daisy's, but I wasn't sure how the process actually worked.

"Let's try the station first," she said. I looked over at her to find her shaky hands clasped together in her lap.

"You know they can't just let him go." I didn't want her to get her hopes up.

"There's no way David is going to make him stay overnight. No way." She sounded like she was trying to convince herself more than anything.

"Okay," I drew out, still not sure it was a good idea. There was no way, friend or not, David was going to let him walk out of there still intoxicated with no repercussions. He was a good man and a friend to our family, but he was no pushover and never broke the law for people. Even for people he loved.

"You want to talk about why you quit your job?" I asked, taking advantage of the situation. I'd gotten a phone call from a co-worker of hers asking if she was okay. When I'd asked why she told me she hadn't shown up for the past week. No call, no show. If one more shift went uncovered, she'd be fired. That was three days ago, and I was sure she hadn't left her bedroom.

"Now is not the time, Tessa," she declared, rummaging through her purse and popping a breath mint.

"It's never a good time," I grumbled. "You got fired from your job, Dad's been arrested, and our family doesn't even talk to each other. What's going to happen next? We go broke, lose the house, and have nowhere to go? Because that's what our future is looking like right now."

"I didn't get fired, I quit. I told Millie I couldn't handle it anymore." Mille was the owner of the pharmacy she worked at. "She understands."

I pulled into the station parking lot and swerved in an open spot. "So are you going to be looking for another job?"

"Not at the moment. We have plenty in our savings account,

and your father is still working. I needed a break. Eventually, I'll get back into the work force. I just need time."

I narrowed my eyes at her. I was beginning to resent my own mother. "It's been months. I'm back at school, and so is Derrick. I know what you're going through, what we're all going through. You're not the only person dealing with this. It's hard, but you can't break down and not live. You can't die, too."

A tear trickled down her cheek. "Don't try to talk logic to me. You'll never know the hurt of losing a child until you're a mother. I miss him every single second of the day. When you two were born, I prayed to God I'd never have to bury one of my babies. But he didn't listen. He only gave me seventeen years before he took him away. Seventeen years! That's nothing." She slammed her hand against the glove compartment and cried out in agony.

I fidgeted in my seat and undid my seatbelt. If this was the past, I would've leaned over, wrapped her into my arms, and consoled her like she'd done for me so many times.

But now? I had no idea what to do with this stranger. She continued to cry, and I finally patted her arm a few times.

"Can you please go see if they'll release him?" She sniffled. "I can't go in there like this."

I knew this was going to happen. "I don't think they'll release him to a minor."

"Just do it!" she shrieked, and my hand shot away from her.

"Fine," I snapped. I should've been more sensitive to her emotions, but she was selfish. She only cared about the fact that she was hurting. I was seventeen and heading into the police station at four in the morning to try to persuade an officer to release my drunk driving dad from his cell because she *couldn't take it.*

"This isn't going to go well," I whispered to myself as I grabbed the door handle and walked into the station's lobby.

"Tessa," a throaty voice said my name, and David moved

around the front desk to me with his uniform on, a phone in his hand, and a worried expression on his face. It'd been months since I'd seen him. "Please tell me you're not here for your dad."

"I am," I said, embarrassed.

"I'm sorry, honey," but I can't release him." He looked past me. "Where's your mom?"

I swallowed hard and clutched my arms to my chest. "She's out in the car."

"Maybe you should ask her to come in."

"Yeah, she's heaving a breakdown at the moment."

"Shit," he hissed under his breath. "I'm sure she's angry at me. Look, I can't let him go. I could lose my badge, and I won't risk the safety of our town. He has to stay in there for the rest of the night. When he's sobered up, your mom can post bail." Great, my mom wasn't going to be happy about this news.

"Can we please bail him out tonight? I'm driving, I'll put him in bed, and no one will get hurt."

"I'm sorry, but I can't let him go anywhere tonight." He paused for a moment. "And it's too late for you to be out. Do you want me to take you guys home?"

"I'm good, thanks." If my mom saw him, she'd probably claw his eyes out.

"I want you to text me when you get home to assure me you've made it there safely. Tell your mom to call me in the morning so I can tell her when he will be released. You don't need to be worrying about this stuff."

"Thanks," I whispered, turning around to leave.

"And Tessa?"

I twisted around to look at him. "Yeah?"

"If you or Derrick need anything, and I mean anything, don't hesitate to call Janis or myself. We're all still family."

"I know." I opened up the door and headed out into the dusk, staying in line with the parking lot lights overhead until I made it back to the car.

The car was still running when I got back in.

"Where is he?" she asked. I looked over at her, blinking a few times, before I realized she was serious. She'd actually believed they were going to let him walk out free.

"He's in the drunk tank. They won't release him until tomorrow."

"That goddamn asshole!" She threw her door open. "I'm going to tell that little prick what a piece of shit he is! No one would do that to a friend. No one!"

"Jesus Christ!" I yelled, and then jumped out of my car to chase after her, which was an easy task because she was stumbling around. I grabbed her arm to drag her back to the car. "If you go in there and act a fool it's only going to make it worse." I shoved her towards the car. "Get in unless you want to share a cell with dad."

She kicked the open passenger door. "They can't arrest me! I've done nothing wrong!"

I scoffed "If you go in there and threaten a police officer, whether or not you know him, it's against the law. Especially right in the police station where there are other officers and cameras."

"Fine," she said, crossing her arms and falling back into the seat. "But you stay away from them. All of them – including Daisy." A deep pit formed in my stomach. She didn't even know about Daisy leaving.

I took a deep breath. "Okay, just please calm down, and we'll bail dad out tomorrow."

"Just take me home, please." She held her shaking hands in her lap and sobbed the entire way home.

CHAPTER 12

TESSA

"Hey babe," Reese said, sitting down next to me.

The first thing I noticed were his bloodshot eyes – which were becoming a usual occurrence, and it put a sour taste in my mouth.

"What do you want?" I grumbled. A few days had passed since the whole incident at his brother's, and we hadn't talked since then. I was perfectly fine with that.

He slapped his hand over his heart. "Awe babe, you're really mad at me? You're the one who took off with my brother, and I had to find out the guy who picked you up from our first party was that fucking douchebag? How do you think that makes me feel? I'm not hanging out with other bitches." He leaned forward to swipe a piece of hair behind my ear. "And you're having other guys take you home ... or wherever you supposedly went."

"You were acting like a maniac," I argued, playing with the wrapper around my water bottle and not looking at him.

"We were drunk and high. Did you forget how you were acting?"

I squinted my eyes, thinking back to that night, but things were still blurry. "I don't think I did anything wrong."

"Look, we were both in the wrong. Give me a chance to make it right."

"How are you going to do that?"

"My dad is going out of town this weekend for a fishing trip, so I'll have the house to myself. You're coming over, and we won't have to worry about my asshole brother barging in and spewing bullshit."

"I don't know if that's a good idea." Actually, I *knew* it wasn't.

"Babe, give me a chance. You've never entirely given me a chance. Not to mention, you owe me for leaving parties *twice* with that guy." Shit, was I ever going to hear the end of that? Reese would apologize and immediately expect me to forgive and forget, but he liked to drag it on for days if someone wronged him. He pressed his hands together in a pleading motion. "Please."

"Fine."

"You're amazing." He kissed my cheek. "Be sure to bring an overnight bag ... unless you want to wear something of mine." He winked, and my back straightened. We'd never spent the night together. It wouldn't be any different than us being at a party except we'd be alone all night, which was a pretty big difference.

"I'm going to make you dinner, try to be all romantic and shit."

"Romantic and shit? You've already made it sound super romantic."

He moved in a rested a hand on my thigh. "You're my girl, Tessa, and I need to start acting like it. I know I'm a dumbass sometimes, but you need to know my feelings for you are real. I don't want to lose you. For as long as I can remember, my life has been one screwed up cluster fuck. I've had plenty of girls," I gave him a look, and he ran his hand over his face. "Shit, wrong thing to say, but it helps make my point. I've never treated any of them like I treat you. I've never invited them to my house or made them dinner. I actually enjoy spending time with you." His shoulder hit mine playfully. "Even when we're clothed."

"Okay, that last part could've been left out," I grumbled "But the rest of it was sweet, thank you." I paused, hesitant about bringing it up. "What about Alexa?"

His brother's words had been haunting me since that night. Did Reese really ruin her? Did he cheat and then try to hit her? I was too afraid to ask. I knew Reese had his flaws, but I hope none of them were that horrifying. I was scared of his reaction. I was afraid to find out the truth. If I did, it would be expected for me to leave him. I would rather be left in the dark than left alone.

Reese groaned in frustration and ran his hands through his thick hair. "Alexa and I are nothing. Our dads are friends, so we've known each other forever. We tried something years ago, but it would never work out between us. We butt heads too much. We're too much alike, and we decided that a year ago."

"Oh, okay." I wanted to ask him more questions, but I could tell he was done with that subject. "When do you want me to come over?

CHAPTER 13

DAWSON

I IGNORED THE LUNCH ON MY TRAY WHILE FOCUSING ON Reese sitting with Tessa. I grinded my teeth and watched him scoot he chair closer to him to grab her hand. My heart pounded when he kissed her full on the mouth.

How the fuck could she forgive him for how he'd treated her at the bonfire? The guy was an idiot, and she believed every word that came out of his lying mouth. She was going to fall apart when he dropped her faster than one of his cigarettes. She wasn't going to be able to handle it.

"He's going to fuck her, ya know?"

I looked over at the sound of her voice to find a girl pulling out the chair next to me and plopping her ass down onto it. She flipped her hair over her shoulder and waited for my answer.

She was hot. I couldn't argue that and was positive there wasn't a guy in the room who would argue with me about it. Her long, dark hair was curled and fell to each side of her large breasts in the low-cut top she was wearing. Large gold bracelets dangled from her wrists, and gold hoops hung from her ears. Her make-up was done, and her lips were the color of a juicy, bright apple.

"What?" I asked.

She pointed over to where I'd been staring. "Your little crush over there. He's going to fuck her and then leave her."

Who the fuck was this chick?

"Shut the hell up," I said, sharply, my throat stinging as her words sunk in. I wanted to deny it, but I knew better. I knew it would happen, and I knew there was no stopping it.

She shrugged her shoulders. "I'm only warning you. Reese loves the game. He loves the challenge."

"She's not a challenge."

She scoffed. "Oh, she is the definition of challenge. I've watched it happen so many times. He finds the cute but broken insecure girls, gives them attention, showers them with compliments and makes them feel wanted. He gives them life when they're about to give up." My jaw set, and as much as I wanted to stop her, I couldn't. I needed to hear what she had to say. She kept going. "There are so many girls here that will rip off their panties and bend over for him with the snap of his fingers. No questions asked. Something about having the bad guy, you know?" I stared at her without answering. "He gets bored with that. He likes the chase. He likes to take their virginity and then brags that he was the man who'd convinced them to give it up. And then he cuts the cord."

"Maybe he's changed," I argued, feeling like a damn idiot. "Maybe he truly likes her and wants to be with her." I hated myself for what I was doing. But Tessa asked me to let her make her down decisions, and as much as it killed me to do it, I wanted to make her happy.

She laughed. "Oh trust me, he's still bending those girls over.

You think he'd go that long without sex? Hell no. He's just discreet about it." Who the hell was this guy? Fucking Casablanca? "He likes to seduce the good girls, turn them into girls like me, and then leave us crying on the sidewalk."

"And what exactly is a girl like you?"

"Used," she answered, her honesty shocking me. "Slutty." She held my eye contact without looking ashamed. "We end up on a search to find another guy to give us that feeling again and not leave us. But that never happens. Once they find out what you are, they'll hook up with you, but you're nothing more than bragging rights to their friends. The guy we thought cared about us was using us."

I slammed my bottle of water down hard against the table. "You don't know shit about her. She's none of those things."

"Not yet."

"If that happens, it's not my problem." My words hit me straight in the gut. It would fucking obliterate me if she gave him her virginity. But I couldn't stop it. She wasn't mine. She was his now.

Derrick had been giving me updates on her during our guys' days. She'd go to his football games with me, but text him the entire time. Instead of going out for pizza or burgers afterwards, she'd meet him at some party and stay out until early in the morning. She never stayed out all night. He told me Reese had come over once, and they'd gone straight up to her bedroom. He didn't know how late he stayed, but it was after he'd gone to bed.

"Right. You've been stalking them the entire lunch period. You don't like him with her because you want her. She probably wanted you before, but you were too pussy to do shit about it. And because of your pussy-ness, she's with him now, and you're jealous, but still not doing shit about it. It hurts to see her with someone else, doesn't it?" Damn, this girl sure knew how to kick a guy when he was down. "Wait until she's fucking him. Imagine her naked in his sheets."

Now she was going overboard. "That's enough," I snapped. "Who the fuck are you, and why are you even talking to me?"

She held out her hand and gave me a red-lipped smile. "I'm Alexa, that douchebag's ex-girlfriend." She tilted her head to a laughing Reese rubbing Tessa's shoulders.

"Sorry to hear that," I answered. "And this sounds like it's a jealousy thing on your part."

She popped the gum in her mouth. "Yeah, you could say I'm jealous of all the girls he shows attention to because I miss that affection, but I'm over him. Him and me, we're like fire and gasoline."

"Again, why are you talking to me?"

"Reese's dad is going on a fishing trip with mine this weekend." She rolled her eyes. "They do it every year even though they should be working. And every year, Reese has a girl stay with him. He makes them dinner, gives them all this romantic bullshit, and obviously gets laid."

If she brought up Reese fucking Tessa one more time, I was going to flip the table over and destroy everything in sight. "Thanks for the info," I said, wanting the conversation to end. "But like I said, it's not my business. Or yours."

She peered up at me through her dark lashes. "True, do whatever you want with the info. She seems like a decent girl, and if someone is willing to save her, they better." She reached out and ran her red-nailed hand over my arm, and her lips tilted into a mischievous smile. "If not, let me know when you outgrow your crush or are up for some revenge sex."

I peeled her fingers off me. People would probably call me an idiot for not taking her up on her offer, but it didn't feel right. I was aching to get laid. I hadn't touched a girl since Tanner's death, but it felt like I was cheating on Tessa anytime I talked to another girl now. Tanner's death had taught me that life was more than having meaningless sex with random girls.

"Thanks for the offer, but I'm good," I said.

She clicked her tongue against the roof of her mouth. "Let me know if you change your mind." She got up from her chair and sauntered away, shaking her ass seductively in the process.

"Dude, what the hell?" Cody asked. I snapped back into reality and noticed Cody and Ollie were still sitting at the table. Shit, they'd heard everything. "If you want to turn her down that's cool, but what about me?" He pointed to himself. "Bro code, you always have to introduce the bros."

"She wouldn't want your goofy ass," Ollie said, shaking his head. "She'd want me."

"You were obviously listening, assholes," I said, breaking into the argument. "Don't you dare say shit to anyone about what you heard." The last thing Tessa needed was getting a reputation for putting out before she even lost her virginity. People were already making speculations about the two of them.

"You know we'd never do that shit," Ollie said. "Plus, I don't think Cody heard a word that was said. He was too busy drooling to pay attention to anything."

Cody threw an apple slice at him. "Screw you, asshole. I wasn't the only one." He looked at me. "You do need to say something to Tessa, though. You need to warn her the fuck away from him. I'd do it, but you're closer to her than we are."

"You've also got the fact that she's in love with you on your side," Ollie added. Put it out there, and I'm sure she'll listen."

"Not so sure about that." I could've stopped her before, but this new Tessa, I wasn't so sure about. I had no idea what was going through her beautiful but torn mind.

"Did you hear about her dad?" Ollie asked.

I nodded. "She's the one who had to bond his ass out," I said, repeating what Derrick had told me. "He's lawyered up by someone in his firm, and they suspended his license. But because of his situation and role in the town, he'll probably get off with probation and not face any jail time."

Everyone knew about it because they'd posted it in the paper. Not much happened in our small town, so when an affluent lawyer got arrested on a DUI charge, that shit made headlines. I was pissed about it, too. They'd put her family through the ringer by running numerous articles about the victims' deaths and now this. The media were fucking assholes.

"That sucks. Out of all of our parents, they'd be the last I would think something like that would happen to," Cody said.

We grabbed our trays when the bell rang and tossed them onto the conveyor belt.

"Now's the time to do it," Cody said, bumping my shoulder and jerking his head towards Tessa.

I nodded and walked away from them. Tessa was standing with Reese beside their table and gasped when I grabbed her hand and pulled her away from him. I heard him talking shit behind us but ignored him.

I walked her into an empty hallway and pressed her against the wall of lockers. I caged her in, my arms going to each side of her head. I'd had enough.

"What the hell are you doing with him?" I asked. "Your rebellious phase needs to end before you do something you're going to regret."

I had asked her the question so many times. At first, I'd tried to convince myself it was temporary, but it was getting out of hand.

I noticed Reese coming towards us from the corner of my eye. I had to act quickly. He stopped a few steps away from us and crossed his arms. He was going to let me have my moment because he knew it'd end up in his favor. He was aware I'd piss her off and she'd run straight into his shady arms.

She sighed, and her eyes looked everywhere but at me. "He's helping me through things and makes me feel better, Dawson. He makes me forget to be sad. I really like him." She paused and took a deep breath. "I think I'm falling in love with him." I stumbled back, my hands falling to my side, and her words stabbed me straight into the heart. "I don't understand what the big deal is. Don't you want me to be happy?"

My pulse was running a marathon as I slammed my hand against a locker. "You think he's going to help you? You think he loves you? Newsflash, he doesn't," I spat. "He's going to break you even more and then step over your crushed body when he's gotten what he wants. He's fucking toxic. His shit will bleed into you and make you more screwed up than you already are." I pointed a finger at a smirking Reese. "I promise you he's not the answer."

Her palms flew out, coming into connection with my chest, and I stumbled back at the force. "More screwed up than I already am?" She pounded a finger into my chest. "I'm glad you didn't want to be with me. You led me straight into his arms, and I couldn't be happier."

"That's a goddamn lie," I fired back.

"Reese doesn't remind me every three seconds how broken I am. He tells me he understands. He doesn't point out my flaws or make me feel bad about myself. He makes me feel good. How can you have a problem with that?"

"You know why! You fucking know why!"

She groaned in frustration and raised her hands in the air. "You've shot me down so many times and now that I've found someone else you all of a sudden care about me? You all of a sudden want me to leave him so you can fix me?" She let out a harsh laugh. "I've moved on. You need to do the same."

That was a low fucking blow. "Please don't have sex with

him. I'm begging you. Hang out with him, watch movies with him, but please don't give that to him. He's using you."

"Wow," was all she said before turning around and stomping down the hallway ... right into his arms.

"Fuck," I seethed, throwing my head back and kicking a locker forcefully.

"You want me to leave you alone?" I yelled when the started down the hallway. She turned around, still in his hold, and looked directly at me. Her face was void of any emotion – like she wasn't even there anymore. Her body was within reach, but her heart had been sucked out. "Have it your way. I'm done. If you turn your back on me and walk away with him, we're done. I'm done with you."

"Then we're done," she said, her voice strong.

She turned back around, and they walked away. I stared at her back, my heart shattering into pieces and stabbing into my rib cage, when she turned around and walked away. I slammed my fist into a locker, feeling skin break when it connected with the sharp metal, before darting out the doors jumping into my truck.

She didn't even try to stop me. She did nothing.

If she didn't want me, why was I fighting to keep her?

CHAPTER 14

TESSA

I was running late, and the sky was dim when I punched in the address to Reese's house into my GPS. I turned down the music, needing silence, and put my car in drive. Anticipation was biting at my nerves. What did he have planned for us? I prayed it wasn't another party. My phone beeped, breaking my away from my thoughts, and I grabbed it from the passenger seat to read the text.

CODY: *You need to talk to Dawson. He only wants what's best for you. Don't be mad at him.*

I tossed the phone back down. None of them had a right to meddle into my personal life. I kept my eyes on the road, and what happened with Dawson in the hallway flashed through my mind. It had felt like all of the air released from my lungs when he said he was done with me.

He was giving up. Even though I had Reese, I never thought

I'd lose Dawson. I'd loved him for as long as I'd known him, but he didn't want me until Tanner died. He'd turned me down continuously and now that he was alone he finally was opening his arms.

That stung.

Jesus Christ, it hurt.

My inner voice kept telling me he was only reaching out because he didn't want to lose my family, the only one he'd ever had, and I was the perfect pawn to keep that.

Reese wasn't always trying to babysit me or make my decisions. He allowed me to be me – the new me. Dawson was trying to save the girl who'd once been full of life, bubbly, and ready for everything. That girl was gone. Reese understood me, and being understood when you're in a dark place is one of the most comforting feelings in the world.

I parked in front of a small one-story house and eyed it from the street. The paint on the siding was chipping off around the windows, exposing the dingy wood, and a few shutters were broken off and falling to its side. The front door was open, a thin screen in its place.

I grabbed my bag, got out, and wrapped my sweater around my shoulders. Music was blaring from the house, and I walked through an open chain-link fence and onto a narrow walkway surrounded by overgrown grass, weeds, and dandelions. I lifted my leg, nearly tripping on a broken step, and jumped up on the porch.

"Hello!" I shouted through the screen. I pulled at the handle, noticing it was unlocked, but I hesitated on whether or not to walk in.

"He ain't going to hear ya over that garbage noise, darling," a struggling voice called out. I looked over to the porch next door to find an elderly man sitting in a chair. An oxygen tube was connected to his nose that led to a large tank. "Be careful. Boys who listen to music that loud are always trouble."

"Uh ... thanks," I said, giving him a friendly wave, because I wasn't sure what else to do. I yelled Reese's name through the screen. No answer.

I clutched the handle in my hand again, ignoring the neighbor's penetrating stare, and walked in. The pungent scent of cigarettes and dust balls smacked straight into me. A ripped, brown curtain blocked the sunlight from entering the room, and a suede couch was positioned in the middle of the room across from a TV perched onto a black stand. A blue and yellow plaid chair sat to the side. Bottles of alcohol covered two black end tables.

"Hello?" I called out again, venturing down a hallway.

The music pierced through my ears when I landed in the kitchen and spotted an iPod plugged into a docking station, but still no Reese.

"Oh hey, I didn't hear you come in," a gravelly voice said, causing me to jump and bump into a cabinet. I turned around and found Reese standing at the back door with a plate in one hand and a beer in the other.

I rubbed my side and shuffled my feet against the floor. "I knocked a few times," I replied, pointing at the player.

"Oh shit, yeah," he muttered, walking around me and turning down the volume with his free hand. He set the plate down on the small table, and I noticed it was filled to the rim with cheeseburgers.

"Are you having a party?" I asked, counting twelve burgers on the plate and waiting for his answer with dread.

He looked down at the tray and back at me. "Nope, just figured you might be extra hungry."

"There's no way I'm eating all of that."

He laughed, grabbed my waist, and brought me into his tight

hold. "When I take the time to cook I make a shit ton of food and save it for the rest of the week."

We ate the cheeseburgers and sucked down a few beers while Reese talked about a few parties coming up and his friend's band. I stayed quiet, nodding my head, and sipped on the beers he kept handing my way. He finally stood up from his chair and shot his arm out for me to grab.

"You have no fucking idea how damn happy I am that you came. I promise you we're going to have a good time tonight. Just you and me," he said, kissing my forehead and dragging me into him.

"Just you and me," I whispered, smiling back at him.

Suddenly, his lips were on mine, and he was grabbing my waist to lift me up on the counter behind me. My head spun as he slid his tongue into my mouth and kissed me roughly. I ran my tongue over his piercing, and his hand shot up to my hair, clasping it while groaning wildly. I spread my legs, allowing him to slide in between them and press his growing erection against my heat.

I moaned at the sensation of him grinding against me, and he took that as an invitation to go farther. He reached for the hem of my sweater and pulled it over my head. He threw it on the floor and immediately unhooked my bra. A cold shiver crawled over my skin, and I shuddered. Reese didn't notice. Instead, he continued to grind against me. He suddenly pulled away, and before I had a chance to ask what was wrong, he leaned down and pulled a nipple in his mouth.

"Oh my God, that feels good," I moaned out, enjoying the tingling sensations swirling through my stomach. I wasn't sure if it was the alcohol, but I'd never felt something so intimate before. He groaned at my response, and I got lost in his touch.

His hands dug into my hips, and he made a move for my legs.

That's when I picked up on what was about to happen and froze. "Wait," I said, stopping him.

He pulled away and took a step back. It took me a few seconds to gain the nerve to look at him. He shook his head at me in disgust when I did.

"Are you even attracted to me, Tessa?" he asked.

My back went straight, and I crossed my arms to cover my bare chest. "What?"

He gave me a blank look before sighing dramatically. "Whenever I try to show you affection you pull away from me. Why? Do you not like me like that? Am I not your type?"

I tried to think of the best way to explain myself. The alcohol was making it hard for me. "I told you I'm not very experienced."

"Are you planning on joining a convent or some shit?"

"Uh, no," I answered, confused.

"Then what's holding you back? Everyone starts out inexperienced, babe. You'll never know how great it is or what you like until you try it. Trust me. It's easy, and amazing when you do it with someone you have feelings for, like I do you." He settled himself back in-between my legs. "I want you. God, I want you so bad. I want to feel closer to you. Everyday, I think about how great it would feel if you gave yourself to me. I'd know you truly cared about me." His hand traveled in-between my legs.

"I guess you're right," I squeaked out, closing my eyes.

He started to rub his fingers in circles, making me dizzy. "I'm not trying to push you, love. I've been waiting so long." He pulled his piercing into his mouth, scraping his teeth against it, while he kept his hand at work.

My vision grew hazy, and this time when he went to pull off my leggings, I didn't stop him.

CHAPTER 15

TESSA

"Hey, it's me," I said into my phone. I adjusted myself against the chilly pillows in my bed and sunk into the comfort of my sheets. "I've tried calling you a few times, but you're not picking up, obviously. Please, just please, call me back," I pleaded to his voicemail. With every missed call, I was struggling harder to keep my cool. Why was he ignoring me? Did I do something wrong? Fear pitted at the bottom of my stomach as a headache split through my skull. This couldn't be happening.

"Screw it," I whispered into the quiet of my bedroom and slid out of my bed. There was no way I was falling asleep until I talked to him. I slammed my eyes shut and sobbed silently. Why did everyone leave me?

I pulled on a pair of sweatpants and threw on a jacket. I snatched all my hair up in one hand, pulled it into a loose ponytail, and walked downstairs and out the front door.

The party was in full swing when I arrived. I knew he'd be there. He'd mentioned it to me the other night, and he never missed a party. That's all he did.

I nudged a few people with my shoulder, dodging them left and right, and spotted a large group of people standing in the living room. I immediately spotted him standing in the middle of the crowd. I blinked a few times, counting to ten, and tried to calm myself down.

"I'm dreaming," I whispered to myself. "Please be dreaming."

I opened them back up and my stomach clenched. Nope, I definitely wasn't dreaming. He had his hands wrapped around a tall busty blonde while he talked to the people around him. He was holding her like he'd held me. He was showing his ownership over her like he'd done to me so many times. A chill hit my spine. Everything we'd done and everything he'd said meant nothing. They were all lies. Stupid bullshit lies. And I'd been suckered into falling for every single one of them.

"Hey Tessa," Maya shouted, noticing me and breaking out of Bobby's arms. I looked up to see her skipping my way before pulling me in for a tight hug. I hugged her back but kept my eyes on him. His entire body stilled at the mention of my name, and his head jerked up to look directly at me. He saw me. He acted like he didn't, but he did.

"Hey," I muttered, pulling away from her.

"Let's go get a drink, girlfriend," she said, grabbing my hand to drag me away. I pulled back from her, and suspicion hit me. Was she trying to help me by not letting me see Reese, or was she trying to protect him?

"I'll be right back," I said.

"Shit," she spat out under her breath, answering my question.

I stomped over to him. He wasn't going to get away with this.

"Are you kidding me?" I shouted. There were so many thoughts running through my head, and I couldn't keep up. I'd never felt so angry, betrayed, and hurt before. I'd officially become one of those girls who created a scene in public over a guy.

"Fuck me," Reese breathed out, dropping his arm away from the girl and pushing her back behind him in a protective gesture. Was he trying to shield her from me? His hands ran over his face, and he shook his head. Was this what it meant to have your heart broken?

I realized that every warning I'd ignored had been the truth. I listened to his lies and lost people I loved. I lost people who cared about me by choosing him. I'd been blind. Every word, every promise, and every touch meant nothing to him, but everything to me.

"Who the hell is she?" the girl behind him screeched, looking over his shoulder and pointing at me. The crowd had parted, allowing me to walk straight to him and create the scene they were waiting for.

"She's a friend," he answered, biting his piercing roughly as his words seared through my heart. *A friend?* He threw his head back and cursed a few times before looking directly at me. "Look, Tessa, we need to talk."

"I've been trying to call you all day," I yell.

He patted his pockets like he was searching for his phone. "Fuck, sorry, I forgot my phone at home." My ribs squeezed when I eyed the bulge in his right pocket that was strangely the size of his cell.

"Okay," I drew, looking around at the curious looks around us.

Alexa was in the corner, her attention on us, and shaking her head at me in what looked like pity. Dawson was in the kitchen, oblivious to what was going on, and playing a drinking game with his friends and a few girls. He helped one of the girls get the perfect aim for her beer pong, and she hugged him when she scored. He'd moved on. I couldn't be mad at him for it. I'd practically shoved him out of my life and handed him to her.

"This probably isn't the best place to have this conversation," Reese said, gritting his teeth and pointing to the gawking crowd. "Call me tomorrow, stop by, and we'll talk."

The girl behind him scoffed and pushed into his back. "What the hell do you need to talk to her about? Is this your girlfriend? You told me you were single!"

"Chill out, babe. She's not my girlfriend," he fired back, grabbing her angry hands and settling them to his side.

She's not my girlfriend.

I'd been so naïve. He'd made me feel like I was the most important person in the world to him. I thought we were in a relationship. I was falling in love with him. I hated love. I wanted to rip love into shreds, shove it down his throat, and let him choke on the emotions until it made him feel as sick as I did.

"You can go fuck yourself," I seethed, taking a few steps forward. My hand whipped back, and I felt the sting of my palm connecting with his face before he had the chance to stop it. The girl behind him shrieked as he fell back into her chest, and she was shoved against the wall. Tears burned at my eyelids, begging to be released, but I refused to let him see me cry. I wasn't giving him, or anyone else, that satisfaction. He stared at me in shock when I shoved a finger into his chest. "You're an asshole, and I hate you!" I pushed him again, causing another shriek, and he finally shoved me away from him.

Fire burned his eyes when he pushed me again. "You need to fucking leave, Tessa," he spat.

Bobby instantly appeared and grabbed his arm to pull him away. "Dude, chill out. Let's go smoke," he said. "Don't do anything fucking stupid."

"He's already done something stupid!" I yelled. "You're a coward, and you're worthless."

"Fuck you, you crazy bitch. Don't get mad at me because I don't want you!"

I charged at him but was suddenly stopped and pushed back. "Tessa, calm the fuck down," the familiar voice said into my ear as another pair of hands helped him keep me still. Rage ate at me. I wanted to hurt him. I couldn't cut Reese emotionally like he'd done me, but I could physically. At least I thought I could. I was pulled into a chair and hated myself when the tears began their course down my cheeks. Dawson leaned down in front of me, placing his palms on my kneecaps, and swiped away loose strands of hair falling from my ponytail.

"Listen to me, baby, you need to calm down," Dawson said, wiping away the evidence of my hurt from my cheeks. "I'm here for you; you know that. I'll always be here. Forget about him, and let's go home."

"You said you were done with me," I sobbed, choking the words out. He'd left me. Flashes of him saying those words lit up through my mind. He'd left me like everyone else. His chest was the next one I pushed back. "You lost your best friend, and now you're looking for someone to fill that void. I get it, Dawson! Trust me, I fucking get it! That's what I did with that stupid jackass." Every word that spewed out of my mouth shocked him and me. Who was this girl? I'd become a monster. "But it's not real, so stop! I'm not going to let you ... or anyone else ... use me again. I'm done!"

"Jesus Christ," he hissed, the intensity of his blue eyes peering down at me. "Use you? Are you even listening to the bullshit you're saying? That guy over there." He pointed to Reese standing with his hands clenched while Bobby still tried to calm him down. "The guy you're crying over, that's what using someone looks like. He used you, not me. I've done nothing but try to help you!"

"Fuck you!" Reese shouted, leaving Bobby before he had the

chance to pull him back and charging our way. "I didn't fucking use her. You don't know shit about what happened between us."

Dawson pushed him away before he got any closer to me. "Oh, so you didn't fuck her for the fun of it and then bail when you got what you wanted?"

"Dawson!" I shouted, humiliated at his accusation.

A menacing smile crossed Reese's lips. "I don't know what you're talking about, pretty boy," he taunted, and Dawson stumbled into my chair when Reese's palms smacked into his chest. He rubbed his chin a few times and looked down at me. "You know why I bailed? You want me to tell all of these people why I freaked out?"

"Don't you dare talk to her," Dawson said, pulling himself up and pushing Reese away from me again. Spit flew from his mouth, and he looked at Reese like he was ready to murder him.

"Dude, not here," Ollie said, grabbing Dawson's arm when he reached out to hit Reese.

"You want to hit me, pussy boy?" Reese said, slamming his fist against his own chest. "Let's see how big of a badass this momma's boy is, shall we? Have you ever punched anyone before?" He snorted. "I bet you haven't and now you're trying to play prince charming boy for the girl who chose me over you. I wonder how it's going to feel to get my leftovers?"

"Fuck this asshole," Cody yelled, appearing at Dawson's side. "Please tell me I can beat this arrogant fuckhead's ass because he fucking needs it."

I'd seen Dawson get into a few fights, but nothing serious. He'd punched a guy for grabbing my ass one year during spring break and another one for calling me a dick tease at a bonfire. But Cody, I'd seen him fight. I'd seen him fight a lot. I knew he'd hit Reese; no questions asked, no over thinking it. That was Cody's release. It was his high to beat the shit out of people.

Dawson shook his head as Reese continued to taunt him. "No

man, this is my shit." He snagged his arm out of Ollie's grasps and slammed his fist into Reese's smirking face, catching him off guard. Reese fell into Bobby's big frame, wiped his bloody lip with the back of his hand, and regained his composure. I gasped, watching him charge back at Dawson and hitting him on the side of his face. A few girls shrieked, jumping away from the fight, while guys crowded around to watch with their phones in their hands recording it. But nobody attempted to stop it.

I tried to watch what was going on, but there was too much commotion. The crowd zeroed in on the two and blocked my view.

"Fuck me," Cody yelled, darting into the crowd. I kicked my legs up and stood up in the chair to see what was going on. I gasped when I saw it. Bobby and another guy had joined the fight. They were holding Dawson down on the ground while Reese kicked him in the stomach.

"No!" I screamed. "Somebody stop him." I jumped down from the chair and pushed through the crowd of people. "Get off of him!" I continued to scream, elbowing lingering bodies before I reached the front of the crowd. Cody and Ollie had jumped in, pulling Reese's friends away, but Reese continued his assault on Dawson. Dawson was on the floor, crouched into the fetal position, as he took each blow. My legs locked up, and I grabbed onto the stranger next to me when I noticed Dawson's bloody face. I looked over at Reese, his face full of rage, and rushed towards him

"Get off of him you asshole," I shrieked, tugging at the back of his shirt with all my strength until Cody pulled me away.

He put Reese into a headlock and slammed him against the wall at the same time his fist met Reese's nose. Reese pushed Cody away and held his hands up in surrender like he knew he was about to get his ass kicked.

"It's fucking over," Reese yelled, grabbing the bottom of his shirt and holding it up to the blood dripping from his nostrils. He yelled at his friends who were still trying to fight Ollie. "It's fucking over!"

I bent down to grab Dawson's hand, and Ollie and Cody helped me drag his limp body up. Tears streamed down my face when I took a good look at him. His face was bleeding and already beginning to bruise. Blood covered his shirt, and his bottom lip was busted. He spat blood onto the carpet and cursed out loud.

"You good to walk, bro?" Cody asked.

"I'm good," Dawson said, staggering a few feet, and Cody stopped him before he toppled over.

"Dude, you ain't cool," he said.

I tried to help them, but Ollie stopped me. "We got it," he said, sternly. They were pissed at me, and I didn't blame them.

Cody whipped around before they headed to the doors and pointed to Reese's friends standing at his side. "You fuckers are pussies for jumping in. You want to talk shit and act like bulldogs, be sure that your Chihuahua asses can back it up. Real men don't jump people; they fight their own fucking battles. Who's the pussy now?" he asked, his attention turning to Reese.

"I think it's time for you to go, and I'd steer clear of any future parties around here," Alexa said, coming to my side. "I didn't peg you as a troublemaker, but I can see it now. Look at you, you've got two hot guys fighting over you. I don't know what it is, I mean you're not even that cute, but I guess the whole innocent thing works. Maybe I'll buy some turtlenecks and try it out."

"What's that supposed to mean?" I asked.

"You need to stop, or it will get worse."

"Stop what?"

"Stop relying on other people to fix your shit. You need to fix it on your own, honey. I'd suggest staying away from our crowd. They're not fans of overly dramatic girls and girl, you're over-dramatic as hell. Stay away from the bad boys, or this is what you'll get every time."

"I'm not overly-dramatic," I said, defensively. "You know nothing about me."

Dawson spit out blood again while he and Reese gave each other the stare-down. I could tell they were ready for round two. I looked over at his friends, both looking like they could go another round as well.

"I'm honestly not trying to be a bitch," Alexa went on, bringing the cup in her hand to her lips.

I snorted. "Could've fooled me."

"I'm helping you. You need to stay away from social events and people for a minute before you get shunned completely. Otherwise, this will happen again. Now get your friends and get gone. I'll get this shit sorted out."

She walked away from me, her knee-high boots stomping into the carpet, and stopped in the middle of the crowd. "Gentleman, this is over," she announced, swinging around in her tight jeans and pointing to Dawson. "It's time for you guys to go." Without listening to his response, she turned to Reese. "And you, leave the room so they can get their shit together and leave. Go clean yourself up because all of you look like pathetic idiots."

Reese's friends scurried away like she was the queen giving orders. Reese slid his arm across his still bloody nose. "Show's over!" he called out to everyone.

"Let's fucking go, Tessa," Dawson yelled, swatting away his friends' hands to help him move. He used the arm of a chair to balance himself and began to walk out of the house. "My keys are in my pocket," he told Cody. Cody grabbed them and hopped into the driver's side.

"Help him in," he instructed us. Ollie came to my side, and we both lifted Dawson into the seat of the cab.

I rummaged in my pockets and pulled out my car keys when

Ollie snatched them from my hand. He looked over at Cody. "We'll take care of your car later. For now, get in."

I nodded, not knowing what else to do. I didn't want to leave Dawson. Ollie helped me into the cab before jumping in next to me.

"Holy shit!" Cody yelled, starting the truck and gunning the gas. "That shit was not cool."

Ollie snorted. "You think? Those dickheads straight jumped him."

Dawson stayed silent beside me. "I'm sorry," I whispered, trying to grab his hand, but he pulled away.

"Not now, Tessa," he snapped, looking straight ahead.

"Please don't hate me," I pleaded.

He shook his head. "I don't hate you. I hate what you've turned into, but I'll never hate you." I flinched at his words. That stung.

"Please ... just let me explain."

"There's no explaining shit. My head hurts like hell. Just stop." He couldn't even look at me, and I didn't miss the disgust on his face.

"You want me to stay at your house tonight, bro, or drop you off and bring your truck to you tomorrow?" Cody asked.

"Just drop me off at my house," Dawson answered, his voice flat. It was a punch to the gut each time we passed a streetlight and I got a glimpse of his battered face. Even after everything I'd put him through, he'd stuck up for me. I didn't deserve him. He deserved someone else, someone who wouldn't turn their back on him for a worthless loser, and someone who wasn't so fucked up in the head they didn't know right from wrong.

I'd done this to him.

I was breaking him because I couldn't fix myself.

CHAPTER 16

TESSA

I KILLED THE ENGINE OF MY CAR AND TOOK A DEEP BREATH.
Different scenarios played in my head about what was going to
happen today. I'd shut my phone off for the rest of the weekend
and stayed in my bedroom. Dawson had canceled plans with
Derrick, and I knew it was because he didn't want him to see his
battered face.

I walked through the parking lot and screeched when a white
sedan sped towards me, the tires squealing. I jumped to the side,
practically on top of a truck, and the car missed me only by a few
inches as a trail of dust followed it. The driver didn't stop or slow
down. I tried to get a good look at the driver or passengers, but
they'd moved too fast. I bowed my head down and went back on
my way, hoping that was an accident. It had to be. No one would
try to run me over me on purpose, would they?

I kept my head down on my way to my locker and hurriedly

dumped my things and grabbed what I needed. I wanted to get to class before anyone saw me. I clutched onto a book in pain when I was suddenly pushed into the door of my locker and the edge scraped into my arm.

"Seriously?" a girl snarled, stopping in front of me and resting her hands on her hips.

I blinked, trying to put a name to the face, but I didn't recognize her. "What?" I asked, rubbing my side.

"Seriously, you stupid bitch, your crazy ass gets kicked out of a party, and you decide to call the cops on everyone? You know what happens to narcs, don't you?"

I stumbled back. "What? I don't know what you're talking about," I said, noticing a few girls joining her side. Maya was one of them, giving me some relief that I had someone coming to my defense.

"That's what everyone is saying," Maya said. I felt my body overheating. "They're saying you hooked up with Reese, no strings attached, and you freaked out when you saw him with another girl. We all saw the fit you threw, then the fight with that other boy, and you got kicked out. Not ten minutes after you left the cops showed up. I thought you knew better than that." Okay, so she wasn't coming to my defense. She was blaming me too.

I shook my head. "I didn't call the cops."

Maya's face fell a little, but she didn't let up. "Seems sketchy, but who knows, maybe you didn't. I want to give you a heads up, though. Reese, Bobby, and some other people were arrested. Half of them were on probation and had drugs on them. Most of them had priors, which means they can't just be bailed out and they'll be in there for a minute. They and their girlfriends are ready to tear you apart."

They needed to blame someone, and they were putting that target on my back. I was the crazy girl who'd caused a scene, started a fight, and left in tears over a guy. Girls wanted payback, and that's what they thought I'd given Reese.

"I swear I went home and straight to bed," I said, my voice breaking. I was afraid of what tearing me apart meant, but it didn't sound good. "I didn't call the cops on anybody."

"Snitch bitch," a guy grumbled, pushing into me roughly as he walked by. "You should've died along with the rest of those kids."

I grabbed onto my locker and squeezed my eyes shut, praying to God I'd just imagined what he'd said. I shook my head and knew that was the truth. I wished I would've died with them ... with Tanner. I wouldn't be in this hell right now.

"Yeah dumb bitch, just because you open your legs up for a guy doesn't mean he's going to marry you," another commented.

"Go kill yourself," another girl added, not only bumping my side, but also turning around to snarl at me with two other girls.

"Angie!" Maya called, pushing the girl away from me. "That's not cool. Be mad at her, but don't say shit like that."

Angie shrugged her shoulders. "I'm grounded for two months because the cops called my parents to pick me up. I can't even go to the winter formal now."

"Angie, you and the rest of your follower cronies need to beat it and take your bullshit threats with you, you brainless bitches," Alexa said, joining my side and eyeing the girls standing in front of me.

"You don't have anything to do with this," Angie spat. "Why are you even sticking up for her? You know she was banging Reese, right?"

"I don't know what she was doing because I mind my own damn business," Alexa argued. "Now go." The girls scurried away. Damn, did everyone obey this girl's commands? Maya still stood awkwardly in front of us, not sure what to do. "And Maya, you know that shit's not cool."

Maya looked at me with regret. "I know," she said, looking down at the ground. "I'm sorry, but we can't be friends anymore. People will think I'm on your side, and Bobby will break up with me."

I nodded, not saying anything back.

Alexa sighed. "God, I hate bullies and the people who follow them. I swear, one gets mad at you, they send their entire army to do their dirty work." I looked over at her. Why was she helping me? I figured she'd be the first person to sign up for the Tessa hating parade. "Anyways, I'd stay incognito if I were you. Good luck." She patted my shoulder when the bell rang and walked away.

I slid down against my locker and fell down to the floor when the hallway cleared out. Taking a deep breath, I opened my legs, and my head fell in between them. What was happening to me? Why was my life turning upside down?

This was when I needed Tanner more than anything. He'd help me through this. I'd tell him what was going on, and he'd help me through it. Or set the people straight who'd been mean to me. But it didn't happen often. I'd had lots of friends at my old school, and I'd never witnessed people act this cruel.

"God," I hissed out to the floor. I smacked my palms against it and raised myself up. There was no way I was getting through the day here alive or at least without a few scratches. People were out for my blood today.

I walked down the hallway, pushing open a door, and headed to my car, but froze when I saw it. A scratch stretched from my driver's door to my trunk that could've only been done with a key. I got closer and saw the rest of the damage. The words *slut, whore, and snitch* were also written. I dragged my finger across *whore,* and a pink residue hit my finger. Nothing better than getting your car labeled with lipstick. At least it wasn't permanent.

I slammed my car door shut, drove it home with the lipstick labels, and parked it in my driveway. I stomped through the front door, going directly to the laundry room, and grabbed a cleaning bucket. Filling it up with water, I latched onto the handle and dumped it onto my car. The pink splotches were still there, but at least I'd gotten the words off. I set the bucket down onto the ground, threw down my phone I'd never bothered to turn back on down I reached my bedroom, and fell into my bed. I rummaged through my drawer and pulled out the prescription bottle with my name on it. I grabbed a few pills, shoved them down my throat, and washed them down with yesterday's water bottle. The medicine kicked in quickly, and I felt relief when my swollen eyes slowly shut, and I traveled to tranquility.

❧

"WHAT THE HECK HAPPENED TO YOUR CAR?" DERRICK asked, walking into my bedroom and waking me up.

"You need to learn how to knock," I grumbled, shoving my pillow over my head.

"What the heck happened to your car?" he repeated, sitting on the side of my bed. "And why are you in bed already? Are you sick or something?"

"Someone keyed it," I answered, shrugging my shoulders. "And yeah, I don't feel good."

"Someone keyed it?" he asked, eyes wide. "Don't you think you need to figure out who that someone is?"

"I don't care who it is." I was actually afraid to find out.

"Did it happen at school? Call them and tell them to look at the cameras."

"It doesn't matter." Even if I found out who exactly was responsible, it wouldn't fix anything. They'd only make my life more miserable if I turned them in. I'd already gotten a preview of it this morning; I didn't want to see how much worse it could get. I knew I had to call the insurance company and they'd make me get a police report, but I'd lie and say it happened somewhere else. Somewhere there weren't cameras. "I'm going to go back to sleep, but let me know if you need anything."

"Okay, feel better."

He left my room and shut the door behind him. I closed my eyes again and fought to go back to sleep, but my mind was racing. There was no way I could go back to school. They'd make my life a living hell. Would they find out it wasn't me? Did Reese hate me? Did everyone hate me?

My mind drifted back to Tanner, and I subconsciously began talking to him. *I need your help right now. So bad. You always knew how to help me.*

◌⁂◌

I woke up to a dark room. I vaguely remembered Tanner in my dreams telling me to come to home and he'd help me. I swung my hand over the side of the bed and felt around on my nightstand until I captured my phone. I groaned at the bright light hitting my eyes.

Six voicemails.

Forty-five text messages.

When did I suddenly become so popular?

I opened up the first text from an unknown number, and my hands shook as I read the words:

You're such a snitch bitch. I'd think twice about coming back to school.

I quickly closed out of it and opened a new one.

Wait until I see you around, you're going to regret it.

I knew it was a bad idea, but I opened up the rest of them. They all said the same things: kill myself, I was a snitch, and I better be afraid next time I leave my house. All of my voicemails were from unknown callers, and I wasn't even going to go there. I hesitated a moment, wondering if Dawson would answer if I called, but I was too scared to find out. He'd given up on me. He had every right to hate me.

My legs felt flimsy when I stepped out of bed and walked to my bathroom. I collapsed to the floor at the same time the sobs started. I stared blankly at the wall across from me with swollen eyes before bringing myself up to look in the mirror to see someone I didn't recognize.

I was nothing but a lost soul.

I crawled across the floor and opened the cabinet underneath the counter. I was at war with my own mind and allowing my stubbornness to take over my inner strength. I searched through the large compartment until I found what I was looking for. I set it down on the floor and went for the half-empty bottle of vodka I had stashed.

I twisted the knob to my bathtub. The mirrors reminded me of what a mess I'd become while I waited for the tub to fill. Stripping away my clothes, I tossed them onto the floor and sunk into the warm water. I was floating. The heat felt good, and I relaxed my head back. My hands slid out of the tub, fumbling for the package, and I set it down beside me. I grabbed the vodka and took a gulp before placing it back onto the floor and grabbing the package next to it.

It was time for a new one. I needed something fresher. I needed something sharper. I'd tried using alcohol to break my habit, but it wasn't working anymore. I needed something stronger. I needed something more permanent.

It took me a few minutes to open the package with my shaky hands. I ran my fingers along the sharp edges but didn't feel anything. I was becoming immune to the sensitivity. I snapped the razor from its holder and ran a finger across the blades again.

It still wasn't enough. I needed to feel completely numb and taken over. I needed the release.

I'd started cutting a month after Tanner died. I wasn't sure how it began, but it helped me. It started on my arms and wrists, but I moved to my thighs in fear of people noticing. I wore long sleeves everyday to hide my secret. I couldn't run a razor through my skin without leaving a mark, just like everything else. Loss, pain, suffering– they all leave a mark on us.

I raised my hand up in front of me and examined my palm and then the back of my wrist. Therein lied my secret. My vice. My parents used alcohol to cope, and I used my own self-destruction. I was the victim and the abuser. The scars weren't deep but they were there. The faint lines reminded me of every time I was weak. I massaged the skin, feeling the build-up of tissue, before gently slipping the razor back over my flesh.

I took a deep breath when I broke through the skin. Why wasn't I feeling anything? Where was the pain? Slicing through my skin didn't cause me pain, no; it gave me ecstasy like a drug coursing through my body. The feeling manifested through me as my remedy. I was cutting my emotions away. The blood would drain me of my hurt. I wanted to cut away the pain flowing through me and take myself to a better place. A place where I didn't lose everyone I loved.

I gasped at the blood falling into the water, washing it turn a light shade of pink, and sunk down deeper in the water, heat building up around my skin. I needed more. I drug the blade back over my skin but harder this time. The water beneath me began to grow darker the deeper I went.

My vision grew shaky as I eyed the blood seeping from my wrist. Everything began to slowly fade away. I was going to see him. He'd make me happy again. My head fell back as dark spots crept from the corner of my lids before my sight grew blurry. My breathing was labored, every exhale taking all of my energy, and I caught a glimpse of bright red before everything went black.

This is what I'd wanted.

This is what I'd craved.

This is what I'd planned.

I'd wanted all the pain to fade away.

And that's exactly what I was getting.

CHAPTER 17

DAWSON

THE RESONATING RINGING WOKE ME UP FROM MY DEEP slumber. I groaned, dragging an arm out from under my body, and stretched it across my bed in the darkness of my room. My fingers hit my nightstand next to me, and I scrambled around until I grasped the vibrating phone in my hand. I cringed at the loud noise and stuck it to my ear without checking the caller ID.

"This better be good," I grumbled into the speaker. I'd had a rough night. My body was still in pain from the ass beating I'd received from Reese and his friends, and I'd been popping ibuprofen every few hours.

"Dawson!" the frantic voice yelled from the other end, and I suddenly felt a large weight fall onto my chest. Something wasn't right.

I clutched the phone tightly in my hand. "What is it, Derrick?" I asked, suddenly becoming fully alert.

"It's Tessa," he answered quickly. "I found her in the bathroom. She's ..." He went silent. I took a deep breath, waiting for the news he was about to give me while praying it wasn't as bad as the thoughts running through my head. But I got nothing.

"She's what?" I rushed out impatiently.

"She's bleeding everywhere. I don't know what's wrong with her."

"Did you call 911?" I jumped out of my bed and flipped the light on while holding the phone up with the top of my shoulder. I grabbed a pair of dirty shorts from my floor and hurriedly slipped them over my legs with shaking hands.

"Yeah, they're on their way."

"Good job, buddy. I'll be there in a few, okay?" I threw on the first t-shirt I found and stuck my feet in my tennis shoes without even bothering to look for socks.

"Okay. I'm scared, Dawson. She's not moving or anything."

I rushed out my front door, nearly losing my footing in the process as rain poured down on me, and hopped into the seat of my truck. I sped down the street while shutting the door and slammed my foot onto the gas pedal. I didn't follow the speed limit as I gripped my hands against the steering wheel while the windshield wipers squeaked back and forth.

An ambulance was parked in front of the house when I pulled up. Their red and blue lights flashed through the chilly night and lit up the entire block. I jumped out of my truck with the engine still running and waited for the EMTs to get through the front door before storming up the stairs.

The purple bedroom was crowded with paramedics, firefighters, and medical equipment. Derrick was sitting on the edge of her bed, his head bowed, and he played with his hands in his lap. Her dad was across from him at the front of the room pacing back and forth as he muttered to himself. I looked around the room for Lorraine, their mom, but she was nowhere in sight.

I took a few steps forward and peeked into the bathroom while being careful not to get in anyone's way. Bile swept its way up my throat, and I swallowed it down as my heart thudded against my chest. Medics shuffled around the space, sometimes bumping into each other, and I caught a glimpse of Tessa's nude, limp body lying on the white tiled floor. A faint red color that resembled blood dripped from her wrist. I looked to the right and noticed the bathtub filled with crimson-colored water.

"Is she dead?" I asked to no one in particular.

I held my breath, waiting for the answer. Darryl continued his pacing, and Derrick stayed silent on the bed. My fear turned into anger, and I kicked my feet against the carpet to hold myself back from charging towards her dad. I wanted to scream at him and to make him feel the pain that Tessa had felt when she'd done that to herself. I wanted the guilt to eat at him every single day if I lost her. I pinched the bridge of my nose and managed to keep my cool. I needed to focus on Tessa, not him. I'd save him for later.

"Is she dead?" I asked again.

"She's still breathing," a voice called out from the bathroom. "And we're trying our best to keep it that way."

"What the hell happened?" I asked Derrick.

"I don't know," he answered, his face pale. "I was up late watching TV and realized she hadn't come down to tell me to get to bed. She always tells me what to do. So I went upstairs to see if she was feeling better, but her room was empty. I noticed the bathroom door half open, so I peeked inside." He shut his eyes and took a deep breath. "She was in the bathtub with her eyes shut. There was so much blood. I tried calling her name, but she wasn't moving."

He'd been the one who'd found her. That pissed me off. He needed to be shielded from this shit. I knew what it felt like growing up with an unstable family and how it haunted you the rest of your life. You may grow up, but you don't forget about that shit. "He paused and shook his head nervously.

"I'm sorry you had to see that," I said, joining his side and pulling him in for a hug. I moved my attention to the EMTs. They worked bandages around her skinny wrist, confirming what I was afraid of.

She'd tried to kill herself. This girl, who'd been so full of life, had decided to end hers. She'd looked so forward to every day with a light of radiance shining around her, but each day it dimmed until she finally decided to pull the plug and let it go black.

They strapped her onto a stretcher and lifted it up into the air. "Everyone step aside," a medic demanded. I followed them down the stairs and outside. Thunder rumbled, and lightning crackled as they hurriedly put her in the ambulance. Streetlights dimmed, and I noticed neighbors standing outside their houses, huddled underneath umbrellas. I grinded my teeth and flipped them off when I got back into my truck. Nosy assholes.

"Please God, let her be okay," I whispered into the emptiness of my cab as I followed the ambulance and rain streaked my windows. I ran through the red lights, stop signs, and kept at their speed. I cried out, smacking my hands against the cold steering wheel in anger and frustration. I blinked as the tears fell down my cheeks.

I wasn't a crier. I didn't cry when my dad got his prison sentence. I was only twelve, but I knew what was going on. There were only two times I could remember crying: Tanner's funeral and tonight. Tanner's death crushed me, but if I lost Tessa, it would do more than that. It would completely obliterate me.

I swerved into the emergency parking lot, got out of my truck, and stormed through the deserted area.

"Can I help you?" an older woman asked when I walked in.

"I'm here for they girl they just brought in the ambulance," I answered.

She nodded and began typing her wrinkled fingers against the keyboard. "I don't have anything yet, honey, but as soon as they know they'll send a nurse out here to update you."

"Thanks." I turned around and found Derrick and Darryl walking in, dripping wet.

"Have you heard anything?" Darryl asked, joining my side. I stepped away from the counter and took a few steps into the nearly empty waiting room. There were chairs, but only a few were taken with people sitting around reading magazines and watching the small TV perched up in the corner.

"No, not yet," I answered, and he flopped down into a chair.

I took the chance to finally take a good look at him. He looked like hell, was in need of a good shave and haircut, and the scent of alcohol covered him. Nausea swirled in my stomach when I realized he'd been driving with Derrick while he was loaded with liquor. I clenched my fist and glared at him. I'd looked up to this guy for years, and I felt every bit of that respect washing away.

We all turned around when the ER door opened, and a young woman walked out wearing blue scrubs with an RN badge connected to her top. She glanced around the room before focusing her eyes on us.

"Are you with the girl they just brought in?" she asked, taking the few steps to us.

Darryl nodded and got up, thankfully without stumbling. "I'm her father."

"She's in critical condition," she said. "The lacerations were pretty deep, which caused her to lose a large amount of blood. She's been stitched up and will most likely be admitted."

"So what's going to happen to her?" I asked.

"Things are looking up," she answered. "We have a fantastic doctor working with her. I need you to fill out paperwork for us while you're waiting, and we'll be sure to keep you updated on her condition."

"Can we see her?" Derrick asked shyly.

She shook her head. "Not at the moment, but as soon as it's okay, I'll let you know." She gave us a sincere smile before disappearing back through the doors.

"What the hell happened to your face?" Derrick asked, sitting back down while Darryl went to pick up the paperwork.

"I got into a fight," I answered, sitting next to him.

"Did you win?"

I pointed to the fading bruises around my eyes. "Not exactly."

"I thought she was dead when I found her," he whispered.

I patted his leg. "It's going to be okay."

"Do you think she really tried to kill herself?"

"I don't know."

"I hope not," he said, his voice cracking. "I saw her car and tried to talk to her. But she said she wanted to be left alone, so I went downstairs. I knew she was sad. I knew it. I should've stayed with her, made her hang out with me, something."

I looked over at him with a serious face. "Don't you dare try to blame yourself for this." He was the last person that needed to feel condemned. I looked over at Darryl. He was on the blame list. He wasn't the only one, but his name was scribbled near the top. So was mine. I'd told her I was done with her. I should've tried harder to get her to talk to me. "What was wrong with her car?"

"It looked like someone keyed it," Derrick answered.

"Someone keyed her car?" Darryl asked, looking up from the paperwork. "When did this happen?"

"Yesterday or earlier. I'm not sure since it's early in the morning or late at night."

"Who did it?" Darryl and I asked at the same time.

Derrick shrugged. "She wouldn't say."

"Damnit," I hissed under my breath. I'd work on figuring that out later, but I had a hunch it was those evil bitches at school. They were another name on that list. I'd heard they were giving her a hard time about that party. I wasn't sure what it was about, but I'd heard whispers and gossip during class. "Where's your mom?"

"She stayed in her bedroom. She wouldn't even come out," Derrick replied.

Fuck. They weren't kidding when they said their parents were out of it.

❧

WHAT FELT LIKE AN ETERNITY PASSED WHILE WE WAITED for any news. I'd picked up some magazines to try and occupy my time, but my mind wouldn't stop racing. I'd overheard Darryl talking to Lorraine, but she never showed.

We all stood up when the doctor came out. He shook Darryl's hand and introduced himself.

"She's stable," he started. "She lost some blood, and we had to perform a small transfusion. Her vitals are fine, and we've stitched up the lacerations, but we are going to admit her for a few days to be sure she doesn't get an infection and the transfusion was successful. I highly recommend she be admitted into a mental health facility upon release." Darryl nodded in agreement. "I'll have a nurse provide you with some additional information."

"Okay, thank you, doctor," he said.

"The nurse will take you to see her if you'd like. I suggest you go easy on her for right now. I know you have plenty of questions you'd like to ask, but let her rest and recover." He fetched a card from his shirt pocket and handed it to Darryl. "Here's my card. Give me a call if you need anything."

"He doesn't want us to ask questions, but I'd like to know what the hell is going on," Darryl said when the doctor left. He looked over at me. "Why would she do this? I can't believe she'd do this to her mother. We're already dealing with losing Tanner."

"You're kidding, right?" Derrick answered before I had the chance to. "Have you been paying attention to us at all? You know, your children that are still alive." Darryl winced at the word *alive*. "Have you even noticed my sister, your daughter, is falling apart? She's practically a walking ad for depression."

His eyebrows scrunched together. "What do you mean?"

"She spends all of her time in her bedroom or hanging out with that pierced lip douchebag."

"Pierced lip douchebag?" Darryl questioned.

"Jesus Christ," I muttered. They didn't even know she was staying out all night with random guys.

"If she's hanging out with bad people, then why aren't you stopping it, Dawson?" he asked me.

"Why aren't I stopping it?" I fired back. "Maybe because her parents need to be there to stop it. Maybe because she feels like she's alone. I've tried talking to her. I've tried helping her. But I can't be the only one. It takes more than one person to make her whole. It's time to do your part."

Darryl's face burned as sweat began to build up around his hairline. "I've been doing my part. Don't tell me how to raise my daughter; you hear me?"

I held up my hand. "Look, don't get worked up. We don't need to be fighting and causing more stress for her. Let's be sane for Tessa, but you need to work it out. Next time, Derrick may not find her, or it will be too late." The thought of her actually succeeding sent chills up my spine and tingles through my chest. I hated even saying those words, but he needed a reality check.

"I'll always be there for my daughter," he replied, guilt bleeding through his face.

I shook my head and leaned back into my chair. I wasn't going to argue with him. I just needed to get to Tessa.

I STOOD TO THE SIDE OF THE ROOM AND ALLOWED DARRYL and Derrick to see Tessa first. They'd transferred her from the emergency floor to a room upstairs. Derrick grabbed her hand while Darryl stood to the side and stared at her sleeping body. He didn't talk. He didn't touch her. His eyes just bore down at her. I couldn't read him. He finally bent down, kissed her forehead, and walked out of the room without saying another word.

I made my way to the bed, and Derrick yawned loudly when he flopped down in the chair next to the bed. "You need to get home and get some sleep," I told him. "I'll text Ollie and have him take you and your dad home."

"Why can't my dad drive?" he asked.

"He's been drinking."

His eyes grew wide. Either he didn't notice, or he didn't want anyone else to know. I was going with the latter.

"I can't leave her," he said.

"She'll be okay. She's going to be sleeping for a while. When she wakes up, I'll call you and get you a ride up here." I grabbed my phone and texted Ollie. I'd called him earlier, telling him the situation, and he said he'd wait up in case I needed anything.

"You promise?" Derrick asked.

I looked away from my phone and up at him. "I promise. Ollie will be outside waiting for you in a few minutes."

He looked at Tessa one more time and leaned down to kiss her cheek before giving me a wave and scurrying out of the room. I sat down in his abandoned chair and grabbed her hand, pressing my lips against the chilliness of her skin. Her skin was pale, making her look drained and lifeless. I cringed at her gaunt appearance, the hair tangled in every direction, and her skinny frame.

"I'm going to fix this. I'm going to bring you back to life and make you happy again," I whispered into the brisk room while machines beeped around me. I slid out of the chair, grabbed a blanket from the couch sitting in the corner of the room in front of a single window, and re-joined her side. It had been a long night, and I knew it was far from being over.

CHAPTER 18

TESSA

I BLINKED, FIGHTING THE BRIGHT LIGHT SHINING THROUGH the small window across the room, and looked around in confusion. What the hell? I glanced around the unfamiliar room. The white walls were bare with a dry erase board on the back of a door, and a poster asking me about pain levels was across from me. I shivered as a cold breeze smacked into me and snuggled into my thin blanket.

A TV hung from the wall with a reality show on mute as an annoying machine beeped beside me. I didn't notice the IVs connected to my arm until I raised them up to rub my pounding head. My stomach knotted, and my head fell back when I saw it. The thick, white bandage wrapped around my wrist brought all of the memories back to me in a rush.

I'd done it.

The demons in my head had won, but they'd tricked me. They didn't take me to Tanner. They'd kept me in hell.

I'd tried to kill myself. God, just saying the words in my head made me sick to my stomach. My eyes closed while I remembered taking the razor and watching it slide against my skin until it was decorated with color. How could I have been so stupid? I was embarrassed, shocked, and a little disappointed that I'd failed. Were people supposed to be happy when they were saved from a suicide attempt? Or were they supposed to feel like total failures? Should I be happy I was here instead of sitting in the morgue, lifeless? I wasn't sure.

I'd told the nurse I didn't want any visitors when she found me awake. Apparently, she didn't care what I wanted because a few minutes later my parents came walking through the door. My mom was in pink pajama pants with her hair pulled into a bun at the top of her head. Her face was swollen from crying. She took a long look at me, her puffy eyes growing wide, and bolted out of the room. My dad stayed a few minutes, tucking his hands into the pockets of his pants, and just stared.

I stayed silent, not sure what to say, until he slowly came toward me. He kissed me on the cheek, whispered he was sorry, and then left the room. I blew out a harsh breath.

They'd never understand. How much pain did you need to go through before realizing you'd never be okay? They knew how I felt. They were using alcohol to mask their pain; drinking themselves away. Their death would come, but it would come slower. Their suffering would be longer and more drawn-out. I wanted the quickest way out. I'd figured out alcohol and Reese weren't working. I needed instant gratification, and I thought the razor would do that. I'd come up short.

I was terrified to see Dawson. I knew he wouldn't be turned away. He'd fight his way into my room, throw a couple of punches, or sneak through my window if he had to.

My elbows pressed into my side, and I tried to hide my wrist when he walked in. I was sure he knew why I was in there, but I didn't want him to see the evidence. I didn't want him to know how messed up in the head I was. He stared down at me, and I waited for him to say something.

"You want to talk about it?" he finally asked, pinching the skin at his throat.

I bowed my head down. "No," I replied in a weak voice.

"You're going to, now or later. You're going to talk about it. It doesn't have to be me, or your parents, or anyone you know. It can be with a therapist, a stranger, anyone, but you're going to talk about it. There's no more harboring it and hiding. You're going to let it all out, baby, so you can start to heal."

His words triggered something in me. I'd been waiting for someone to say those words. I'd been waiting for someone to tell me how much they cared ... how much they wanted me to be whole again.

I cleared my throat and watched him take a seat next to me. "I ached in parts of myself I didn't even know I had," I said. "It didn't matter how many times I told myself it would get better or how many drinks I sucked down to help me forget. I would still go to bed every night feeling the pain. I'd lay there for hours wondering if I'd ever be happy again and fighting with myself for the answer."

A single tear dripped down my face. "It was like I had good and bad running through me. I had a devil on my shoulder, telling me to cut away my pain, or it would last forever. And an angel on the other side insisting I give it time and things would work out on its own. That someday I could numb myself enough that I wouldn't feel it anymore. But the longer it took, the dimmer that angel's list got until she eventually faded away. And that devil was jumping up and down in his victory. I was being punished for not helping Tanner. No one else saw the hell I was in. I felt hopeless."

He leaned forward and tried to grab my hand, but I pulled away so he wouldn't see the bandages. "Baby, you're going to feel the pain of losing Tanner forever, and we both know there was nothing you could've done to save him. You have too much to live for, and it would kill us if you were gone as much as it killed you losing Tanner. That's selfish." I shook my head. "Are you kidding me? You can't take that beautiful smile away from the world. You can't take that caring heart away from everyone. You're the glue for your family. Even Tanner knew that. We can't lose you. We want you here, demons, flaws, and all."

He grabbed my hand quickly before I had the chance to pull away. I winced at the pain, and he immediately loosened his grip. "Why didn't you tell me?" he asked, looking at the bandage.

"Because I'm fucked up, Dawson. I'm fucked up in the head, and it's embarrassing. I see you all the time, and you're coping fine. I saw you at the party with those girls who were happy. That's what you deserve. I'm tainted. I'm a emotional mess, and I'll always be this way. I can never make you happy. I'm the suicidal girl who can't deal with her own problems."

He kept my hand in his. "You're not fucked up." I gave him a look. "Sure, you've got some shit to sort out, but everyone's got their demons, baby. I'd rather be with someone who can share them with me than let them explode later. You're not that suicidal girl. You're the girl who attempted to do it because she felt like she had no other options. Actions don't label you. After this, you'll be the girl who ate dinner or the girl who watched TV. You're not tainted, you're not fucked up, and you're going to get better. And there's no one else I'd want to fight demons with more than you."

CHAPTER 19

DAWSON

I LEFT TESSA'S ROOM AND SLUMPED DOWN IN A CHAIR IN the waiting room. My head dropped down between my knees, and I covered it with my hands while trying to shake off the headache pounding through my skull.

"Dawson," a soft voice said, breaking me from my trance, and I slowly raised my head.

"Nice of you to finally show up," I snarled, leaning back against the chair and crossing my arms across my chest.

It was an asshole thing to say. I knew it. I was being an asshole to everyone who played a part in Tessa's unhappiness. I knew Daisy lived in Atlanta, so it had to have taken her hours to get here, but I didn't give a fuck at the moment. I didn't want to tell her about what Tessa did, especially since she didn't bother to tell her she was moving thousands of miles away, but I figured seeing her would lift Tessa's spirits. That's all I cared about.

Daisy looked better than when I last saw her before she left. We had a falling out during Tanner's funeral, and we haven't talked much since then. Anger built up inside of me when I looked over to see a guy sitting down next to her.

What the fuck?

"And you already have a new boyfriend. That was pretty fucking quick," I spat.

Tanner had been her first and only boyfriend here. They'd constantly talk about marriage and how many kids they were going to have. Tanner had even brought up that he was planning on proposing after graduation. How could she have moved on so quickly?

The dude jumped up from his chair and barreled towards me. "Hey, asshole, what the fuck is your problem?" His face was red, and I noticed the clenched fists at his side. Everyone's attention in the room turned to us to see if a fight was about to happen.

"Dude, I have no problem with you. Just be careful with this one." I tilted my head towards Daisy, who was staring at me in shock. "She treats people who care about her like total fucking shit. I wouldn't even put myself in that predicament if I were you, man. Just giving you a heads up." It was a low blow, but I needed to get my anger out, and they were just there at the wrong time.

"I'm sorry, Dawson," she whispered, truly looking that way.

I wasn't the one she needed to apologize to. I wasn't the best friend she turned her back on and left. "I don't want your apology. Today isn't about you for once, okay? This is about Tessa and her accident."

"Accident?" she asked, looking at me baffled. "She tried to kill herself. That is not an accident."

I pulled myself up from my chair. Maybe I was wrong calling her here? "Don't try to talk to her about that shit tonight. If you would've stayed around or at least answered her phone calls, you'd understand that Tessa hasn't been in the right state of mind lately, so it was an accident. She's in room two eleven if you want to see her. If you do, don't fucking upset her more." I moved around her new guy's large frame, stalked across the room, and smacked open the door to the stairway.

CHAPTER 20

TESSA

DAWSON STAYED AT MY SIDE FOR HOURS, AND WE WATCHED TV in silence. He interlaced our fingers and would occasionally swipe his thumb across my bandage. He moved out of the way when a nurse would come to check on me, but as soon as they were finished, he was right there again.

After awhile, my eyes started to feel droopy, and I let my exhaustion take over. He was gone when I woke up, and I hoped I hadn't been dreaming of him here. I pulled the blanket further up my body and looked up at the TV at the same time a knock came from the open door. I stayed still, expecting Dawson to come around the white curtain that blocked my view of the hallway, but my heart skipped a beat when I saw her.

"Hi," she said nervously, fidgeting with her hands while slowly walking into the room and sitting down. I blinked, certain the meds they had me on were giving me hallucinations. I'd tried calling her a few times after she'd left for Atlanta but got nothing. I'd finally given up after two weeks. I didn't have anything to say to my best friend who'd abandoned me. I'd been there for her every time she needed me, but she couldn't return the favor.

I focused my eyes on the TV and ignored her. Why was she here? I didn't want her to be here. She needed to leave me the hell alone like she had for months. She couldn't come in here after ignoring me and want to act like she was worried now that I'd hit rock bottom. That's not how friendships worked.

"What happened?" she asked.

I finally turned my head to take a good look at her. She looked good – like she was starting to get back to her old self. She'd gained weight, had her hair brushed, and was even wearing some makeup.

"I tried to kill myself, obviously," I spat out angrily. Maybe she'd leave if I acted like a total bitch.

She winced at my hostility. "I know that, but why?"

"I just couldn't deal with it anymore," I explained, raising my IV-covered hand and rubbing my temples to ward off a headache. "It just became too much for me to handle."

She looked at me sharply. "You couldn't deal with it anymore?" I knew my old best friend well enough to know when she was about to go on a tangent, and she was about to go on a tangent. "I didn't want to deal with it, either, but you can't just go off yourself because you can't deal with real life anymore. That's not how it works."

I crossed my arms across my chest and rolled my eyes. She had no idea what I'd been going through. "Whatever," I muttered in exhaustion.

She shook her head at me. "I'm serious! There are so many people that love you, and it would kill us to lose you too."

She'd hit a nerve. "Screw you, Daisy!" I screeched, pointing at her. "Not everyone can run away from their problems and leave their best friend. I had no one here for me!"

She looked at me like she'd taken a slap to the face. "I'm sorry," she said, sadness in her voice. "That was insensitive of me."

"For which part?"

"Everything," she answered, surprising me. "For leaving without saying goodbye, ignoring you, and for what I just said. I'm sorry." A small tear dropped down her face, and she pushed it away with her finger quickly.

I took a deep breath. "My twin was gone, then I lost you, too. My parents are practically catatonic. They just move around like freaking zombies everywhere, refusing to take care of Derrick and me. I felt so damn alone, and I wanted to be with him." It was as of a load had been broken off my shoulder at my confession. They drooped as a sob tore through my chest. "I knew he could make me feel better."

She nodded in understanding. "I know it sounds easier, but think of everyone it would hurt if you did that. Your parents, your little brother who depends on you, me."

I sighed loudly. "I know."

A nurse knocked on the door before walking in and looking between the two of us. "Sorry to interrupt, but visiting hours are over," she informed, coming to my side and checking my vitals.

Daisy nodded. "Thank you for coming," I whispered to her. "Even if we only had a few minutes, I was hoping you would."

"Me too," she said, sending me a shy wave and walking out of the door.

I was happy she'd visited, but it still wasn't the same. We didn't hug or laugh like old times, but it was better than nothing.

The nurse handed me a few pills before asking if I needed

anything. I shook my head, and watched her leave when the phone rang. Derrick had left his phone for me in case I needed anything. Dawson lied and said he couldn't find mine. I knew he didn't want me to see all of the hurtful texts and calls that were still coming. I looked down at Dawson's name flashing across the screen, and a tiny smile spread across my face.

"Hey," I answered, putting the phone to my ear.

"Hey babe, everything going okay?" he asked. "I'm sitting in the parking lot about to head home, but wanted to know if you needed anything before I left?"

"No, I'm good, thanks. I guess visiting hours are over."

"Did everything go okay?"

"With what?"

"Daisy."

"It did."

"Good. I want you to know I texted her and told her you were in the hospital, but no one forced her to come. It pissed me off when she left, but she still cares about you, Tess. Don't forget that. We all care about you. You're not alone."

"Thanks," I muttered. I was beginning to get that now. I should've earlier, but my thoughts had been taken over by my hurt from losing Tanner, my anger towards my parents, and my weakness to latch onto anything that would make me feel better.

"Now get some sleep, beautiful. I'll be up there in the morning. Call me if you need anything."

"Goodnight," I said.

I tried to get as comfortable in the bed as I could after hanging up and shut my eyes, but my mind was racing. I was terrified of what the next day was going to bring. There would be questions that I wasn't ready to answer yet. People thought I was crazy ... psychotic ... unstable. I could tell from the way they looked at me, and the pity looks from the nurses only hurt worse.

I'd overheard my doctor discussing transferring me to a mental inpatient mental health facility upon release.

There was no way that was happening. No way in fucking hell.

CHAPTER 21

TESSA

I was released from the hospital three days later.

Daisy had visited me once more, along with her parents, which was slightly awkward. Dawson showed every day, but my parents were nonexistent. They were probably drowning themselves in bottles of liquor instead of thinking about their child in the hospital.

Dawson wouldn't answer my questions about whether people were talking about me at school, or if they even knew. He'd only shrug and say it didn't matter before changing the subject or the TV channel.

I was being transferred to the mental health facility today. I'd tried to fight it, but there was nothing I could do. I wasn't a legal adult yet, so my parents held all the power, and shipping me away was easier than coming to terms with what I'd done.

The doctor lectured me on destruction of self-harm and how

difficult it was to break yourself away from it. It was easy to relapse. Cutting wasn't like a drug that could've gotten taken away or tested for. It was something that was disposable at all times; a razor, scissors, or a curling iron. The thought of going to a psychiatric ward scared the living shit out of me. As much as I wanted to jump out of the window and make a run for it, I knew I'd never get better on my own. I'd go home, be well for a few days, but as soon as something went bad, he was right, I'd probably go back to cutting. There was no way around it. I didn't know how else to deal with my problems. So I'd agreed to go and prayed I wouldn't regret it.

There was one advantage of deciding to go. It would delay me going back to school. They'd labeled me *a tattle-telling whore* before. I could've only imagined what they were saying about me post suicide attempt. I was sure it was something along the lines of *wrist-slitting suicide bitch who'd been admitted and also liked to call the cops to get people in trouble because she was a slut.*

Oh, what a lovely reputation to have.

"Special delivery," Dawson called out. He came into the room with a duffel bag strapped to shit shoulder and a bowl of food in his hand. He set the bag onto the chair and handed over the bowl. My mouth instantly watered at the beautiful sight of biscuits and gravy.

"Thank you," I say, opening up the bowl and taking a large bite. "You packed a bag for me?"

He smiled at me proudly. "I sure did, and I think I did a pretty kickass job at it."

"Did my mom help you?"

"Nope, I told her I could handle it."

I could tell he was covering up the fact that my mom probably didn't even offer to help him. "Please tell me you didn't go through my panty drawer?"

He grinned, and I threw a napkin at him. "I didn't think

you'd want to run around commando, so yes, I did, and you have a very nice collection, I might add."

I flipped him off. "Very funny, perv." I tried to think of the last time I'd done laundry, hoping there were a few decent pairs in there.

"That's a compliment, babe. I think I got everything you'll need. They gave me a list yesterday. I figured you'd want to be comfortable, so I packed some sweat pants, t-shirts, and sweaters. I grabbed your hair and body stuff from your shower, but I couldn't bring any heated products." His eyes left me and looked down at the floor.

"That's fine, I understand." The Dawson I knew could barely pack a bag when the football team went away on weekend games, let alone an entire week for a girl.

"Oh, and some make-up, I'm not sure if I got everything you needed, but I tried."

"Thank you," I said, taking another bite and groaning. "God, this tastes so much better than the hospital food they've been feeding me." He gave me a look. "Okay, fine, what little hospital food I've had." Dawson had snuck me up food for almost every meal so I wouldn't have to eat the freezer burned cheeseburgers and cold mashed potatoes.

"Derrick wanted to be here, but I told him he couldn't miss school," he said.

"What about my parents?" I asked. "Do they need to be here with me when I get discharged?"

He shook his head and ran his hands through his hair. "They were up here earlier when you were sleeping and signed your release forms because they have prior commitments."

I rolled my eyes. "Of course they do." I was sure they had prior commitments with a bottle named Jack.

He clapped his hands. "But, I told them I'd take great care of you." His thin lips gave me a smile.

"You're taking me?" I asked, shocked. I wasn't sure how the process worked. "They're not taking me in an ambulance or a van with padded walls or something?"

"You need to quit watching so many movies. Yes, I'm taking you."

I looked down in shame. I hated him seeing me like this. I'd been in love with Dawson since freshman year, even when I was with Reese, deep down I still wanted him. I fought it, but no matter what, when I went to bed at night, he was the one I thought of. So him seeing me like this was embarrassing.

"So get dressed whenever you're finished eating, and we'll head out," he added.

I finished my food knowing that security in my new place probably wasn't going to allow Dawson to sneak me in some tacos. I pulled myself out of the uncomfortable, lumpy bed and grabbed the bag from the chair slowly. I cringed, feeling a deep pain in my wrist when I lifted it and started walking towards the bathroom to get dressed. I shook my head when Dawson asked if I needed a nurse to help me.

I grabbed the first articles of clothing I found and didn't bother to look through the bag. I glanced in the mirror before heading out and noticed how terrible I looked. I'd taken a shower yesterday, but I didn't have a blow dryer or anything, so my hair looked like a rat's nest. Circles gathered underneath my vacant eyes, and my skin looked clammy. My reflection was gross. Never in my life had I felt so ugly. I was finally noticing what a mess I actually was.

"Ready to go?" Dawson asked when I walked back into the room.

"They're really going to let you take me?" I asked, skeptically. "Aren't they scared I'll like skip town or something?"

He laughed. "Tessa, you're not a convict on your way to prison."

"Pretty much," I grumbled.

"The doctors said you agreed to get help." He wrapped his arm around my waist. "They didn't peg you as a runner, plus I can outrun you." He carefully grabbed my hand, and I didn't miss the way his fingers brushed against my bandages. I looked up at him, and he gave me a small smile. He grabbed my bag with his free hand and led us to the elevators. "I'll come visit you." We stayed silent on the way down to the first floor, and I fidgeted nervously. He helped me into his truck before getting in and taking off down the road. "Everything is going to be okay."

"Do you know how long I'm going to be there for?" I asked, biting my fingernails nervously.

"Your parents said possibly a week or two. It depends on how well you make progress."

"Oh."

His palm cupped my knee. "Which I'm sure you'll do in great."

"Does everyone think I'm crazy?" He shook his head. "Be honest."

"The people that matter don't, and no one gives a shit what the others think." His hand moved to grab my hand, and he kissed it softly. "You've been going through a rough time, we understand. I just wish we could've gotten you help before this happened. You scared the shit out of me, so no more, okay?"

"It won't happen again." I hoped so.

"Damn straight it won't. You start to feel like you want to cut, call me. I'll come over, I'll talk to you, I'll just sit there with you while you deal, but you call me."

I nodded in response. The fear that I was about to be admitted was growing stronger with every passing mile.

We pulled up to a normal-looking one-story brick building. There were no bars to block people from escaping through the windows, or electric fences to shock the runners. Crazy people weren't running around the yard or planting their faces against the windows mouthing, "*Help me!*" It looked like a doctor's office or a nursing home.

Yeah, he was right. I'd seen *way* too many movies.

"If you need anything, anything at all, you call me. I'm going to put my name on the list. I'm so proud of you for doing this," he said, killing the ignition and settling back against the ripped seat.

A tear trailed down my face. "Why are you proud of me? I'm a coward, a freak, and I'm headed to the nuthouse."

"No, you're not."

More tears released. "Yes, I am. I tried to kill myself. I'm mentally fucked up, Dawson." How many times did I have to explain this to him?

"You're not fucked up. You have some issues, and you're getting it taken care of. If you didn't get help, it would get worse, and then you would become mentally fucked up. It's not unnatural for you to feel this way. You're depressed, and we need to make you better." Was I depressed? I'd never wanted to say that about myself. I was empty, and I'd been lying to myself. I tried to believe that sucking down booze and being with Reese was the right coping mechanism. I'd used them both to block out the irrational, self-destructing feelings – because you can't feel like shit if you feel nothing.

"Depression isn't something to be embarrassed about; you hear me?"

I scoffed. "Says the guy who's not depressed."

A sympathetic look crossed his face. "They'll give you medicine to help. It's a chemical imbalance in the brain. It doesn't mean you're weak."

"Meds?" I covered my face with my sweaty palms. "Dead God, I truly am crazy."

"There's no difference between someone taking a pill for high blood pressure, or any other medical condition, and someone taking one for depression. Your body, or brain, isn't producing properly, so the medicine will help that." He opened a plastic bag sitting in the middle of us and handed over my favorite candy bar. "Now eat up. I don't think they're going to be so lenient on me sneaking you in the good shit."

I chuckled lightly, unwrapped the candy bar, and ate it hurriedly.

๏๛๏

THEY WOULDN'T LET DAWSON PAST THE FRONT DESK, GIVING me an even bigger desire to flee. The thought of going through this alone terrified me. I had courage with Dawson by my side, handing over candy bars, and giving me words of encouragement, but alone? That was a different story.

"I'll find out when I can visit, and I'll be here at the first opportunity," he told me. He strapped my bag over my shoulder, pulled me forward, and kissed me on the cheek. "You'll be fine."

I nodded, unable to hold back the tears as reality sunk in. I was getting institutionalized. Sure, it was temporary, but that didn't stop me from feeling like I was a lunatic. A year ago, I would've laughed in someone's face if they'd told me this was going to happen. It's crazy how your entire world can fall apart when you lose someone you love. Everything you believed about yourself, all of the strengths you thought you had, was truly tested.

I waved goodbye to him as a short and plump woman wearing a long skirt and jacket waited on me with a clipboard in her hand. I followed her through a set of double doors, pulling my bag tightly against my stomach, and tried my hardest to shut-up the devil telling me to make a run for it. She stopped at a shut door, and I followed her inside. The room was small with only a computer sitting on a small desk and a chair sitting next to it.

She grabbed my bag from me and threw it onto the desk. The sound of the zipper being pulled down made me jump. "Do you have any sharp items in here? Pills, drugs, anything of that nature?" she asked.

I shook my head, playing with the ends of my hair and shuffling my feet against the tiled floor. "No, not that I know of. I didn't pack it."

She shuffled through the bag and checked everything to make sure I wasn't attempting to smuggle anything in. "Have a seat." I did as I was told. "How are you feeling?"

"Uh, okay." I was actually terrified.

"Do you feel like harming yourself or anybody else?" I shook my head, biting into my lip nervously. "Good. It's only standard procedure for me to ask you these questions."

"Got it," I muttered.

We went through all the required questions before we left the room and I followed her down a long hallway. I looked in every direction taking in the people. Some were sitting around a table chatting. Others watched TV or were reading. Everything seemed sane so far.

She turned around the corner and stopped in front of an open door. "This is you."

My feet felt heavy as I walked into the room. It was definitely different than what I'd imagined. The walls were white, but not padded. There were no restraints on the two twin-size beds or tools to perform a lobotomy. Everything looked, well, normal.

I examined the beds. The one closest to the door had a white blanket spread across it with a single pillow. My gaze moved to the one by the window. A bright pink comforter was laid out with a stuffed unicorn propped up against the pillow. Unless that was how they welcomed new patients, I had a feeling I was going to have a roommate. And that wasn't a good feeling.

I gulped and set my bag down onto the white bed.

"Let me know if you need anything," the woman said. I turned around, forgetting she was even there, and nodded before she disappeared.

I unzipped my bag and began dragging clothes out. Dawson had done a pretty decent job. He'd packed comfortable clothes like he'd said. I found myself grinning and running my hands over the soft fabric of the oversized sweatshirt with *Thomas* scrawled across the back. Dawson's football number was stitched underneath it. He'd been telling me he wanted it back for the past year, but I lied and told him I lost it. He probably wouldn't have taken it from me anyways. He'd thrown a few books and magazines in there. I started putting things away when I noticed something drop onto the floor. I slowly bent down and picked up a folded paper with my name written across it before opening it up.

Tessa,

I hope they don't confiscate this letter before you get the chance to read it. If it did get confiscated and you're the person who took it, it would be pretty shitty not to let her read it. Just saying.

I know I told you I'll always be here for you. I want you to know I meant every word of that. Every single word. You're not going through this alone, and there's nothing, nothing you could ever do that would make you lose me. Nothing. You're not crazy. You're Tessa, who's dealing with some shit so she can go back to the amazing person she is.

You're my forever. You're my always. The sadness you're feeling, it's only temporary. I'll help you feel whole again. I promise.

I love you,
Dawson.

I re-read the letter. Then read it again. And again. Tears laced my eyes. I hurt him. I didn't miss the bruises still lingering on his face, they were fading, but they were still there. I didn't bring them up because I was terrified he'd remember all the pain I'd caused him and give up on me. He'd realize I wasn't worth the hassle. I'd chosen Reese, turned my back on him, and then watched him get beat up. So I stayed silent, in fear of losing him again.

I wiped the tears off my face before folding the letter back up with shaking hands. I picked up a pillow and slid the letter underneath it, silently praying no one would find it. I wasn't sure if having letters was against the rules or not.

"Hey there," a wispy voice called out. I turned around to face a tall girl around my age. Her jet-black hair was pulled into a large, side-braid. She was wearing a black velour sweat outfit that looked expensive. She was gorgeous even without makeup. Her lips were full and profound, almost looking artificial, but not too dramatic. The girl looked like a model. What the hell was she doing here?

"Looks like we're going to be roomies. Please tell me you're not a kleptomaniac?" she asked, kicking a leg out and eyeing me.

"No," I drew out.

Thank God." She walked around me and sat down on her bed. "The last girl they stuck me with stole my shit, denied it, and then got away with it." She shrugged and held up her hand. "I'm sorry, but Hello Kitty slippers do not just grow paws and walk away during a trip here. They want to, but they just can't."

"Oh." I wasn't sure what else to say. The girl seemed pretty chipper considering the place we were in.

"I'm Elise," she said, kicking up her feet, showing off her fuzzy purple slippers.

"Tessa," I replied, sitting across from her on my own bed.

"What are you in for?" she asked.

I rubbed my arms, wondering if I should be honest or not. "Isn't that kind of personal?" This wasn't prison. She didn't need to know my background to find out whether I'd shank her in her sleep.

She shrugged her shoulders and flipped her braid behind her shoulder. "I get it, this is your first rodeo, but trust me, we'll all find out sooner or later." I stared at her in horror. "They'll probably make you do group with us, which is a total fucking drag."

"So what happens now? I mean, what did they do when you first got here?"

"You'll probably meet with a counselor, and she'll figure out what meds you need to be on."

"Great," I muttered. "Just freaking fantastic."

৩৯৩

I focused my eyes on my fidgeting hands. As soon as I got settled in yesterday, I was taken to see my therapist. She was nice and not too pushy. It took me a minute to get warmed up to her, but she managed to get me to open up about my cutting, Reese, and my parents. I told her why I'd started and how I was using alcohol to fight myself from it. My cutting wasn't as frequent when I was hanging out with Reese, and that's why I believed I was falling in love with him. I'd believed his presence was fixing my problem.

"Sorry we didn't see you much at the hospital," my dad said when I finally looked up at him. "And we weren't able to bring you here, but we've been preparing for this visit."

He and my mom were sitting across from me with their fingers laced together. I eyed them skeptically, scanning them, and picking up on the change. The smell of alcohol wasn't overtaking my senses, and they looked like they'd both actually showered this morning.

My dad was wearing a button-up shirt and slacks. His blonde

had been cut and was styled to the side. The scruff that had been building on his face was shaved clean, and the expensive watch my grandfather had given him was strapped around his wrist. I inhaled a deep breath, pinching my hand to be sure this was real, and took a long look at my mom. A bright red sweater was accessorized with a white wool scarf hanging loosely around her neck. Black booties covered her feet and hit the top of her ankles to meet dark blue jeans. Her blonde hair was pinned back with a red barrette.

They looked healthy.

And sober.

I was happy they were sober for the day, but that didn't make up for the months they'd been gone. "See me much?" I repeated, baffled. "Mom came for like two seconds, and you managed to make it five minutes before you left. That was it." They might've looked put together, and their blood wasn't streaming with liquor, but one day of good parenting didn't make up for the countless ones they'd abandoned me.

Dawson had asked me to take it easy on them. So did my counselor. But I couldn't. The pent up anger was too much to hold back. I hated how they were sitting there acting like they were the victims. They could act like that when Tanner died, but I was the victim now. I was the girl left out to hold my own when I barely had working legs.

"We understand why you're angry with us," he said. "Nothing we've been doing is acceptable. Our lack of parenting is disgusting, and there's no way we can ever make that up to you or your brother. But please, we ask that you forgive us ... give us another chance." His green eyes glazed over. I could sense the regret flowing through him trailing through the room with the wind and hitting me directly in the chest. "I promise you things are going to change. We've thrown out every bottle of liquor in the house, and we've been attending AA meetings daily since you were hospitalized. We know that's not much yet, but it's something. We didn't come see you because we're trying to make ourselves better, and we knew we had to give you time." I stared at him, watching his face twist in agony while he rubbed his eyes roughly.

"We're so sorry, sweetie," I looked, shocked at the sound of my mom's soft-spoken voice. "You needed a mother, you needed a friend, and I wasn't there for you. I had no idea Daisy had moved." She shook her head and tears glistened her cheeks. "And then I tried to forbid you to see the best friend you'd already lost."

"How does this make you feel, Tessa?" my therapist asked, finally cutting into the conversation. She'd been silently sitting in the corner of the room.

My throat burned as I fought with my answer. I was too scared to reveal my pain. When you've been hurting for so long, fighting to hide it from other, eventually that pain sinks in and refuses to resurface. With them, it becomes more of you – deeper and deeper – until it's a permanent mark in your body.

"Good," I finally answered to the quiet room, keeping my head bowed down.

"We weren't aware of what was going on," my mom told the counselor. "She'd always been a good girl. She seemed like she was coping. She wasn't crying all the time, changing her wardrobe to all black, or listening to heavy metal."

I shook my head, and the sobs came through. "I didn't cry because I numbed myself. I numbed myself with alcohol, razors, scissors, anything I could that would put my pain somewhere else," I replied. There was no heavy metal or dark eyeliner because that wasn't enough. That wouldn't make me paralyzed. I needed not to feel.

My dad squeezed my mom's hand when another sob escaped her. I should've felt bad for them. I shouldn't have lashed out, but I couldn't stop myself. I wanted them to endure the guilt, suffer through the pain, and realize they were wrong. I hoped the guilt would eat them up, consume them, and they'd change for good. This was their last chance.

※

Two excruciatingly long days had passed before a visitation day. I was beginning to get the hang of things. I met with my counselor every day then go to group therapy, which was terrible like Elise had said. After we finished everything, we'd get free time to hang out in the rec room. It wasn't fun, but it wasn't horrible either.

"Holy hell," Elise said, stopping my movement into the rec room by grabbing my arm. "That guy is some serious eye candy." I looked up to see she was referring to Dawson. He got up from his chair when he saw me and waved. "And he belongs to you? You little sex kitten. I'm sure you'll be having more fun than I will. Daddy dearest isn't very thrilled to visit me for my latest stint in rehab."

I shook my head at her while keeping my eyes on Dawson and took a deep breath as I made my way over. His hair was dripping water at the tips from the snowflakes I saw drifting through the window. Seeing Dawson waiting for me at that moment was one of the best feelings in the world. I noticed a man Elise plopping down in a chair across from a man wearing an expensive suit. He didn't get up to hug her, and neither one of them smiled.

"Hey," Dawson greeted, wrapping his strong arms around me to pull me into the warmth of his coat. I inhaled his scent, wanting to take it with me to replace the harsh odor there. Everything smelled like bleach. He held onto me for a few seconds before letting go and holding me out at a distance to look at me. "You look good, baby."

"Thanks." I fell down into the chair beside him. "It's not as bad as I thought it would be."

He scooted his chair closer to me and grabbed my hand. "See, I told you. Your parents said you're doing awesome. We can't wait to have you back home."

I shut my eyes. "I miss you guys too." I was ready to get out of there. I missed my own bed. I missed my family. I missed him.

"And we're planning a huge welcome home party."

My head flew up. "Please tell me you're kidding."

"Nope."

I shook my head back and forth a few times. "Absolutely not. People don't have welcome home parties for getting out of places like this. That's not happening."

He held a hand up to stop me from arguing. "I'm kidding, I'm kidding." He paused, a slow smirk spreading across his face. "Maybe."

I groaned and rested my head down onto the table. "I will seriously hurt you," I muttered. "Have you been to school?" He nodded as I dragged my head back up. "And?"

An eyebrow rose. "And what?"

"Do people think I'm a psycho freak?" I rushed out.

"I don't know. I don't talk to anyone besides Cody and Ollie."

"What about Reese? Have you seen him?"

The mention of Reese made him flinch. "I don't give a shit about that asshole. And you shouldn't either."

"I don't." I wasn't lying. Reese had shown me his true colors, and they were the shitty ones.

"Do you know when you're going to get out of here?" he asked, changing the subject. Reese was a sore topic for the both of us.

"No, but they said I'm progressing well, so I'm hoping by the end of the week," I answered, repeating what my therapist had told me. She recommended I still do outpatient therapy to keep me on the right track when I was on my own.

"Did you get my note?"

My stomach fluttered. I had the damn thing memorized. "What note?"

His face fell. "Did you unpack your bag?"

"Yeah."

"And you didn't find anything?"

I shook my head. "Clothes? And thanks for the make-up, you did well for a newbie."

"And nothing else?" He rubbed the bottom of his stubbly chin anxiously.

"Like what?"

"Like a note."

"Nope," I said, watching his brows draw together in confusion. His face reminded me of a child who'd just dropped his entire ice cream cone on the floor. "*Yes*, I got your note."

His hand flew to his chest. "Seriously? How can you play with a man's emotions like that?"

I fidgeted in my seat. "I didn't know you'd get so upset."

"A man writes a letter giving his undying love to someone and that someone acts like they've never received it, that kind of thing messes with your head."

"Your undying love?"

"You know what I mean. Every word in that letter is true. You don't have to say anything back yet because I want you to focus on getting better. But I wanted you to know how I feel and what you have to come back to. I want you to realize your importance to not only me, but to everyone lucky enough to know you. Get better, get home, and we'll get through it."

I nodded, and butterflies swam in my belly when he leaned forward to kiss my forehead.

"Please tell me that dude has a twin," Elise asked, clasping her elbow through mine when we left the rec room. Dawson and I talked effortlessly until they announced visiting time was over. He'd kissed me goodbye, telling me he'd either visit me the next family day or see me at home, whichever came first. Being with him just seemed so easy.

People say they don't want easy love. I don't understand that. Didn't they want someone they could talk to for hours? Someone who'd be there during the rough times in life? I wanted easy. Easy was a good fix for me.

I shook my head in response to Elise's question. "A brother?" she asked. I shook my head again. "A cousin?"

"Nope, sorry girl."

She threw her head back. "The hot ones are always either taken or arrogant assholes."

She was another person who'd helped me with my recovery. She'd taken me under her wing and made me feel not so crazy. She knew my story, and I knew hers. She was raised by nannies, and her dad worked all the time. She hated him and abused herself and other shit to get his attention. She didn't tell me everything, but I found out she'd been raped, and her father insisted she was lying about it to get attention. Elise despised him for that and was doing everything in her power to fight against him. I told her she was only hurting herself, but she didn't care. I guess you have to forgive someone before you can stop using yourself to hurt them.

"Don't let him go, girl. If you do, I'm going to hunt you down and kick your ass. That's not an easy thing to find," she said.

"What?" I asked, looking up at her.

"Whens someone sees you for you, don't let that go. I haven't had one boyfriend who looks at me like that or doesn't see me as the slutty rich girl who tries to act out. His eyes lit up when he saw you in the freaking nut house." She laughed when I gave her a look. "He sees you behind the bullshit, behind the slips, behind the girl who tried to kill herself. He sees you. He knows the real you, and he's not letting your thoughtless actions diminish his love for you. And that, girlfriend, is someone you need to keep. That is someone who's not going to let you *not* keep him either. He'll fight for you until he can't fight anymore. He'll be there for you until the moment he takes his last breath."

"Wow," I said, shocked and looking over at her. "That was pretty deep."

"Yeah, and that's about all the deepness I have in me. Now come on, it's movie night."

"What's the movie?"

"Marley and Me."

"Isn't that movie really depressing?"

"Yeah, whoever is the movie picker around here should be fired."

☙❧

"I'M GOING TO MISS YOU," ELISE SAID, SITTING ON HER BED and watching me pack. I pulled out Dawson's letter from underneath my pillow and gently pushed it into the pocket of my jeans. Every night before I went to bed, I read it. Elise begged me to let her see it, but I wouldn't. This was my secret, the piece of me that made my heart feel whole again, and no one else was getting a sliver of it.

I slumped down onto my bed. "I'm going to miss you too."

"What's wrong, girl? You're about to be out of here, what's the long face for?"

I was terrified. It was easy to walk when someone was there holding your hand every step of the way and leading you with words of encouragement. But it was a hell of a lot harder when you were doing it on your own. You're balancing yourself, fighting off everything flying your way while trying to remain sane. I wasn't sure if I could do it.

"How do you know when you're fixed?" I asked her.

She looked up at me and grabbed the unicorn on her bed, gripping it against her chest as her face fell. "I'm probably the wrong person to answer that, but I don't think anyone is ever fixed. You break a lamp, and it shatters. You can glue it back together, but you'll always see the cracks and the superglue will always seep through them. I think we're the same way. We can come in here, get help, and feel like we've been fixed. But we'll always have those cracks and the chance of us breaking again is likely. The important part is the quality of glue we have. It's the bond that leaves us put together. You don't have good support, your foundation breaks, and you're back to sweeping up the pieces and trying again. Girl, you'll always be cracked, but you've got some good glue; you've got people who love you. Stick with that, let it stick with you, and I think you'll be okay."

"What about you? Why do you keep coming here?"

She shrugged. "I'm not strong enough to win my battle yet, and I don't have soldiers on my side."

"What do you mean?" She crawled to the edge of the bed and looked directly at me. "Look at those scars. Each one was a battle with yourself that you lost. Same thing with me. Every pill I popped and every guy I had random sex with, I lost. Every time you pick up that razor, you lose again. Every time I pop a pill or spread my legs, I lose again. We give them the victory. He'll keep winning over and over again until you stand up and tell it to go fuck itself. Now, go home, throw away those piece of shit razors, and be happy. I'm not ready to do that yet. I'm still angry."

"I can't believe you're not begging to get out of here."

"I know it's fucked up. That's why you're going home and I'm staying."

I felt sorry for Elise. She was beautiful and strong-willed, but she was out for revenge. She hated everyone around her, and I didn't blame her. She lashed out at them by lashing out on herself. She'd run her dad's name through the dirt with her bad behavior and let him suffer the bad appearance of his company. She'd be the problem child they talked about in the news because that was her way of hurting him.

She got up and hugged me tightly. "I better not see you in here again, or I'm so beating your ass," she laughed. "Now, go home to your boyfriend before I break out of here and kidnap him for myself."

I chuckled. This was the first real friendship I'd had with another girl since Daisy. I'd never thought that I'd be meeting one of my newest friends in a mental institution, but she already knew my dark secrets, and I knew hers, so we'd always have that bond.

"You have my number. You better call me," I told her.

She was getting out next week. She said they never kept her too long. Like me, she wasn't crazy, she was just pissed off and wanted to be free of the world.

She laughed. "You'll be the first to know when I bust out of this place."

CHAPTER 22

DAWSON

"Nice to see you finally decided to make an appearance at home," my mom said when I walked into the kitchen.

"I've been staying at a friend's," I answered, yawning. I'd been helping the Bensons out with Derrick as much as I could, working, and going to school. I was exhausted, so I'd either been crashing on their couch or coming home late.

"And what friend might that be?" she questioned, taking a drink of coffee.

"The Bensons."

Her lips pursed as she tilted her head to the side. "Have you been feeling okay?"

Her question caught me off guard. I paused for a second before answering. "Uh yeah?"

"That friend is dead," she pointed out bluntly, shocking the shit out of me.

"I know. I've been helping his parents out with their little brother." Jesus, did she think I was going all *Sixth Sense?*

"That's sweet, honey," she said, smiling and creeping me the hell out. Something was about to happen. I knew it. "Don't forget about your dad's hearing."

And there it was. All of the sweetness, the honeys, the no-bitching. All of those were because he needed my help. My dad's hearing was in two weeks, and I was supposed to be preparing for what I was going to say. She wanted me lie to get him out. But I didn't want him free. He didn't deserve that luxury.

I groaned and kicked my feet against the floor. "Mom."

"You have to do this. We need your dad back home," she argued.

I took a deep breath, and my throat constricted. "You need him." I knew what would happen if he got out. He'd be on his best behavior for a few weeks, get my mom's hopes up, and then bail again. Then I'd be the one to pick up the remains of his cyclone. It'd happened too many times for me to trust him.

"Don't start this shit, okay. Just be there and keep the attitude at home."

"Doesn't he have an attorney you pay to do that for him? Why do I have to be there?" I couldn't keep up with the endless amount of attorney bills that were racked up so she could see him again.

"His lawyer is working on it, but having family support is a huge part of his release. We need to show he's a family man and will stay out of trouble when he gets out. If they see he has a son that needs him ..."

"I don't need him!" I shouted, rolling over her words angrily. "We're doing pretty damn good without him here."

"He's your father."

"He is nothing to me! Just because we share blood doesn't mean he's my father or means anything to me! What he did was wrong and you know that, Ma. Do you really think the victim's family isn't going to show up and fight against his release? He's selfish, and he will always be selfish." My arm shot out, and I gestured to the pile of bills sitting on the table next to an open checkbook. "He knows you're paying all of these attorney fees with money we don't have, but does he care? No. He cares about himself and himself only. That's not a father!"

"Just do it for me, please," she begged.

"I'll think about it," I lied. I wasn't going to allow him to kill my excitement today. "I have to shower."

She nodded, choosing not to argue with me. She wanted to stay on my good side so I'd do what she wanted.

I went to my bedroom, grabbed some clothes, and hopped in the shower. The water sprinkled down my face. I turned the knob to make the water hotter, an attempt to cool down my anger. I despised that motherfucker. I used the washcloth and scrubbed my skin as I cursed to the water. I needed to calm down. Today was her day.

She'd been in the rehab center for a week, and she was finally coming home. The doctors said she was progressing well. That didn't surprise me. Deep down, I didn't think she'd wanted to kill herself. She'd only wanted the pain to stop and was also panicked about going back to school after those bitches did a witch-hunt on her. I had to resist the urge to confront all of them when I walked down the hallway. Tanner's death might've planted the seed of hurting herself in her head, Reese's actions watered it, and the threats of the others bloomed it.

I got out of the shower, dried off, and headed back to my bedroom at the same time my phone rang. "They just left to go get her," Derrick said excitedly when I picked up.

"I'll be there in ten."

I quickly dressed, rushed out the door, and made a pit stop at the local bakery before heading over to Tessa's. I walked into the kitchen to find Derrick filling bowls with chips and candy. A *Welcome Home* banner hung from one side of the room to the other, and pink and yellow streamers were taped to the walls.

"Good job, kid," I said, giving him a pat on the back.

"Thanks," he replied, grabbing a handful of canned drinks from the fridge. "She's going to love this."

"Or punch us." We weren't throwing her a party per se.

"They're here!" Derrick yelled, ducking behind the kitchen island. "Get down Dawson, or she's going to see your goofy ass and you'll ruin everything.

I ducked down, balancing myself on my heels, and pointed at him. "Watch your mouth."

"Dude, I'm fourteen." I shook my head at him and was bout to tell him that didn't mean shit, but the front door creaking open stopped me. Her parents shouted as they came in, most likely to alert us they were here.

Derrick looked at me as the voices and footsteps grew closer. "Surprise!" we yelled, throwing our hands up and coming up from behind the island.

Tessa stopped and looked at us with wide eyes. "You didn't have to do this," she said, smiling. Her blonde hair was twisted into a braid at the nape of her neck. She was wearing a black pair of leggings with a loose sweater. I smiled in satisfaction over the fact that I'd packed that outfit for her.

"Of course we did, sis," Derrick said, walking around me to give her a hug. "It's good to have you back."

I took my turn to hug her next, grabbing her around the waist and bringing her into me. "I knew you could do it," I whispered in her ear.

"Thank you," she muttered into my shoulder. "It feels good to be home."

I looked over her shoulder at her parents standing in the corner of the kitchen. Her mom's eyes were watering, and she wiped them with the sleeve of her blouse.

Derrick clapped his hands. "I ordered some pizzas, and Dawson brought a cake," he called out. He grabbed the stack plates sitting on the table, handed them out, and opened up the pizza boxes.

"I know you said you didn't want anything big, but I figured this would be okay," I said, grabbing a slice of pizza and handing it to her.

She nodded. "The people I care about are here. That's all I needed."

⚜

TESSA WRAPPED HER SWEATER TIGHTLY AGAINST HER TALL frame as we walked out her front door and into the cold bite of winter. She eased herself down onto the wooden swing hanging on the front porch. I bent down in front of her and covered her shivering body with the blanket in my hand.

"You warm?" I asked, standing in front of her while waiting to see if she needed another. Her parents had set a heater out to warm up the porch, but it was still chilly. She nodded, and the swing suspended as I pushed my weight onto it. She pulled off half of the blanket and tossed it over my lap. The mug in her hand went to her scarlet lips as she took a small sip of hot chocolate.

"So, what happens from here?" I asked, balancing my feet onto the ground of the porch. I leaned forward to gain momentum, and the cold wind hit our backs when I rocked us forward.

She shrugged. "They suggested I go to outpatient therapy a few times a week."

"I think that's a good idea."

She bit her bottom lip and scraped her teeth across it. "I don't know. It's like everything is happening so fast."

"You did therapy at the rehab center. I'm sure it's the same thing, only this time you can curl your hair before you go," I joked, patting her leg over the blanket.

She gave me a weak smile. "That might be the only advantage."

I tucked my hand underneath the blanket to grab hers and interlaced our fingers. "They are there to help you. That's all that matters. If you want me to come with you, I will."

"It's just ..." She paused, looking at the tranquility of the night. "It's embarrassing."

"I keep telling you not to be embarrassed around me. Face mask, remember?" She nodded. "Look at me." Her head slowly turned, and her face illuminated in the dim porch light. "Don't you ever be embarrassed around me, okay? I've seen you sweet, happy, and full of life. I've seen you hurt, emotional, and thoughtless. And I'd never want a different you. Even when I said I was done, I wasn't. I never stopped thinking about you, looking out for you, or loving you. And I don't intend to when you make your next mistake. It's okay to have a breakdown or a lapse of judgment. Shit, we've all been there. We've all had those moments where we feel like the world is falling out from under us and the easiest thing to do is to jump. Don't be embarrassed because you're human."

"You have no idea how much that means to me," she said, the porch light dimming in and out of her face as we swung back and forth. "Just you being here means so much to me. I was a bitch to you. I said hurtful things, and you're still here. No matter what, you're here. And I'm sorry for what I said. I know you're not using me because you lost Tanner."

I let out a sigh of relief. Fucking finally she realized my love for her had nothing to do with losing Tanner. I wanted her when Tanner was still alive. I ached for her every time I saw her. Tanner or no Tanner, I wanted her.

"When's your next appointment?" I asked.

"I'm supposed to start tomorrow. They made an appointment with a local therapist and gave me her information. They don't want me to break the habit or have enough time to change my mind."

"Are you planning on going?"

She shrugged. "Probably. Maybe."

"Maybe? There's no maybe about it. You're going."

She groaned, kicking her feet up on the swing, and causing us to jerk back. "Geez, when did you get so bossy? If I recall correctly, that's my place."

"Sometimes you've got to let someone else steer."

She rolled her eyes. "There can only be one chief, and that's me, buddy."

I laughed. "Sometimes the chiefs have to consult with the other Indians," I pointed to myself. "And they give her advice."

She groaned and threw her head back. "Fine, you can be in my tribe."

"Appreciate it. I better be getting home." I wanted to give her time. She hadn't had a moment to herself in over a week. "If you need anything or want to talk, my phone will be by my side all night."

She nodded, biting her bottom lip. "Why are you doing this?"

"Doing what?"

"Why are you doing this? Why do you care about me going to therapy or how I'm feeling. I know you said you love and care about me, but why now? All of the sudden you're in love with me?"

"All of the sudden?" I repeated. "My love for you isn't all of the sudden. I didn't wake up one morning and have this giant epiphany about my feelings for you. Hell no. I've had these feelings for years. I fell for you the moment I met you. You were this amazing, exuberant girl who was immediately nice to me – the new guy. Then as the years passed and I got to know you more, the stronger those feelings grew. By our junior year, I was certain I was completely head over heels for you. Now, I'm positive I'm in love with you."

"But why are you just now telling me this?"

I cringed. I dreaded telling her this, but I had to. "I made Tanner a promise that I'd never date you ... or tell you about the promise."

"What? That little asshole,"

"It was before I met you, and I've regretted it every day."

"Yet you still hooked up with other girls?"

"First off, there weren't that many girls." She gave me a look. "I swear! I don't get why people always assume just because you're hanging out with someone you're banging them."

"Because usually people are," she said, taking another sip of cocoa.

I shook my head and tried to hold back a smile. "*Anyways,* those *few* girls didn't mean anything. They were filling the void. I thought maybe, just maybe, I could find a girl that would make me feel the same way you did, but no one compared to you. It was an endless search, but I didn't want to break the promise to your brother."

"So what? You're going to say you love me, but can't do anything about it because you promised Tanner to leave me alone?"

I felt like shit. Tanner was my boy and my best friend. I was about to break the one thing he wanted from me. I was going against his honor.

"I'm done letting a promise I made years ago impact my decision and feelings for you, but you're still in recovery. We'll take it slow, let you take time for yourself, but I wanted you to know I do love you." She opened her mouth to say something, but I stopped her. "You don't have to say anything. In fact, I don't want you to yet. I know you love me, but you tell me when you're ready, okay? I want you to love yourself before you love anyone else."

Tears dropped from her lashes. "Look at you, Mr. Romantic," she said, giving me a smile.

"I aim to please, babe."

She pushed my side. "I appreciate your honesty and *finally* telling me why you kept turning me down. I seriously thought you weren't attracted to me."

"Are you shitting me?" She shook her head. "I wasn't attracted to you? Did you miss every time my eyes would follow your body? You're fucking gorgeous. But the thing is, you're not only the most beautiful girl I've ever laid eyes on, but you're also the girl that gets me, and that's more attractive to me than anything. Those other girls, they don't know about my family shit or how eating shellfish makes me sick."

"And puff up like a marshmallow," she added, grinning.

"See, no other girl knows that. Just you. And I want to keep it that way. It's you and only you who knows the real me. Shit, even my mom doesn't know who I am."

"And you're pretty much the only guy besides Tanner who knows me."

"Let's keep it that way, shall we?" There were so many questions I wanted to ask her about Reese. Did she sleep with him? If not, how far did they go? Did she tell him she loved him? Did she love him? Jesus fuck, I was jealous of the biggest douchebag in town.

"Okay, I should probably go. You need to get your beauty sleep, babe," I said, trying my hardest to shake away those thoughts. I'd been with other girls. I couldn't be mad at her for anything she did before we got together. But the thought still made me sick to my stomach.

"They gave me sleeping pills to help me for the next few days, so hopefully that helps."

"Did they put you on anything else?"

She nodded. "An anti-depressant until I feel better."

"Make sure you take those."

She saluted me. "Got it, doctor."

I grabbed her chin, kissing her gently on the lips before pulling away. "Come on, I'll walk you in." I got up and held my hand out for her to grab.

She shook her head. "I actually want to sit out here a bit longer. I think I need some quiet me time."

I nodded. "Okay, but not too long, it's cold out."

CHAPTER 23

TESSA

THE BRISK WIND HIT ME WITH EVERY STRIDE AS I SWUNG back and forth, but that didn't stop me. I felt free. The past week had been a soul-searching, heart wrenching, and insane reality check for me. My legs shot out to stop my movement, and I pushed back on the swing so I could get a glimpse of the stars lighting up from a distance. They were so beautiful, so free, and no matter how much darkness surrounded them, they still shined. I wanted to be like that.

The doctors told me I was masking my pain with the combination of cutting and alcohol abuse. Alcohol abuse. I'd chastised my parents for doing the same thing I was guilty of. When the fog in your head begins to fade and grow clear, you look at things in a different perspective. You start see the real world honestly. You notice things you'd missed, the bad decisions you'd made, and you start to think of healthy ways to fix them.

Dawson and my parents threw all of the alcohol out of the house, so that wouldn't be a problem. I shivered at the thought of throwing all of my razors out. There was no way I was refraining from shaving. No freaking way. I'd deal. I'd fight with myself every time if I had to, and this time, I'd make sure I won. Then there was Reese. I hadn't talked to him since the night of our fight, and I didn't feel the need to reach out to him. My blood boiled just thinking about him.

Dawson told me he loved me. I knew he ended the letter he'd given me with it, but it wasn't the same. People signed birthday cards with love. They told people they love them at the closing of a letter, but there was something different about hearing it in person. It was more gratifying. I'd read the words, but emotions didn't fly through them. But when I heard him say it, the words falling from his lips, my entire heart had lifted, and I truly believed it. I loved him too. I'd lied in bed for years wondering what it would feel like to hear him tell me that. It was better than I'd imagined.

But now, I felt like I didn't deserve his love. I'd accused him of using me. I'd accused him of wanting to be near me so that he wouldn't lose my family. I'd accused him of being an opportunist. But I was wrong. Dawson had no family, and I knew losing us was killing him. It wasn't about him being alone. It was about being surrounded by the people he loved.

I took one last look at the sky before getting up with the blanket still wrapped tightly around my body and went inside. Derrick was sitting on the couch, and a movie was playing on the TV.

"Hey sis, wanna join me?" he asked, looking back at me over the couch. "This is the part where the zombie eats the guy's brain. It's awesome."

"As much fun and not gruesome that sounds, I'm going to head to bed. I've had a long day."

He nodded in understanding, and I realized how much he'd grown up in the past year. Not just physically, but mentally. My baby brother was maturing into a grown man.

"I'll see you in the morning," he said. "I'm expecting a good breakfast. Dawson has been feeding me frozen pizzas and hot wings all week."

"And you have a problem with that?"

"Eh, it's cool at first, but a guy can only have so many slices of pizza before he starts sneezing out pepperonis."

"Okay, that's sick," I said, holding my hand up and curling my lip. "I'll see what I can do."

I grabbed my bag sitting at the bottom of the staircase and walked upstairs to my bedroom. I flipped the light on and looked from side to side. Nothing seemed different. I changed clothes and then began unpacking. I made it to the bottom of the bag and took a deep breath as every muscle in my stomach tightened. I could do this.

I scooped up all my hygienic products in my arms and carried them into the one room I was terrified of. My bare feet hit the cold tile, and I looked down, expecting to see bright red bloodstains, but there was nothing. I looked at the bathtub and sink. Nothing seemed out of the ordinary. There wasn't a trace of red residue anywhere. The only remains of the night were in my head.

I dropped the items onto the counter and leaned back against the wall. Images of that night raced through my mind. I remembered being in the bath and staring down at the blood dripping from my wrist in captivation. Flashbacks came next – the color red flashing in my thoughts, seizing my vision. I slumped down against the wall, the back of my legs hitting the cold floor, and the tears fell faster than my trembling hands could wipe them away.

But the tears weren't sad ones. They were tears of relief.

Tears of revival – of me bringing myself back to life. My pain would no longer consume me. I would no longer numb myself. I was done being succumbed. I'd allowed the toxicity of my life to seep out when I'd cut myself and it had drained my body clean. I was getting a fresh start.

I wasn't sure how much time passed while I sat there, staring at the sink in front of me, but I finally got up and balanced myself against the wall. I pulled the thin elastic out of my hair and ran my hands through the strands to loosen my braid. I stared at my pale skin and ran my hand against the smoothness. I was becoming me again. There were still circles under my eyes, but they were fading. I still had a few blemishes near my chin, but that was okay. I didn't look at the mess of a girl in the mirror now. I just saw me.

I peeked down at my wrist and started unwrapping the thin white cloth. I'd been changing it twice a day since leaving the hospital. It wasn't necessary anymore, but I still wanted to hide my scars. The new indentations on my skin were harder to hide when they were fresh. I knew I wouldn't be able to hide behind my long sleeves anymore. I winced, still feeling pain from the stitches that had just been taken out, and traced the line of the built up scar tissue. They incisions were small, but they'd always be there.

My legs shook as I undressed and stepped into the shower. I ran my fingers across the sharp blades of the razor I'd grabbed from a drawer.

"You helping me was a figment of my imagination," I whispered, warm water streaming down my body. I gripped the handle and slowly brought the razor up to my legs. The first swipe was the worst, but the second was more comfortable. When I finished, I tossed the razor to the side – acting like it wasn't there anymore.

I twirled my wet hair into a ponytail when I got out and

grabbed my phone before sliding into the comfort of my soft sheets. I had a text from Dawson telling me goodnight and sweet dreams. I texted him back with a smile on my face, took the sleeping pills I'd been given, and drifted off to sleep without tossing and turning for hours.

❦

"Rise and shine, sunshine," Dawson's deep voice called out, waking me up. My eyes flew open, and I winced at the sunlight flooding my bedroom. I drug my arm over my eyes and groaned.

"Why are you here this early?" I grumbled.

"You have your first therapy appointment today," he explained, plopping down onto the edge of my bed.

"I know this," I said in dread. I thought I could blame it on oversleeping this morning and get out of this today. I didn't want to open myself up to a new therapist.

"And I'm here to make sure you don't try to play hooky." He knew me too well.

I kicked his leg from under the comforter. "I'm not going to play hooky. I'm getting up, so get out."

He fell down next to me, and I peeked over at him with one eye. He clasped his hands comfortably behind his head and leaned back against my headboard. "Not happening babe, I'm taking you."

"They don't confiscate your driver's license if you try to kill yourself."

"You can drive, but I'm still coming with."

I shoved my face into the pillow. "You know, you seriously suck."

"I seriously don't," he replied, chuckling. His hand smacked the bed. "Now get up, chop chop, we've got things to accomplish."

"Fine, but you're buying me breakfast."

"If that's what it takes, I'll buy you the whole damn menu."

I took another quick shower and threw my hair into a ponytail without styling it. I got dressed and walked back into my bedroom to find Dawson lounging on my bed watching TV. I stepped into a pair of boots, and he followed me down the stairs.

࿇

"You ready for this?" he asked when we pulled up to the building.

"Do I have a choice?" I replied, taking a sip of hot chocolate and dropping the last bite of a donut in my mouth.

He shook his head. "No, not really. But you never know, you may love it here. This doctor may become your new best friend."

"What a story to tell. How'd you meet your best friend? Oh, she was my therapist." I unbuckled my seatbelt. I let him drive because I was going to be too nervous to pay attention to the road. "I'll call you when I'm done." I grabbed the door handle, and my feet hit the pavement. I circled around the car but immediately stopped. "What the hell are you doing?"

"I'm coming in," he explained, falling in step with me.

"I'm sure you have better things to do."

He shook his head. "Nope, I lead a pretty boring life. I'm also conserving gas, saving the environment, going green. It's the thing to do."

"Whatever, I know you're doing it so I won't bail."

"Yeah, that too," he said, laughing as he kept up with my speed and followed me into the building. "I'll stay out of the way, and you can act like I'm invisible."

"Do you have an answer for everything?" I asked, stepping into the elevator.

He slid in next to me. "When it comes to you, hell no. You're the most confusing, unable to find that missing puzzle piece person in the world. But I'd like to think I'm pretty good at solving problems. At least that's what my kindergarten teacher said."

"Oh really?"

"Yeah, but I think she had a crush on me."

I shoved his arm. "When did you get this annoying?"

The elevator doors opened, and he followed me out. "I've been this way forever. You were just too blinded by your infatuation with me you never realized it."

I snorted. "Okay, now you're going overboard."

I knew what he was doing. He was trying to drag the nervousness out of me. And it was working. He escorted me to the office suite I'd been given and opened the door because I was too chicken to do it myself.

"Babe, you got this," he whispered into my ear, squeezing me gently and taking an open seat.

I nodded, swallowing the nausea wanting to escape me, and stopped at the front desk. The lady behind it slid the window open. I told her my name, and she handed me a clipboard with paperwork attached.

I eyed the waiting room that was similar to every other doctor's office I'd been to and took the seat by Dawson. He snatched the clipboard from my hand and held it away from me when I made a grab for it.

"I got it," he said, patting my leg. "You just relax."

"You do know that's my personal information, right?"

"Yep," he said, grabbing the pen and filling out my name and address. I kept an eye on the form to make sure he was answering everything correctly.

"You even know the medication I'm on?" I asked in annoyance. "You nosy little shit."

"I do my research. The only thing I don't know is when you had your last period," he said, and a tingling swept up my back. "I can't believe they even need to know that here. Unless it really is true that those things make girls go ape-shit."

"Okay, give me that back. And we don't go ape-shit."

"Just tell me. I'm a big boy. I passed Sex Ed with flying colors. I know girls bleed for a week. It's strange, but I guess it's possible."

I rolled my eyes and crossed my legs. "You're right, but they don't talk to guys about it."

"But I'm not just a guy." The ball of the pen hit the paper. "Let's just say in progress."

I made a grab for the paper, snatching it before he had the chance to stop me. "Very funny," I said, narrowing my eyes at him. I snatched the pen from him and filled in the date in question.

⚘

"Hi Tessa," a woman greeted me with a smile. I smiled back before following her down a hallway and into an office. She motioned towards a black sofa propped up against the wall. "Have a seat." My knees almost bucked as I did. She shut the door before pulling up a chair across from me.

She was young, giving me a sense of relief that she would understand me, and slender with bright red hair that was pulled back around her crown with the bottom hairs left down. A green sweater covered her top and was paired with black pants. She looked at me through thick frames and set her hands on her lap. I shifted around, the leather of the couch squeaking beneath me. The room was inviting. A box of tissues sat on a table.

"It's nice to meet you. I'm Lina," she said. "Let's get to know each other, shall we?" I nodded nervously. "Let's start out with you telling me a few things about yourself."

"Like what?"

"Anything. You can tell me your favorite color, your favorite book, things that annoy you, or how you're feeling right now. You can tell me anything."

"My favorite book is *Pride and Prejudice*. My favorite color is purple. And I'm nervous and utterly terrified at the moment."

She smiled brightly. "Let's change that then."

I left my therapy appointment feeling freed and reassured that I'd be okay. I knew my problems wouldn't be mended from one appointment, but it was nice to be able to get everything out. There were things I was too embarrassed to talk to with Dawson or my parents. I didn't want them to feel sorry for me or think I was crazy. But Lina seemed to understand me.

CHAPTER 24

DAWSON

I wasn't going to push Tessa about her appointment. All that mattered was that she'd shown up. If she wanted to share with me, I'd be there to listen. But if she didn't, I'd still be her wall – a place for her to lean on.

"Do you want to watch a movie or something?" she asked while I followed her up the stairs. She wasn't intentionally trying to be sensual, but her hips swayed from side to side with every step she took, and I couldn't take my eyes off her.

"Sure," I answered, clearing my throat. "I'll even let you choose one of your cheesy ones." Watching TV with Tessa had always been a pain in the ass. We'd argue over what to watch, over the remote, and she'd always end up winning in the end. The girl was hard to say no to.

She halted in her step to look back at me. "I don't watch cheesy shows."

I snorted. "Baby, you watch movies about vampires who are still in high school. You know that's not normal, right?"

She shrugged her shoulders. "What? They've got fangs and an education to go with it. That's a complete package right there."

"You do realize they're dead?"

"Obviously, we can't all be perfect."

I laughed. "Just in case you forgot, I don't sparkle, so please don't get your hopes up."

She whipped back around, ignoring my comment, and headed into her room. "I'm sure you have glitter in your veins somewhere," she replied, laughing as she makes herself comfortable on her bed.

I shut the door behind me to block out the noise of Derrick's video games, fell down beside her, and grabbed the remote to turn on the TV, but it was immediately snatched out of my hand.

"You said I could choose," she said, flipping the TV on.

"Go right ahead, vampire-it up," I replied, wrapping my arms around her waist.

She stared at me while I dragged her across the bed and situated her at my side. I bent down and pressed my lips to her shoulder as she shifted to make herself comfortable. Her chin rested on my chest, and she looked up at me through thick lashes as her lips slightly parted. She shocked the shit out of me when she lifted herself up and smashed her mouth against mine.

The thrill of her lips hitting mine crawled across my skin, lighting me on fire. I wasn't sure if it was a relief that we were no longer off limits to each other ... or because of everything we'd gone through, but there was something different with this kiss – it was more intense than anything we'd ever shared.

My mouth flew open, and I immediately tasted the sweetness of chocolate while drifting into another world. Her tongue slid against mine, and her breathing quickened as my hand traveled underneath her sweater. She groaned, her hands winding around my back, when I stroked her smooth, bare skin.

Damn ... how I wanted to push her onto her back and run my lips down every inch of her body, but I couldn't. She gasped when I pulled away and looked down at her nervously, gulping. My brain screamed at me, calling me an idiot and telling me to keep kissing her. But I ignored it. I had to know.

"Did you sleep with him?" I asked.

Her back stiffened. I'd detonated a bomb against the mood, but I couldn't stop myself from thinking about my conversation with Alexa. My stomach curled at the thought of him touching her.

"What?" she asked, averting her eyes.

"Did you sleep with him?" I repeated.

"Reese?" I nodded, my pulse pounding when she broke out of my hold and rose up. She scooted backward, her back hitting the headboard of the bed, and rubbed her hands down her arms. "I don't think this is the best time to talk about that."

"You're right. It isn't. There will probably never be a good time to talk about it, but let's get it over with so we can move forward." I shifted and settled down in front of her. I opened up my hand, gently palming her cheek, and stroked my fingers against it. "I won't think any different of you when you answer, okay? Tell me, and I'll never bring it up again." I was a glutton for punishment.

I swear a couple minutes passed before she answered.

"I did," she finally said.

I nodded slowly, feeling my muscles pulsating underneath my skin. I wanted to scream at her, but I couldn't. That asshole had preyed on her weakness when she was down. I wouldn't do the same.

"Are we stopping because of that?" she asked, apprehensively.

"No," I answered.

"Then why?"

"I'm not like him. I'm going to let you work your shit out before you stress about having sex. I want to wait until you're ready to take that step." As much as I wanted to peel back those leggings and feel how good it felt to be so intimate with her, I had to hold back.

"What if I'm ready?"

"You're not ready." Her mouth opened to argue, but I kept talking. "We're not ready, baby. Us having sex will change things, and you're already going through enough changes. I'm not going to leave you or go hook up with other girls. I'll be here watching vampire shit every damn night if you want."

"I know sex will change things, but I'm okay with that. I know you're not like him."

"Do you regret having sex with Reese?" I asked.

She hesitated before answering. "Well, yeah."

"Exactly, I'm giving you time. Take it."

"But we've known each other for years," she argued.

"I know, but this kind of relationship is new to us."

She tipped her head back against the headboard. "When did you get so un-sexual. I thought you were some sex god or something."

I chuckled. "Sex god? I'm far from a sex god. I'm not saying we can't mess around." I rested my hand on her thigh before slowly elevating it.

"Okay, maybe you just suck a little," she said, biting the edge of her lip.

"Just no sex," I said, moving my hand higher, feeling the soft cotton of her leggings against my palm.

"No sex," she repeated, smiling.

I grabbed her feet and slid her down the bed until her head rested on a pillow. "Thank you for giving me this chance and not being pissed at me because I didn't have the guts to do this a long time ago," I whispered, moving back up and hovering my lips over hers before kissing her hard.

My hand went back to exploring her silky skin underneath her sweater as she kissed me back. A shallow breath released from her when my fingers traced the underwire of her bra. The fabric felt rough against my fingertips, like a thick lace, but I had to see for myself.

She lifted up on her elbows, as if she was reading my mind, and reached behind her back to loosen her bra. I took in a breath as she grabbed the bottom of her shirt and swiftly pulled the sweater over her head. My eyes fastened on her bare stomach, taking in her ivory skin and the cups of her bra hanging loosely along her plump breasts. I licked my lip at the peek a nipple and used both of my hands to slide the thin straps down her arms before tossing it on the floor.

The only thought in my mind was giving her, this girl I'd been in love with for years, pleasure. I cupped her breasts with both hands and massaged them gently. They fit in my palms perfectly. "Is this okay, baby?" I asked, looking down at her.

She nodded, brushing her arms up and down my arms as they moved against her.

I bowed down and tenderly took a nipple in my mouth. It hardened against my tongue, and she gasped at the same time her back arched up into the air.

"Yeah, that's definitely fine," she said, breathlessly. I mentally gave myself a huge high five. I'd thought about doing this for years. Every time she sauntered around in her tiny bikini, every time we relaxed on her bed and my fingers ached to touch her, it was finally happening. I gave her breasts my full attention and felt her squirm underneath me. "More," she said.

She wanted more, but I wasn't sure how far I could go without wanting to plunge myself into her. I dipped my hand down, her legs instantly parting, and I rubbed her through her thin leggings as I kissed her deeply. Her hips withered and eyes looked at me with such passion it stole my breath. She moved in sync with my hand, and I slowly dipped it down underneath her waistband. She wiggled out of them without hesitation and took her panties with them.

She was perfect lying there completely nude and offering me every inch of her. It was pure fucking bliss, and there was no more holding myself back from something I've needed for years. I ran my fingers between her legs and grinned at how wet she was. A soft moan released from her when I caressed her soft folds before slowly sliding one finger inside of her.

She was tight, so damn tight, and I waited for her to get adjusted before inserting another finger. I grabbed her hip while she started moving in motion with me. My pace was slow as I took in each moan and sigh from her. I never wanted this moment to end.

I knew she was close as her body began to tremble and quickened my speed as she grew wilder until I felt her tense around my fingers. Every ounce of stress from the both of us melted away as she let go and I watched her.

"Holy freaking shit," she whispered, throwing her arm over her face. "Really?" I leaned forward to gently kiss her on the lips. "That's what you've been keeping from me?" she asks against my lips. "You seriously suck."

I grinned when I pulled away and stuck my fingers into my mouth, sucking on them. Her jaw dropped. "No baby, soon you'll find out how good I actually do suck."

Heat fires up her cheeks. "Well ... I guess I can't wait for that day."

I chuckled while getting up from the bed and situating myself under my pants. There was no hiding this erection. Tessa noticed but was too shy to say anything about it, which was fine with me.

I wasn't expecting anything from her today. My enjoyment was getting her off and watching her come apart on my fingers.

"It wasn't like this," she whispered.

I grabbed a pair of sweatpants from a drawer and handed them to her. "What do you mean?" I asked, sitting down next to her.

She leaned down to pull her shirt up from the floor and put it on without her bra. "It wasn't like this ... or that ... with him."

And there was the goddamn mood killer.

So long hard-on. I rubbed the back of my neck. I didn't give two shits what it was like with him.

"With you, I feel so much more comfortable," she went on. "It's like I belong here and only here with you. My mind doesn't race with anxiety while I question every move you make. With Reese, it was like my body couldn't enjoy anything because it knew you should be the only one touching me. My body saw it as him trespassing."

I ran my hands over her silky tresses. "Because he was, and do you know what we do with trespassers?"

She looked up at me, her nose wrinkling. "We kill them?"

"Damn straight. Violators will be shot."

She laughed, burying her head in my chest. "Oh God, that was so cheesy."

"Really? I thought it was pretty original."

"Don't quit your day job, babe."

Her grin made me grin. If my cheesy ass jokes could get her to crack a smile, I'd be cheesy all damn day. "But you know it was the same way for me. Those girls were trespassers, but I'd suggest you not kill them. I don't think you'd do well in prison." She rolled her eyes. "I'm serious. I slept with other girls, but it's not like I actually saw them."

"Then what did you see? Ghosts?"

"No, smart ass. This might make me sound like a huge

asshole, but I didn't see them, *see them*. I imagined they were you. Why do you think I never had a serious girlfriend? When my eyes would open and reality sunk in, I'd realize they weren't you, and I couldn't give another girl my heart when you already had it. So I'd leave and come hang out with you."

"After you'd had sex with them?" She gave me a dirty look. "Gross. I'm not sure if I should smack you for that or slip you some tongue."

"First, I told you I've only had sex with a few girls, but I'd prefer the tongue."

She bent forward and kissed me softly on the lips. "That will have to do for now." I kissed her back, moving my lips to her cheek, and then nuzzling her neck. "I wish we could've done this years ago."

I pulled away, balancing myself with one arm, and looked down at her. "Me too, babe."

"If Tanner were here right now, I'd go kick him in the balls."

I laughed. "He was doing it to protect his baby sister."

"Baby sister? I'm two minutes older than him." She paused, her face suddenly falling. "Or I was."

I tapped her nose with my finger. "He would've been happy for us."

"I know. You were the only guy he trusted me with. I bet if you would've asked him to date me, he would've been okay with it. Sure, you might've had to deal with a few punches to the face, but he would've been okay."

I chuckled. "You're right. Deep down, I knew I'd eventually get the balls to do it, but I thought I'd have more time to do it."

"I like how you're always trying to be the good guy." Her lips twitched into a small smile. "And now that I've gotten my orgasm, can we watch one of my cheesy shows? I'm behind, and my DVR is about full."

I threw my head back in fake horror. "I guess."

She giggled when I tickled her side and started to change the TV channels. "Here you go."

I looked at her in shock when she handed me the remote. It wasn't that easy to win with her. Actually, I'd never won the remote from her. "What's the catch?" I drawl out. "Is this some kind of boyfriend test where the guy has to pick the right movie or the girlfriend gets pissed?"

"Nope, this is the part where I realize that I don't always have to be in charge." She paused, taking a deep breath. "Anyways, I think I'll be a nice girlfriend today, I can't even believe I'm calling myself that, and let you choose the show. Are you sure the medicine isn't giving me hallucinations?"

I laughed. "If so, we're both crazy then. I like the girlfriend version of Tessa."

"That's a really low standard if letting you watch shows makes me the best girlfriend ever," she laughed.

"Oh, that's just the icing on the cake with you, babe." I flipped through her DVR list, putting it on her vampire romance to make her happy. If it meant watching bloodsuckers walk the hallways of their high school with my girl, I had no problem with it.

She gave me a bright smile and turned her attention to the TV. She made herself comfortable in my arms, and thirty minutes later, I heard faint snoring coming from her. I tightened my hold on her and kissed her hair.

CHAPTER 25

DAWSON

"Are you sure you want to come?" I asked Tessa as we both buckled our seatbelts.

She nodded as I started the car and turned the heat on high. "I'm sure," she replied, rubbing her hands together in front of the vent. "I can ask my parents to come with us if you want?"

"I appreciate it, babe, but I'm good." The less witnesses the better.

Tessa was going to regret coming. I was sure of it as I slowly backed out of the driveway. Snow blanketed the trees, covering the rooftops, and the roads were icy. The windshield wipers squeaked back and forth, disposing of the large falling flakes.

My mom asked me to ride with her, but I refused. Today was going to change how she looked at me, and there was no way we'd survive a ride back together after it. She'd probably leave me on the side of the road stranded to freeze to death.

I cautiously kept my hand on the wheel and my eyes on the road. There weren't very many cars out, so thankfully the roads were clear with the exception of the snowplows.

"You know everything is going to be okay, right?" she asked. "Do what's best for you."

I nodded in response but stayed quiet. I appreciated her gesture, but my mind was racing. Was I going to regret what I was thinking about doing? Would my mom hate me forever?

"Quit trying to make everyone else happy and think of yourself for once," she went on. "This decision will affect your life too."

"I'll never stop trying to make you happy," I threw back.

She grinned widely and slapped her hand against her chest dramatically. "I wasn't referring to myself, you can keep making me happy all you want. But other people ... screw 'em. If they don't want to see you happy, then it's all you and me, babe."

"It's you and me," I repeated, merging onto the interstate and driving at a steady speed. Tessa pulled her phone from her bag, plugged it into the stereo, and soft music streamed from the speakers. She kept the volume low, only giving me enough to help me relax.

The drive took us twice as long as it normally does, but we anticipated that and aren't late. Snow crunched underneath our boots as Tessa's glove-covered hand clasped mine tightly. She tightened the scarf around her neck and snuggled into my side as we trudged through the parking lot. We entered the building through double doors and went straight to the courtroom.

The first face I saw was the one I didn't want to. She was still in her seat, and a tissue was clasped in her hand. I still recognized her from my dad's sentencing. My mom forced me to go with her then. I remembered how I'd kept all of my attention on her that day as tears flowed down her face the entire time. When the judge had finally read my dad's sentencing, a woman held her up while she cursed at the jury.

I didn't blame her. I never will. He should've gotten more time for killing her husband. It didn't surprise me that they'd be here ready to fight against my dad's release.

I led Tessa to the other side of the room, and we slid along the bench in the row behind my mom. "Hey ma," I said from behind her, wrapping my arms around her shoulder and kissing her cheek.

She patted my arm with a shaking hand. "Thank you for coming. I've been trying to get ahold of you all morning to make sure you'd be here."

I didn't want to talk to her this morning, so I crashed at Cody's last night. That didn't stop her phone calls, though, which started at five in the morning. I'd finally sent her a text letting her know I'd be there after the sixteenth call. "Sorry, I had my phone on vibrate during the drive. I wanted to keep my eyes on the road."

She gave me a weak smile. "That's fine, honey. You made it here. That's all that matters." She glanced over at Tessa and gave her a head nod, resulting in a friendly wave in response. "I've been praying this works out in your father's favor. If they accept his parole, his attorney said he could be home in the next sixty to ninety days. Our family will be back together as one." I couldn't stop myself from shuddering at the desperation in her voice. She was delusional.

A side door opened, and everyone's attention went to my dad coming in. His feet were in shackles, his hands were cuffed, and two guards walked him to his seat. He had the same outfit on as he always had. His hair was cut short, the ponytail gone, and the goatee was nonexistent. He'd cleaned up in hopes it'd make him look like a better man.

He could look a certain way all he wanted, but that wouldn't change him from being the piece of shit he was.

My mom blew him a kiss, and he nodded at her as I fought down the bile rising up my throat.

We stood up when the parole board walked in with file folders gripped in their hands. We didn't sit back down until they did. They all looked straight at my father, then to his attorney, and then to the prosecution like they were doing a prescreening.

There were seven of them. An odd number to be sure a final decision would be made.

I looked down in shame as they started going through the details of the crime and tried to recreate the scenes in my head. They weren't pretty. My father had gone into a bank with his friend to rob it. They demanded money and then shot the security guard. My dad somehow only got charged with manslaughter because he testified he didn't mean for the gun to fire. The trigger was pulled as they both struggled to fight for the gun.

I hated that he didn't get charged with more. He'd gone into that bank with every intention of robbing it and had a gun with him to be sure nothing got in his way of doing that. Sometimes the law let people off the hook to easily. Sometimes they went too hard on people who didn't deserve it. Our law system was fucked up.

The prosecution argued that my dad was a danger to society. He had a long rap sheet of convictions and incarcerations. He'd been in and out of prison since he turned seventeen. I hardly knew the man. I owed him no empathy. He did something despicable, so I had every right to feel the need for him to deal with the consequences of his crime, blood or not.

How was she expecting me to stick up for a man I hardly knew? A man who'd done nothing but hurt my family for as long as I could remember?

The victim's family stood up for the chance to argue his release. His wife was the only one who spoke. She talked through sobs about how confused her children still are when they ask where Daddy is. She looked at my dad dead in the eye as she explained how hard her family is having trouble paying their bills and had to move in with her parents because she can't afford a home with only her income.

My dad's lawyer finally approached the bench and began his argument. He boasted about my dad's good behavior and how he was working in the kitchen to provide *nutritious and well-cooked* meals to his fellow inmates. He was apparently the fucking Chef Boy of Prison. He also brought up the bullshit apology my dad had given the day of his initial hearing. He'd tried his hardest to put up a halo above his head.

I had to give the attorney credit. He was doing a damn good job. My mom was definitely getting her money's worth ... our money's worth ... every thousand of it that should've went towards our bills.

"Would anyone like to speak on behalf of the defendant?"

My mom jumped to her feet at the question and pulled a piece of paper from her pocket. She head it in front of everyone with tears in her eyes. She begged them to release him because he needed to be home and was having her own financial difficulties. She pleaded that he'd learned his lesson and would never break the law again. She wanted her family back. I needed a father. My hands turned into tight fists, and I had to fight back the urge to snatch the paper from her hands when she brought up the shooting and how I lost Tanner.

She was fucking using that to get her way. My loss was the sharpest key to his chains. One fist loosened when Tessa took it in hers, and the other dug into the wood of the bench in front of me.

My mom closed her statement by telling the courtroom I'd like to speak next. I took in a deep breath as all eyes went to me.

Even though I knew it wasn't going to happen, I'd prayed last night that she wouldn't involve me. That she wouldn't ask me to do this. I'd hoped her seeing my father would cloud her train of thought, and she'd forget I was even there. I gulped as I pulled myself up, slid between the people sitting in my row, and walked to her side. I didn't look at her as I opened my mouth and did what I'd contemplated doing since she brought this day up.

"I don't think my father should be released from prison," I said.

Shock struck through the room with different reactions. A hard sob tore through my mother's chest as she took a step away from me as if I was now poisonous. The victim's wife gasped but there was a different light in her eyes now. I pointed to the stranger who'd wanted me to defend him and took a good look at the man I never wanted to know. The veins in his neck protruded, showing through his skin, and I could tell he was holding back every ounce of anger to keep up with his good guy act.

"This man has done nothing but destroy not only my family and other's. He won't change." I avoided the crowd and looked straight at Tessa. Her eyes met mine, and she gave me a nod of support. "He's been released before. He swore up and down that he was a changed man. That *changed man* robbed a bank and killed an innocent man – a father, a husband, a son. My mother is right when she says I've had a tough year, and I wish I did have a father, but that man isn't anyone I want in my life."

CHAPTER 26

TESSA

DAWSON HANDED ME TWO HEAVY TRASH BAGS FULL OF clothes. "Can you take these to your car?" he asked.

We'd drove straight to his house after the hearing in hopes of beating his mom before she got here. He threw all of his belongings into bags.

I'd never forget the rage on his mom's face when Dawson didn't vouch for his dad. I was just as shocked as everyone in the room. He'd told me he was thinking about going against his mom's wishes, but he wasn't sure what to do. He was stuck between doing what was right and doing what wouldn't hurt someone he loved.

His dad's parole was denied, and his mom stomped out of the courtroom behind him screaming that he was kicked out of her house. I'd wanted to slap her in her face and tell her to wake up.

She knew Dawson had nowhere else to go and he'd given her most of his money to help pay the bills.

I took the bag from him with a comforting smile and walked outside. I unlocked my car before hitting the trunk release and was careful not to slide on ice as I tossed them into the trunk. I jumped at the sound of tires squealing next to me.

"Was this your idea?" Dawson's mom yelled, jumping from the car and slamming the door shut behind her. She marched up to me with both hands latched to her hips.

I should've known she'd blame this on everyone but herself. "I don't know what you're talking about," I replied, looking away from her. I'd only met her a few times. She wasn't around much, but she'd never been rude to me before.

"Did you tell him not to help his father out?" Venom spewed alongside her words, and I took a step cautious step back.

I tightened my scarf with shivering hands. "I didn't. Dawson makes his own decisions, and I support whatever makes him happy."

"And you don't think I want my son to be happy?" she snapped back.

"It doesn't seem like it."

She winced at my response. It probably wasn't a good idea for me to get on her bad side, but I was always going to stick up for Dawson. It was my turn to be his wall. He needed me now. "I'm sure your family's stuck up and rich influence had nothing to do with it," she replied sarcastically.

"No, they didn't. No one did."

She shoved her finger my way. "Listen here, Ms. Goody Two-Shoes, we all know your high-profile daddy spent a night in jail for joyriding while drinking, so maybe you shouldn't look down on people for making mistakes. People deserve a second chance."

Tears pricked at my eyes. I agreed what my dad did was

wrong, and I understood second chances, but Dawson's second chance to his father wasn't mine to give. It was his, and it wasn't the second time his dad had fucked up. That man had let him down his entire life.

"You can stop right there," I snapped, my voice as cold as the snow around us. "Don't you dare talk about my family and our struggles. I understand you're upset with Dawson, but you should support him, not lash out because it didn't go your way. He's always made you a priority in his life. Now is the time for you to do the same for him."

"You think I'm going to support him when he's the reason Phillip got more time?"

My shoulders slumped. I'd been hoping my words would wake her up, but she was still asleep. "More time?" I repeated, disgust rolling with my words. "He got sentenced to that time for a crime he committed. Every person in the victim's family was there, and they weren't going home without a fight. If I were you, I'd go apologize, tell him to unpack his bags, and make things right before you lose him and have nobody. He didn't only do that for himself, you know?"

Her eyes grew like fire. "You stupid little bitch," she snarled.

"Ma, get away from her," Dawson yelled, warning clear in his tone. I turned around to find him standing on the porch with more bags in his hands. "Leave her alone. She had nothing to do with this. If you want to be pissed at someone, be pissed at me." He walked down the stairs, tossed the trash bags in my backseat, and stood in front of her.

"I didn't know I had to spell shit out for you! You went in there and made it worse instead of doing what I said and telling them you needed your dad."

"Newsflash! I don't need him!"

"But I do!" She slammed her finger in his chest. "Don't you

get that, you selfish brat? I need him! You have the girl you love."
She moved her finger to point it at me angrily. "Why can't you
want the same for me?"

"It's not like that," Dawson said.

"Save it," she interrupted. "It doesn't matter anymore. Get
your shit and get gone. You're not welcome here. I'll be in my
bedroom until you're finished collecting your shit." She stuck her
hand out. "Keys." Her voice was completely void of emotion. The
woman only cared about herself.

All of the color drained from Dawson's face, but he quickly
got himself together and fished the key ring from his pocket.
"Here." He unclipped the key and placed it into her hand. "I love
you, Ma. No matter what, I want you to know that."

"Good luck," she said before walking past him straight into
the house.

I waited until the door slammed shut behind her before
stepping into his space. "Dawson," I whispered.

He held out his hands, stopping me. "Please get in the car
and turn on the heat. You shouldn't be standing out here in the
cold. I need to grab a few more things then we can go."

I nodded and watched him go back inside before getting in
my car. My hands shivered as I turned the heat on high, took of
my hands, and ran them back and forth against each other. I
jumped when the passenger door a few minutes later and
Dawson slumped into the passenger seat, a sorrow look on
his face.

"Just drive," he whispered, stretching the seatbelt across his
body while I did the same. "I need to get the hell away
from here."

I backed the car out of the driveway and carefully turned
onto the street. "What are you doing to do?" I finally asked when
we were almost to my house.

He shrugged. "I have some money saved up – not enough to

rent a place yet, but I'll ask for extra shifts. Until then, I'll ask Cody or Ollie if I can crash at their place. If not, I'll stay at a motel or something."

"What about staying with us?"

"Appreciate the offer, baby, but I don't think your parents will go for that."

"Why? You've spent the night there hundreds of times."

"That's when I hung out with your brother and wasn't dating you."

"So? There's no difference."

He chuckles. "There is a big difference."

It was a few days before Christmas. I wasn't letting him stay at some motel or with a friend. I liked Cody and Ollie, but there wasn't enough room for Dawson to stay with them. He needed to be with his family for the holiday, and we were his family.

"My parents love you," I went on. "We can at least ask. What's the worse that can happen? They say no? If they do, we'll come up with something else." I carefully turned the corner but had to correct my wheel before we slid into the other lane.

Dawson tilted his head towards the window, and a circle formed around his mouth from his breathing. "This is fucking humiliating," he muttered. He hated asking for help or handouts.

"We're past humiliating ourselves in front of each other, remember?" I grinned over at him. "I've seen you act like a drunken fool and fight Tanner over the last White Castle cheeseburger."

That granted me a weak smile from him. "I told you not to bring that shit up. You promised."

"*Oh please,* just like I told you not to bring up my terrible face mask experiment."

He chuckled, shaking his head. "We're one destructible pair, aren't we?"

"Yep. The good thing is that we know everything about each other, flaws and all, so nothing can surprise us."

"But are they flaws if I love them?" he asked.

I looked over at him grinning. "No, I guess they're not."

CHAPTER 27

TESSA

I sat in the recliner while watching Dawson spread out blankets on the couch in the living room. He grabbed a pillow and situated it before falling back against the cushions. We told my parents about what happened, and they offered him a place to stay. He was apprehensive at first, and I thought he wasn't going to take it out of embarrassment, but they wouldn't take no for an answer.

My parents had been working hard on their recovery. They hadn't taken a sip, to my knowledge, of alcohol and were home with us every night. Things weren't as perfect as they used to be, but they were getting better than what they'd been after Tanner's death.

I got up from the chair to sit down next to him. "Has your mom called yet?" I asked.

He shook his head. "I checked my phone a few times and turned it off an hour ago. I'm not waiting around for a call I know it's coming."

I sighed and allowed my head to fall on his shoulder. I knew he was going through a whirlwind of emotions. He'd lost what little family he had, and the only belongings he had now were in trash bags. "Maybe she'll change her mind."

"She made her decision and turned her back on the only person who's ever been there for her." His voice grew harsh. "I was the one who begged for more hours at work to help with the bills, and in return, she'd give that money over to him. There were weeks we'd go without groceries because his commissary was more important. We were living off leftover pizza from my work and peanut butter sandwiches. Everything has always been about him, and that's never going to change. I knew if he got out, it would only get worse. He would use her and use her until he broke down every piece of her. At least now he can't do that."

His hands wrapped around my waist, and I relaxed myself as he situated me on his lap. He glanced down at me, and I shivered at the feel of his fingers brushing my hair away from my eyes.

"You're always helping people," I said. "You're amazing, incase you didn't already know."

"I help the people I love," he replied.

I took in a deep breath when he tilted his head down to kiss me. I lightly pressed my lips against his before pulling away. He needed to know. I stood up and looked at him nervously, watching his eyes focus on me before I lifted a leg and brought myself back down to straddle his lap.

I rested my palm on his chest. "You know I love you, right?" He needed to know this. "I know you said you wanted to wait until I loved myself before we got intimate, but I need you to know where my head and heart is. It's you making me this happy.

It's you who I want to be with for the rest of my life. I love myself
... and I love you."

The bright smile passing over his lips made my stomach
flutter. Goose bumps spread across my skin when his lips hit my
chest. I sighed, enjoying the feel of him raining kisses along the
edge of my camisole. I hooked my arms around his neck and
leaned in to give him better access. He pulled my top down with
his teeth and squeezed my breasts together.

I moaned out in ecstasy, trying my hardest to keep my voice
down. Who was this girl? That girl who'd been nervous about her
inexperience was now melting in his arms and begging him
for more.

His hands roamed down to my waist, his fingers digging into
my flesh, and he pushed my top up and over my head. He
brushed each side of my breast in hesitation, waiting for me to
give him the green light. There was no way I was putting a stop to
this. I wanted him just as much as he wanted me. Maybe more.

I quickly unsnapped my bra, giving him all of the permission
he needed. There was nothing more attractive than watching the
expression on his face when my breasts dropped as my bra fell to
my lap. His hands went to my hair to bring me closer to his lips,
and he kissed me urgently. I allowed him to release all of his
frustrations with me. He breathed in the gasps escaping my lungs
and massaged my breasts as I started to grind against him. Our
tongues danced together as I got lost in him.

I hastily pushed his shirt over his head and leaned back to get
a good look at his bare chest before running my fingers across the
smooth, rippled skin. I outlined the contours of his muscles and
bent down to take his nipple between my lips. He bit into his lip,
his eyes pinching together, and his hand dived back into my hair.

I loved that I was making him feel this good, and the fear of
my inexperience was evaporating. He moved my hand to palm

my breasts and took my nipple in his mouth. I reached down to unbuckle his shorts and yanked them down.

That's when he stopped me. "Tessa, we can't do this here."

"Everyone's asleep," I assured. *Please don't stop. I need this. We need this.*

He cursed underneath his breath when I grinded against him again. I could feel him through his boxers. He was hard and ready for me.

His head fell back as I kept rocking against him.

I grinned. I won.

He slammed his hips up, and we moved in harmony with each other. I leaned forward, resting my hands on the top of the couch for support, until I got the perfect angle of his cock hitting the perfect spot.

I gave him a dirty look when he pulled away *again.*

"We're not having sex for the first time on your parent's couch while we're trying to be quiet," he said around heavy breaths.

I chewed on the bottom of lip. "Then what can we do?"

A mischievous grin spread across his lips. "Lay down, baby." I took one arm off the couch slowly, balanced myself, and laid down. I took in a deep breath and waited for what was coming next.

He untied the waistband of my bottoms and slowly dragged them down my legs. His eyes hooded as he ran his hands over the red fabric of my panties. He spread his fingers out, using each one to touch me in a different spot before kissing me over my panties.

It was the most intimate experienced I'd ever had.

My heart pulled at my chest as all of my blood shot to my core. I was nervous but anxious at the same time. His arm reached back to grab a blanket and he pulled it over us at the same I felt the weight of his body on top of me.

"I thought we weren't having sex?" I muttered, swallowing hard at the feel of his naked body against mine.

"We're not," is all he answered.

I tilted my head in confusion, but didn't get the chance to keep asking questions because he kissed me hard. I released a gasp into his mouth as our tongues lapped each other's, and the intensity burning through me grew hotter. He broke away to rise up on his elbows and looked down at us underneath the blanket. He reached down, and I jumped at the feel of his erection sliding against my heat.

"Is this okay?" he asked. I nodded – even though I wasn't sure exactly what *this* was, but I was perfectly fine with wherever *it* was going. He groaned. "Thank god."

Our bodies created this perfect, comfortable rhythm, and he stimulated me with his cock without ever slipping inside the place I wanted him the most. The friction of our bodies, of the part of him I'd never experienced until right now, awoke every sensation inside of me. I met his every stroke with excitement as our momentum built.

I watched his muscles tense when he lifted himself up to get a better angle. Pressure built up inside of me and I felt like a balloon ready to burst. I spread my legs wider and got completely lost in him until I felt weightless underneath him while crying out my release.

"That was amazing," I panted out, looking up at him. He looked ... pained, and it only took me a few seconds to figure out why. I could still feel him hard against me. "Oh shit, carry on."

He laughed and grinned before going back to work, his pace quickening, and he groaned deep from his chest before I felt something warm hit my stomach. I noticed the thin, white substance when he dipped the blanket down.

"Sorry," he said with a weak laugh. "I didn't know where

exactly to go. You felt so damn good I didn't have the time or strength to pull away."

I grinned. "It's fine." I wasn't sure why, but I liked it. I rubbed my hand down my stomach and played with the sticky substance between my fingers before spreading it over my skin like lotion. I wanted the evidence of him being there to last forever. He bent down, grabbed his shirt from the floor, and wiped my stomach clean. I tried to get my breathing under control as he grabbed my panties and put them back on for me.

"I have a feeling your parents won't be very happy if they find us down here naked," he said, continuing to dress me because I didn't have the energy to do it myself.

"I love you," I said when he finished.

"And I love you," he replied, kissing the top of my head.

You know that feeling when you're really sleepy – not exhausted, just sleepy, and when you finally get the chance to snuggle into the comfort of your sheets? It feels like the best place in the world and you'd never want to be anywhere else.

That was what being with Dawson felt like.

☙❧

"Shit!"

I woke up at the sound of the loud voice and pulled away from Dawson's chest.

"Damn, this couch is uncomfortable as shit," he groaned. "But I did sleep pretty well."

I peeked up at him while yawning loudly. "Me, too. I haven't slept that well in forever." I snuggled in closer to him. "I didn't even take my sleeping pill."

He chuckled at the sound of my stomach growling. "Come on, let's get you something to eat."

Cold air wrapped around my body like a cloak when he

flipped off the blankets. I felt the weight of him rolling over me as he got to his feet and then helped me up.

"Good morning, children," Derrick sang out when we walked into the kitchen. Him and my dad were both sitting at the table with a plate of food in front of them. Derrick used the back of his hand to wipe milk from his upper lip and then revealed a large grin on his face. "My bad if I woke you guys up."

I spotted my mom at the stove pouring pancake batter into a pan. I played with my hands and waited for her to say something about us sleeping together on the couch, but I only got a smile.

"Good morning, I hope you guys have an appetite," she said, cheerfully.

Derrick dropped his fork on his plate. "So does that mean I'm allowed to have girls stay over now? There's this girl in my Science class who's seriously smokin'. She wants me."

"Shut it, twerp," I warned, smacking him in the back of his head and taking the seat across from him as he forked a mouthful of eggs into his mouth.

"What?" he asked, eggs falling from his mouth. "I'm just looking for equal rights in this place."

"I'm sorry," Dawson said. "We were talking and must've fallen asleep." He took the seat next to me. There was no way my parents could've missed the blush hitting my cheeks as I thought about what we'd done last night. It sure as hell wasn't talking.

"You guys were on the couch and had a long day, so I'll let it slide," my dad answered, lifting his mug and taking a long drink before going on. "But we will have to set some ground rules now that you're staying here."

"You're going to be staying here?" Derrick yelled in excitement. Dawson nodded. "Swaaaweeet."

My mom handed over pancakes while they went over the rules with us. No hanging out behind closed doors. The birds and bees talk came next, which was no only embarrassing, but completely ruined my appetite. They set a plan for all of us to go through Tanner's room together so Dawson wouldn't have to sleep on the couch.

"Looks like we have a new member in the fam," Derrick said. "I'll take it."

"You were always a member of our family," my dad replied.

Everyone smiled.

CHAPTER 28

TESSA

SNOWFLAKES FLOATED FROM THE CLOUDY SKY, AND I SMILED brightly as I watched the winter wonderland form in front of my eyes.

I loved snow on Christmas.

If there was anything I looked forward to every year, it was waking up to a cold and frosty morning and watching the cascade of snow paint everything in sight. Tanner wasn't able to be here with us for Christmas this year, but he was in spirit. I know he made sure he sent snow down like butterflies from heaven to let me know I wasn't alone.

"Can we get to the present unwrapping part now?" Derrick asked, storming down the stairs and plopping down on the floor next to the Christmas tree that was decorated with bright golds, dark reds, and flashes of green. White lights wrapped around the branches.

My dad started to pull down the stockings from the fireplace. Everyone had one, including Tanner and Dawson. I'd written a letter for Tanner on Christmas Eve and slid it in there for him. In it, I promised to do it every year.

I took in the view one last time before turning around and sitting on the couch. I hummed along with the Christmas music spilling through the speakers while looking over at Dawson. His arm slid around my shoulders, and my body drifted across the leather until I was in his arms. I made myself comfortable while Derrick began passing out the presents.

I was happy when I saw the presents being handed to Dawson. We all wanted to make sure he didn't feel left out. The holidays were going to be hard for him. His mom still hadn't reached out. I even called her myself and left a voicemail inviting her over for the holidays, but nothing.

"What's this?" I asked, holding up the long rectangular box in front of me. A red ribbon was wrapped around it and tied into a small bow at the top. I looked up to find my parents and Derrick leaving the room.

"Open it," Dawson insisted, eagerly nudging me with his elbow.

My heart pounded against my chest as I untied the bow, dragging the ribbon off, and set the box in my lap before slowly pulling the lid up. I gasped as bright gold sparkled against the sunlight peeking through the room. I stared at it in awe while tracing my fingers against the chain link bracelet.

"It's beautiful," I whispered.

Dawson grabbed the box and carefully pulled the bracelet out. His hand captured my mine, and I waited for him to clasp it around my wrist, but he didn't. Instead, he turned it over and pressed his lips against my scars.

I quickly pulled away.

"What's wrong?" he asked.

I looked down at the hideous lines embedded in my skin. "They're ugly." They made me feel ugly.

"They'll heal."

I shook my head. "They'll always be there."

His face softened. "Baby, everyone has scars they don't want people to see, yours just happen to be more visible than others."

"Yay me," I muttered.

He grabbed my wrist again. "Scar tissue is stronger than regular tissue, Tess. That means that these marks right here are some of the strongest parts of you." He kissed my skin again.

I couldn't hold back the tears as he wrapped the bracelet around it before clasping it together. I held out my hand and stared at it in excitement. The links looped together in the middle of the bracelet.

"It's a knot bracelet," he explained.

"A knot bracelet?" I questioned.

"It symbolizes two people coming together. We're weaving our lives, embarking on a new journey, and no matter what happens we'll never meet the end. We'll always look around and meet each other."

I sniffled as I admired my wrist and brushed my fingers along it. "I love it. Thank you." It covered my scars perfectly. When I looked at my wrist now, I wouldn't see the flaws in my skin that reminded me of when I was in such a dark place. Instead, I'd see gold glistening against my skin that showed me I had promise and happiness in my future. It'd remind me how much I was loved.

"I like the symbol," he went on. "I was thinking we'd get our wedding bands engraved with the them when the day comes, too." I flinched in surprise. He chuckled. "What? Did you think I wasn't going to make you my wife someday? Baby, I'm never letting you go as long as you'll have me."

Butterflies swam through me, and I closed my eyes to savor

this feeling. "I'll always have you." I didn't realize I was crying until I felt his fingers wiping them from my cheek.

"What kind of wedding do you want?"

"I'm not sure." I wasn't thinking clearly. I was still hung up on the fact that Dawson was telling me everything I'd been dreaming about since I was a teen sporting braces.

"There's no way you and Daisy didn't act out fake wedding days."

I smirked. "Nope." I leaned back in his arms as he gave me a look. "Okay, *maybe just* a few times." He grinned at the fact he was right. "What kind of wedding do you want?"

"Any one that will make you my wife."

I looked up at him in annoyance. "Seriously? How can you even have an answer that perfect?"

He laughed. "I've held it in for years, waiting for you to bring it up."

I nudged his chest playfully, and he grabbed my face to kiss me. "God, I love you."

"And I love you."

He grabbed my wrist and kissed it above the bracelet. "Merry Christmas to the most amazing girl I somehow landed."

CHAPTER 29

TESSA

My head spun and the back of my throat burned. I wrapped my hand around the door handle like I was on a roller coaster hanging on for dear life.

"I can't do this," was what I'd been repeating in my head all morning but with one look at the parking lot I changed my mind.

I couldn't do it.

The courage that I'd spent days building up had stayed at my house, tucked into my bed, and wasn't coming out.

My family and I had stayed in the majority of winter break, hibernating together, with the exception of piling up our snow gear and sledding for a day. I'd visited Daisy on Christmas when she was home visiting her parents to catch up. She'd told me about the guy Dawson had argued with when she came to the hospital. They were dating and he was helping her move on from her loss of Tanner. I was happy she was happy. Dawson apologized for acting like a dick.

They gave my mom back her job at the pharmacy, and my dad's law firm gave him another chance. That didn't mean he still didn't hear the snide remarks about his arrest, but he still managed to keep his head up. Just like my suicide attempt, he knew it would never go away and we needed to ignore it.

The county decided to tear down the wing of classrooms where the shooting had occurred and built a new one on the opposite end of the school. It was going to take a year to complete, which meant I'd never have to walk those halls again. I was okay with that. I didn't want to relive that nightmare. I didn't think I'd be able to manage to keep my cool when I put my books into my locker and Tanner wasn't next to me.

"You'll do fine, babe," Dawson assured, turning the car off.

I didn't reply because I was too busy watching the groups of people walk across the parking lot towards the doors to our school. Different scenarios of what would happen today had been playing through my mind. Did they know? They had to know. Would they point and make fun of me? And Reese ... I'd have to face him. Did him and his friends still want revenge for the party incident?

The people in that building had hurt me. I couldn't blame them for everything. I'd already been standing on the ledge with a pounding heart contemplating whether to take the job, but their words and actions struck me, causing me to lose my balance and fall.

"I changed my mind. I can't be here." The words rushed out of my mouth.

My parents gave me the option of homeschool for the last semester so I wouldn't have to do this. That would've never happened in the past, but they were still fearful of me hurting myself again. I'd wanted to be strong when they asked me. A large part of my recovery was moving on and facing my fears. These people, this school, they were one of my fears. They might've pushed me down, but I wanted to drag myself up and charge back with full force. That was until I was actually facing them head on. Everyone is mighty until it's time to step into the ring.

"It's too late," he said, turning in his seat and looking at me. "You know I'm not going to let anything happen to you. Go in there, stomp your hot ass down the hallway, and let them know they can't fuck with you. If they think you're intimidated, they'll jump on you like hyenas, but if they think you don't give a shit, they'll tuck their tail between their legs and find someone else to fuck with. The game isn't fun if your prey isn't scared."

"Let's just hope I don't freak out," I said, exhaling through my nose

"You're not going to freak out. Do you know how amazing you've been? Your doctor even told you your recovery is phenomenal. You think your parents, the doctor, or I would let you come back if we thought it was bad for you? If we thought you couldn't handle it?"

"Fine," I groaned like a child. "Let's get it moving then because you know how much I hate being late."

I finally pulled down on the lever to the door. I took a deep breath, stepped one foot out of the car while taking another breath, and pulled the second one out. Dawson grabbed my backpack from the backseat for me and then came to my side to take my hand.

The stares hit us as soon as soon as I got out.

They knew.

Oh, they definitely knew.

There were looks of concern, hate, understanding, and empathy. They were all different, but that didn't stop each one feeling like a punch in the gut. Dawson's hold on my hand tightened and I kept my head down as he led us down to the hallway to his locker.

"I'll just go get my stuff," I said, turning around to leave, but his grasp on me didn't let go, and I was pulled back. "Okay, I guess I can wait for you to get yours and then we'll get mine." He didn't want me out wandering the halls alone. I felt like a child who couldn't leave without her babysitter. I didn't like it.

He opened his locker and handed me a notebook. "How did you get this?" I asked, looking down at the cover and seeing my handwriting.

"I moved your stuff out of your locker and into mine," he explained, shrugging and grabbing a few more books.

"How did you know my combo?"

He grinned sheepishly. "I bribed the office clerk with donuts."

"Look at you, Casanova," I mocked.

"Keep your phone on you, okay," he said, shutting the locker. "And if anyone tries to talk shit, hit 'em with the right hook."

I laughed. "I was thinking more along the lines of a choke slam."

He pulled me into his side and chuckled. "Now that's my girl."

❧❦❧

"Can we talk?" The familiar voice startled me. I turned around to find Reese standing behind me at our table with a food tray in his hand. I gulped, trying to remember all of the speeches I'd planned to give him when I saw him for the first time but nothing was coming out.

He'd let his dark hair grow out, and it was pulled back into a ponytail. A baggy sweatshirt covered his chest, and he bit down onto his lip piercing. He didn't look at anyone else at the table.

He just kept his dark eyes on me like he wanted me to fall under his trance again.

I broke away from his stare at the sound of the chair next to me screeching against the floor. "I can't believe you even have the nerve to talk to her," Dawson sneered, standing up and circling around the table to get into Reese's face. Ollie shot up to stop him before he made it all the way.

"Dawson, stop," I said quietly, keeping my voice low in fear of causing a scene, but it was too late. I should've known everyone would be watching Reese and me, waiting for our next conversation and hoping there would be a blowout.

Tough shit for them.

They weren't getting that from me.

I'd started first period timidly sitting at my desk and not making eye contact with anyone. I heard the snickers, the whispers, and the flat out rude comments, but I ignored them. Second period, my anger started to surface, but I kept my cool. By third period, I was flipping off every single person who'd ever pissed me off. If I couldn't lash out on them, I was at least telling them how I felt figuratively.

"There's no way in hell I'm letting this asshole come near you," Dawson said. Ollie stumbled back when he pushed him away to get to Reese.

"Not here," I hissed. Dawson stopped and looked over at me, reading the look on my face, and took a step back. He slid his hands into his pockets and waited for my next move. My attention went back to Reese. "We're not doing this here."

Reese gripped his tray. "I've tried calling you, but it says your phone is off." I threw my phone in the trash and changed my number the day I got home. "I didn't know how else to get ahold of you."

I looked at him straight in the face. "I don't think there's anything we need to talk about."

"I need to apologize." My throat grew thick. I didn't want to hear his apology. I wanted him to leave me alone. "I need to explain myself."

"Dude, you don't have shit to explain to her other than the fact that you're a fucking loser," Cody snarled, his lip curling up in disgust. "And we already know that. You're a pussy who hurts girls and has his friends fight for him."

"I didn't have them do shit," Reese fired back. The tension in the air grew thicker. "And you don't know shit about me and Tessa."

"Fine," I said, cutting into their argument. "Stop by my house after school and we'll talk."

"I'll be there," Reese said.

"Five minutes. That's all I'm giving you."

He nodded and walked away.

Dawson sat back down. "You don't have to do that," he said. "I'll tell the asshole to get fucked."

"I know I don't have to, but I think I need to," I answered.

⚜

MY STOMACH WAS A TWISTED BUNDLE OF NERVES THE REST of the day. The stares continued, but thankfully the insults had stopped. I guess they'd gotten word of my middle finger response. Dawson was right about them not having fun if the person they're making fun of isn't crouching in fear.

Dawson was waiting at our locker at the end of the day. He handed me my bag with a kiss on the cheek. "Everything go away? Your elbow sore?"

I laughed. "I actually had to drop kick a few, but other than that I'm fine."

He kept laughing as I grabbed my notebooks and slid them into my book bag. "The gossip has already moved on." He grabbed my hand after slamming the locker shut. The feel of his fingers interlaced in mine helped me relax my nerves as we walked down the hallway.

"Oh really?" I rolled my eyes at the same time he nodded. "I doubt that."

We walked down the salted sidewalks, and I noticed the shadows of our breath hanging through the air. "I guess some freshman is pregnant with the quarterback's baby."

"I don't think that one is going to take all the attention off me. There's always a pregnant girl in school."

"You're right, but it gets better. Quarterback boy has a girlfriend."

"Surprise, surprise," I muttered.

"And that girlfriend is the older sister of the pregnant one."

"And shit just got real," I joked before getting serious. "But I'm done with the gossip. Who knows what the real story is."

Gossip was a bitter, ugly bitch. Something that was always created out of jealousy and spite for people who wanted to bring others down. They were resentful of them, insecure, or just hated their own lives that they needed to drag someone down in order to bring themselves up.

My car beeped when Dawson unlocked it, and I carefully got into the passenger side without busting my butt on the ice. Dawson put the heat on high, and the ice-kissed windshield began to defrost. He was careful on the way home, and I was surprised when we pulled into the driveway to see Reese's beat-up car sitting idly in front of my house. The windows were down, and he was smoking a cigarette.

"I can still tell the asshole to get lost," Dawson said, the veins in his neck pulsating.

I shook my head. "No, I need to talk to him." I kissed him on the lips before opening my door.

"How about I stand on the porch?"

I slapped his shoulder. "No."

He sighed dramatically. "God, I hate it when you get all bossy. Just let me take one swing at the guy and then I'll let him talk to you."

He held up his hands at the look I gave him. "I'm sure he feels bad about what happened at the party. No need to have any more fights."

"I could care less about what he did to me. I got a few bruises, but no big deal. That shit heals. I want to punch his arrogant face in for what he did to you. The heart takes more time to heal than a few bruises."

"I'll be okay," I reassured.

We both got out. Dawson kept his eyes on Reese as he headed toward the house. I waited until he went in before I pulled on Reese's passenger side door handle. After a few pulls, I finally managed to get it open. The same stench still lingered, and he still hadn't taken the time to clean out his car. It was actually worse. Blankets were laid out on the backseat like he'd maybe been sleeping there. Cans of soda and beer along with chips and food wrappers were scattered across the blankets and floorboard.

He his cigarette out the window and then lit another.

"You know those things will kill you," I said, sitting down.

He lifted the cigarette and shrugged. "They're harmless."

"I thought the same about you."

He coughed around the cigarette, my words surprising him, and dragged it from his mouth. "Damn, you're not going to go easy on me, are you?" I stayed quiet and looked out the windshield. He scratched his head while trying to come up with what to say next. "I see you and pretty boy finally got together. I knew that shit was bound to happen."

"I didn't agree to this so you could talk about him or my relationship."

He nodded in understanding. "You look happy."

"I'm getting there."

"I'm happy for you, love, I really am." Low music playing from the stereo interrupted our silence. "Look, I wanted to talk to you so you'd know I'm not that guy."

"And what kind of guy is that?" I asked. My voice cracked with anger as I shot him a disgusted look. "You used me. You acted like you liked me, took my virginity, and then dropped me like a bad habit. You also humiliated me in front of a room full of people and then had your friends jump the guy who stuck up for me. So please tell me what kind of guy does that?"

He let out a sharp breath and smashed his cigarette into the ashtray. "I know, fuck." He groaned. "You scared the shit out of me." He paused and lit another cigarette. "I saw them."

"You saw what?"

"Your scars."

My eyes grew blurry as I looked at him in shock. "What? How?"

"I woke up earlier than you when you spent the night at my house. Your arm was out of the blankets and spread across your pillow. I thought I was imagining it at first until I saw there was more than one. I've been through shit and gotten myself out of it. I knew you had problems, but I didn't know they were that bad ... bad enough that you'd try to kill yourself. I knew what it was like being in a dark place. I cared about you, but it scared me. It scared the fuck out of me. So I fled. It's what I do because I'm a coward. I run away and hurt people because I'm a piece of shit."

My heart dropped, but that didn't mean I forgave him. "So you didn't use me from the beginning?" I mocked. "I highly doubt that."

"It was all for fun at the beginning. I won't like about that. You were hot and a challenge." I scoffed, realizing what I felt for Reese was never love. I'd just been infatuated with the attention he gave me.

"So I was just a game to you?"

He shook his head. "When I got to know you I realized you were more than that – more than some rich girl pissed at her parents and going through shit. You were hurting, really fucking hurting, and I thought maybe I could be the guy to fix you. But I'm too fucked up myself to try to fix anyone. I would've done nothing but hurt you more. So I ran."

"But took my virginity first."

"Yeah, that was bad judgment on my part and I'm an asshole for that. I'm not the kind of guy you date. I'm not the kind of guy you bring home to your parents and talk about your future kids. I'm the in-between guy. I let you drink your thoughts away, fuck you, let your wild side come out, and then let you go on your way. We may talk afterwards, have random hook-ups here and there, but it was never going to go past that."

"So why did you even want to talk to me? Why are you here?"

"I wanted to see how you were doing after," he paused, like he was afraid bringing it up would set me off. "Whatever happened. You don't have to talk about it. I wanted closure with us. I don't want you to hate me. I've tried to apologize to your guy, but he's got a stick up his ass."

I nodded in understanding. I'd thought I wanted closure as well, but now that I was facing him I realized I'd never get that from him. I had to get closure from myself because I'd been the one to make those decisions. I was the one who allowed myself to get manipulated. He wasn't who I had to forgive for my heartache. It was me.

"Fine, I don't hate you. Is that the closure you wanted?" I ignored the part about Dawson. There was no way he'd let Reese try to bullshit him with an apology.

He looked at me baffled. "There's no way it's that easy."

"It actually is." He continued to stare at me, his eyes wide and mouth slightly hanging open. "Does this mean we're going to be hanging out and being best friends? No. But I'm not going to go on and be upset anymore. What happened, happened. You can't take it back. I can't take it back. There's no correcting the damage."

"I guess you're right. But I do want you to know one thing."

"What?"

"When I told you I liked you, I did. I'll be honest that I wasn't in love with you, but I did like you. You're an amazing person. I want you to know that. I'd never feel for you like that pretty boy jackass does. I'm glad you have him to make you happy now."

"Thanks." I paused. "And you too ... with whatever."

He laughed. "Babe, there ain't no making me happy, but I find my own ways to make it work."

I nodded and grabbed the door handle. "Take care of yourself, Reese."

His shoulders slumped. "You too."

I got out and walked to the door without looking back.

Did I hate Reese? No.

Did I want to be around him again? No.

That ship had sailed. Reese had taught me who I didn't want to be. He'd taught me that not everyone in your life was meant to stay there and that every decision you make impacts your future.

I was grateful for that.

I'd forever remember it.

CHAPTER 30

DAWSON

I stood at the open doorway to Tessa's bedroom while trying my hardest to hold in my laughter as I watched her attempt to zip the luggage on her bed. She fell forward, her stomach smacking against the top of the back, and tried to grab the top handle to drag it off the bed. The thing weighed almost as much as she did.

"You stupid thing," she muttered, wrapping her arms around each side and dropping it down onto the floor, nearly taking herself down with it. She pushed the bag upright, cursed at it a few times, and grabbed the handle to stand it up straight.

"You ready to go?" I asked, unable to hold back any longer. "Or do you want to kick the bag's ass some more?"

She jumped at the sound of my voice and turned around to look at me. "Funny," she said, waving her hands toward the bag "I could've used some help."

I chuckled. "It looked like you had it covered."

She flipped me off. "I'll probably end up disposing of your body in it at the side of the road anyways."

A wicked grin slipped over my lips. "I don't think you'd do very well in prison, babe. You do know they don't allow curling irons in the big house, right?"

She scrunched up her nose and looked at me in annoyance. "I'm still debating whether or not it's worth it at the moment."

I placed my hand over my heart. "Promise to make it quick. We've had a long run, but I knew you'd eventually kick my ass to the curb."

"Literally," she added, her pink, glossy lips smirking into a smile.

I pointed at her. "You really scare me sometimes."

She shrugged. "That's the point. Boyfriends need to be terrified of their girlfriends and basically be their servants. Now get my bags, Mr. Thomas."

"If you didn't have a smile on your face at the moment, I'd truly be terrified of you and all of your one hundred twenty-five pounds." I laughed and stalked forward, stopping in front of her. She squealed as I lifted her up in the air and tossed her down onto the bed. I jumped on top of her and relished in her laughter as I looked down. "Plus, you wouldn't want to pleasure yourself for the rest of your life."

Her blue eyes peeked up at me as she laughed. "That's your argument for your life? That the pleasuring you give me would be gone?" She shook her head. "You really need to work on your persuasion tactics. Boyfriends can easily be bought at any store alongside the interstate. They have signs everywhere advertising it."

"Yeah, I think that's the best logic. There's nothing better than the real thing."

She smiled and wrapped her arms around my neck. "I shall keep you then."

I smiled back, my eyes focusing on the beauty in front of me. The mass of sunshine colored hair hung loose and sprawled out against her comforter. She thought I saved her, but the truth was that she saved me too. She'd been doing it for years. I had the strength to help her get through her tough time because she'd been helping me build mine through the years.

I twisted a tendril of her hair and leaned down to give her a peck on the lips. "And I shall keep the promise of pleasure." I lifted myself up and grabbed her arm to bring her with me. "We need to get going through, so rain check?"

"We're about to be together for a week without my parents, there will be plenty of *rain checks* we're going to be cashing in." She ran her hands through her hair to fix the messiness before kissing me and then getting up to grab her bag.

"I've created a monster," I said, slapping her ass, causing her to squeal.

I'd been trying to take it slow with her, but she wasn't making it easy on me. She'd sneak into my room late at night and torture me until I couldn't resist any longer. I couldn't complain about it, though. The feel of her skin intoxicated me and left me with a hangover every morning. The taste of her lips drove me wild, and the feel of our bodies sliding together consumed my every though after she went back to her bed.

But we still hadn't gone all the way yet. We'd been close a few times, but I'd stop us, pissing her off. I didn't want our first time to be a quickie while we were too scared of being caught.

At first I'd been terrified of her parents finding out and throwing my ass out on the streets, but I had a feeling they weren't dumb to what was going on. There were times Tessa would fall asleep or we'd end up in each other's beds the next morning.

"And please tell me you're finished packing," she said, eyeing my duffel bag sitting on the floor.

"I am," I answered, waiting for what I knew was coming.

"I told you to borrow one of my bags," she said. "There's no way you've managed to fit everything you need in that thing."

"You tried to get me to use purple leopard print luggage," I pointed out. "You know I've told you purple does not go with my skin tone, and what would all my friends think if I strolled down the street with a leopard print bag wheeling behind me?"

"If you're with your girlfriend, you're allowed to hold feminine looking bags and accessories," she answered, grabbing a pair of sunglasses from a drawer and tossing them into her bag.

"Uh ... what?" That was the first time I'd ever heard of this rule. In fact, I didn't think the rule even exists.

"They'll obviously know it's mine, and it will make you look like a gentleman."

"On another note," I said, sliding my hands into the pockets of my cargo shorts. "I hope you packed plenty of bathing suits in that pretty pink luggage of yours."

She grinned, biting the edge of her bottom lip. "Actually, I thought we'd go skinny dipping."

I smirked back. "Woman, you kill me."

She laughed, elbowing me in the side, and I kissed the top of her forehead. "We both know I'm not much of an exhibitionist."

"And I'm not into other guy's seeing my girlfriend naked, so I'm very happy about that." There were guys I knew that loved it when their girlfriends dressed sexy or wore skimpy clothes. They liked to show them off to their friends like they were some trophy. Not me. I wasn't with her to win a 'which guy has the biggest balls contest.' I'd rather guys not know what I was getting. I didn't want their corrupted eyes to be mentally fucking my girlfriend.

"We better get going," I said, grabbing her suitcase and rolling it into the hallway. I followed her as she skipped down the stairs with her other bag on her shoulder.

"I still don't get why I'm not allowed to go," Derrick whined when we got downstairs where him and his parents were waiting for us.

"Come talk to us when you're order," Darryl said. "Until then you're not going anywhere without adult supervision."

"Dawson is an adult. Why can't he be my chaperone?" he argued, looking over at me for help. I loved the little guy, but I wasn't playing babysitter on this trip.

"Not happening," Tessa said, shutting him down for me and ruffling her hand through his hair. "Let me know how much you want me hanging around when you have a girlfriend."

"A girlfriend? He already has two," I said. Derrick's eyes grew wide as he flipped me off.

Their parents laughed as Tessa eyed me skeptically. "I knew you were going to be a bad influence on him," she joked, her eyes turning back to her brother. "You keep following this guy's advice, you're in for a bad ride."

"What?" I asked, feigning innocence. "I give kickass girl advice. I landed you, didn't I?"

"That was just luck," she replied, shaking her head.

"He really does," Derrick said, jumping to my defense.

"The fact that he has two girlfriends states otherwise," she argued.

"Do you have everything you need?" Darryl asked.

We nodded. "Yep," Tessa chirped. "The GPS is in my car. I also brought a few maps, so we're good to go."

"Maps?" Derrick asked. "Do people know how to read those things anymore?" He looked over at her. "Do you even know how to read one?"

"I'm sure it can't be that hard," she replied. "If the GPS dies or the car gets stolen, we'll know where we're going."

"Riiiiight," he drawled, causing her to roll her eyes. "If someone steals the car, they're most likely taking your bags with it."

I'd officially moved in with them almost four months ago and hadn't heard from my mom once. I didn't go back for the rest of my shit. She'd shut my phone off, but thankfully I was old enough to start my own plan. I still kept my guy's days with Derrick once a week.

They followed us outside to the Jeep. "You kids be safe," her mom said. "Keep us updated where you are every few hours and let us know when you've made it. If you get too tired, don't push it. Stop at a hotel and get some rest. You have all week to get there."

We nodded and gave them hugs goodbye before loading our bags into the car.

"I can't believe this is our senior spring break," Tessa said, snapping her seatbelt across her body. "This is definitely not how I'd imagined it."

I nodded in agreement and snagged my sunglasses from the visor. There was no way in hell I would've imagined I'd be dating Tessa and headed to Florida alone together. Damn, shit had really changed.

"Are you excited?" I asked, starting the car.

"Yes and no," she answered. I felt the mood shift as I put the car in drive.

I looked over at her. "No?" I ask. "Why no?"

"I'm nervous," she said, her voice trailing like she was lost in thought. We'd been talking about this trip for a month, she'd never mentioned being nervous about it.

"Baby, you have nothing to be nervous about," I said.

"Daisy has this new life," she muttered.

Daisy was still staying in Atlanta, but her and Tessa were rebuilding their friendship by talking on the phone a few times a week. Tessa had nothing to worry about, but I understood her anxiety. She didn't trust people as much as she once did. She didn't like going out to social events or being around people. After everything that had happened to her, I couldn't blame her. She hung out with the boys and me sometimes, but I knew she couldn't have enjoyed it that much.

"What's wrong with that?" I asked. "You have a good life. Both of you have changed for the better."

"I'm scared there's no room for me now. She has all of these new friends, and I'm just sitting here with nobody."

"You have me," I said softly.

That granted me a smile. "Boyfriends don't count."

"Oh baby, I beg to differ," I said, winking. "I'd like to think we count for a lot."

"Anyways," she drew, wanting to keep the conversation serious. "I don't know if she's going to be like the old Daisy. Her new boyfriend is the complete opposite of Tanner. The total and complete opposite."

"Maybe that's a good thing."

"He's the son of a porn star and basically lives in a mansion all by himself. What if I'm not interesting enough for her? I'm this small town girl from Indiana and now she's hanging out with all of these rich kids from a big city whose parents have sex for a living."

"Daisy will always be your best friend. Sure, she might've made some new friends, but you have seventeen years on them. It's pretty damn hard competing with that."

"I guess you're right," she mumbled, grabbing a bottle of water from the bag seat along with a plastic bag. She set them down on her lap and started to drag out smaller bags of chips, cookies and candy.

"You do know we're only going to be on the road a few days?" I asked, watching her open a bag and pop a Sour Patch Kid into her mouth. She then grabbed another, leaned forward, and dropped one into mine. My mouth puckered at the sour taste before swallowing it down

"It's a road trip. You can't have a road trip without the necessities," she said, taking a drink of water before biting into a cookie. "With that being said, I think it's time for a jam session." She grabbed her iPod from the glove compartment and plugged it into the radio. Taylor Swift came streaming through the speakers, and I looked over at her grinning face as she started to sing along.

"Uh babe, I thought we were having a jam session?" I asked.

"We are ... what the hell do you think this is?" She pointed to the radio. "This." Then to herself dancing goofily. "Is a jam session."

"A jam session with Taylor Swift? I'm not a twelve-year-old girl. I can't jam out to Taylor Swift."

"That's awfully mean to Taylor," she said, frowning. I kept my stare on her, and she rolled her eyes. "Fine," she said, frowning while changing the song.

"One Direction? Really?" I asked at her new selection.

"First, I'm surprised you actually know who they are. Secondly, you said you couldn't jam out to Taylor. One Direction are boys. You can relate."

I snatched the iPod from her hand. "You just eat your snacks and let me be the DJ."

She saluted me and popped another Sour Patch Kid. "Fine, but please, no honky-tonk music."

I chuckled. I was a country music guy. "I'll keep it main stream for you, babe."

"Thanks, there are only so many songs I can take about Old Blue sittin' on the front porch while a guy strums his guitar."

I hit the playlist I'd created on her iPod and put it on the same song I'd listened to after she had her anxiety attack, Blake

Shelton's *Mine Would Be You*. It reminded me of her every time I heard it.

Tessa was my favorite anything. I'd experienced my highs with her, and she'd been by my side for my lows. We were each other's backbones that held each other up with every move.

"I actually like this song," she said, lifting her bare feet up onto the dashboard and moving her head to the beat.

❦

"WHY DOES IT FEEL LIKE WE'RE DRIVING ACROSS THE planet?" Tessa asked, groaning and flipping through playlists we'd already listened to a dozen times. "I've already finished two books on my Kindle and am about to go stir crazy." She grabbed her hair at the nape of her neck and braided the yellow strands loosely, letting it fall over her shoulder when she finished.

I honked my horn and flipped off the car edging their nose in front of me in an attempt to cut me off. The interstate was backed up with cars heading south.

I pointed to the GPS screen. "Looks like we're almost there. Quit being anxious because you're making me anxious."

"You get anxious when I get anxious?" she asked, looking over at me and tilting her head to the side.

"Unfortunately, my emotions seem to reflect off yours."

"Really?" I nodded. I read and felt every high and low she'd gone through. If she'd get distressed, I'd feel myself grow with worry. My nerves would tick endlessly wondering what she was so uneasy about. "Sorry, that's probably not very fun for you."

"Eh, not really."

She started to go on but stopped when I pulled up the drive to the address listed on the GPS. "Are all of these kids freaking loaded?" she asked while we both gawked at the monster of a house sitting in front of us.

I parked behind an SUV sitting in front of the garage and took the home in. Large white columns were the focal point of the two-story house. Tall, uncovered windows made up the majority of the front along with stucco and concrete. It was one of the nicest houses I'd ever seen, and I couldn't believe I was about to spend a week in it.

"Sure looks like it," I answered, moving my attention from the house to her.

She was turning into a nervous wreck – fiddling with her bracelet until it settled perfectly to hide her scars. The center console hit my side when I leaned over to her to brush a strand of hair from her face.

I kissed her chin. "Baby," I whispered. "If you feel uncomfortable or want to leave, let me know. We'll find somewhere else to stay or go home, whatever you want." She gave me a small smile. "I want this smile to stay here at all times." I kissed her lips when her smile grew. "And a bikini if that's okay."

She pushed my side and let out a tiny laugh. "I guess let's do this," she said.

I waited for her to grab the door handle before stepping out of the car. The front door flew open at the same time my feet hit the cement, and Daisy came skipping down the driveway to us wearing only a bikini and a black wrap around her waist. She smiled brightly when she reached us. Her looking happy made me happy. She wasn't the broken girl who'd run away because she couldn't handle real life anymore. I knew Tanner was looking down happy that she'd found someone to make her happy.

I spotted the guy who came with her to the hospital coming up behind her – checking her ass out in the process. He loved her. I was sure of it. I'd apologized for my asshole behavior when Daisy came home for Christmas, but I still felt bad about the whole ordeal.

The humid and sweltering air hit me as I grabbed our bags while Tessa circled the car to meet us.

"Hey guys," Daisy greeted. "How was the drive?"

"Traffic sucked," Tessa complained. "But we had plenty of Taylor Swift to keep us trekking."

The guy behind Daisy laughed while shaking his head. "I feel for you, bro."

Daisy pulled Tessa into a tight hug. "You look amazing girl," she said.

"Thanks," Tessa replied, hugging her back briefly before retreating back to my side.

Daisy pointed to the guy behind her. "This is Keegan." She pointed to me. "And this is Dawson." She stopped to grin. "Oh wait, you two have already met, but I figured a formal introduction might be necessary. No punches or threats please and thank you."

"She's a troublemaker," Keegan said, wrapping his arms around Daisy's waist.

Tessa was right. He was the complete opposite of Tanner with this dark hair covered by a baseball cap and the tattoo.

He shook Tessa's hand before shaking mine. "It's nice to finally meet you two," he said. His attention went straight to me. "Sorry about the shit at the hospital. We had a long drive and we're all tired. Everyone was on edge."

"No worries, man," I replied, waving off his apology. "I would've done the same if I dude was being an ass to my girl." Shit, I wanted to punch myself for it. I didn't like to act like an asshole to girls. I wasn't into that shit.

"You had every right to be," Daisy said. "I handled the situation terribly and was acting like a selfish brat."

"That doesn't mean it's okay for him to act like an ass," Tessa argued. She'd already busted my balls about this a few times, but

I didn't mind. She wrapped her arms around my waist and rested her head in the crook of my neck.

Daisy eyed us in curiosity as a smile spread over her lips. I knew she wasn't going to be against me dating Tessa. She grabbed Tessa's hand and pulled her away from

"Come on, girl," she said, grabbing Tessa's arm and pulling her away from my hold. Keegan stepped forward, grabbing a few bags while I grabbed the others, and we trailed behind the girls to the house. "There are people I want you to meet."

I sucked in a breath when Tessa looked back at me in apprehension. She didn't like meeting new people. Hell, she was just starting to get comfortable with adapting to the people she'd been close with before. I gave her a nod, assuring her she'd be fine, and she nodded back. She trusted me.

We walked through the front door into a large foyer and then in the living room where three people were sprawled across the couch. One girl was at the end paying attention to her phone. Another girl was halfway lying on top of a guy as they laughed about something. The girl on her phone screeched and jumped off the couch when she noticed us. She pulled the other girl off the guy's lap.

"Fuck Gabby, forewarn a guy before you do that shit," the guy on the couch said, grunting and holding his stomach, resulting in the girl laughing in reply.

Daisy pointed to the short tan girl who'd been alone on the couch. "This is Gabby." Her finger went to the other red-haired girl. "And this is Cora and her boyfriend Lane."

"I'm Dawson and this is Tessa," I said. Tessa wasn't too weak to introduce herself, but I wanted to help her deal with her stress.

"Are you guys dating?" Gabby asked, her eyes skimming down me. "Because girl, he is fine."

Tessa laughed as she nodded. My hand reached out to grab hers and I squeezed it tight.

"I knew it," Daisy shouted, jumping into the air and pointing at us. "Although, I'm a little mad you kept it from me for so long."

"He's living with me," Tessa pointed out, like it was obvious.

I'd planned on only staying with them for a month until I could save up enough money to get my own place. I thought I'd feel like a bum living with my girlfriend's parents, but now it felt like home.

"And sneaking into your bedroom at night?" Gabby asked.

"Leave her alone, Gabby," Cora warned. "You're going to scare her off." She looked at us. "Sorry guys, she doesn't have a filter." Gabby smirked proudly. "Let me show you your room. I'm sure you want to get settled."

"This place is amazing," I said, following them down the hallway, our luggage in tow, as I admired the large ceilings and marble floors.

"Thanks," Cora said, "it's Lane's parents. They don't mind us coming down here."

"I'd be here all the time if I could," Tessa muttered.

We followed Cora up a flight of stairs, stopping at the end of a hallway, and she opened up the door to a bedroom. A huge bedroom that was nearly as big as my mom's house. A king sized bed sat in between two large windows, giving us a perfect view of waves crashing down against the sand.

"This bed looks more comfortable than my own," Tessa said when Cora left. She plopped down on the bed and snuggled into a pillow. "Can we just stay in here all vacation?"

I kicked my shoes off before climbing in next to her and kissed the sensitive spot on her neck, tasting the sweetness of her skin. "I have no problem with that, baby, but I think that would be pretty rude."

She moaned. "Is it weird I like spending all of my time with you? I mean, I know people call girls like that needy, but what if that's what I want to do?"

"Who gives a shit what other people think? You're not needy if I want to hang out with you just as much. Those guys, the ones who bitch about girlfriends being needy, aren't in love. They're not planning anything long-term. They're just looking to get laid. When you find that girl, the one you're in love with, the one you want to spend the rest of your life with, you'll never see her as needy, because you need her as much as she needs you. Maybe even more."

I moved in closer, running my lips over the smooth skin of her neck, before sucking on it gently. She wrapped her arm around my back, and I groaned at the feel of her fingernails running down my back underneath my t-shirt as her mouth dipped down to catch mine. Our tongues collided, and I reveled in the delicious and intoxicating taste of her.

She jumped when a bang came from the other side of the door. "All right kids," Daisy yelled. "It's time to hit the beach."

"Rain check number two?" I asked, situating myself before rising up from the bed. I stood at the edge and held my hand out to help her up.

She groaned while unzipping her suitcase, and I opened my duffel in search for my swim trunks. "I'll get dressed real fast," I said, turning around and heading to the attached bathroom.

She reached forward and grabbed my hand to stop me. "Come on, it's not like we've never seen each other naked," she said, biting into the edge of her lip.

She was right. We'd seen each other in our most vulnerable stages, touched each other in our most sensitive places, and felt our bodies slide against each other's ... but it's usually been in a bed where we're tucked underneath the blankets with the lights off.

I rested my hand on the curve of her hip. "You sure?"

She answered me by lifting her tank over her head and throwing it down on the floor. I licked my lips at the sight of her perfect, round breasts that were pushed up by a pink and white bra. My breathing heightened when she unhooked it and allowed it to fall at her feet.

I couldn't take my eyes off her. "You are so fucking perfect," I whispered. I'd felt them before. I'd sucked on them before. But this moment was different. We weren't scurrying around to get our highs before we were interrupted. We had time ... I liked time.

Her pouty lips formed a wicked smile as her hands went to the button of her jean shorts. She took her sweet time unbuckling it before sliding the zipper down. I gulped, my eyes watching her every move as the shorts fell to her feet.

She stood there in front of me in a pair of tiny panties. I had to fight the urge to trace every dip and curve of the perfection in front of me because this was her show. I was allowing her to call all the shots.

Her fingertips slid underneath the strings of her panties before she slowly let them join her shorts. My knees felt weak, nearly threatening to give out, and my mouth watered as I watched her step out of them. She was gorgeous in every single way. I'd won with her. I didn't know what I'd done in some past life to deserve her in this one, but this was the best reward a man could get.

She spun around to give me a view of her full, rounded ass and bent down to grab her bikini from her suitcase. My fist went to my mouth as I sunk my teeth into the skin. My cock ached with need while I watched her play out her seduction game. She pulled one the bottoms one at a time, and I frowned at my view being taken away.

"I'm going to need some help with this one," she said, turning back around to face me with the top in her hand. "Dawson." Her loud voice broke me out of my trance, and I gave her my attention.

"Huh?" I asked.

"I asked for help with my top."

I cleared my throat. "Yeah, I … I can do that." My legs felt like they were sinking into quick sand as I erased the distance between us.

She held the strings up in the air as I stood behind her. "I need you to tie these," she explained. I took a deep breath while looping the strings together, twisting them into a knot, and then running my hand down her spine, resulting in goose bumps scattering over her skin. She gasped when I grabbed a handful of her ass, smacking it lightly before cupping her breasts underneath her top. She fit in my hands like she was made specifically for me.

"You're so damn perfect, baby," I growled into her ear while massaging her breasts, using my thumbs to play with her nipples at the same time. Electricity spun through my veins, and I could feel myself growing harder with every stroke. I'd never been so turned on just touching a woman. Never.

But she wasn't just anyone.

She was Tessa.

My Tessa.

Every kiss, every touch, every moment felt ten times with her. It wasn't a race to get her clothes off and get laid. No, every time was special and symbolic. I was excited that eventually I'd know every sensitive spot on her body and what her favorite position was when I was inside of her.

She rested her head along the crook of my neck, and I shivered as her hot breath hit my earlobe. "That feels amazing," she whispered, arching her back forward and moving deeper into my touch.

I slid my hands down her stomach at the same time she spun around to face me. Her eyes grew wide as she looked down at my erection underneath my shorts.

"Your turn," she said.

I was hard as a rock. "You do see what you're getting yourself into?" I asked, raising a brow.

She nodded with a smile, and my cock twitched with excitement. "Oh yeah," she said eagerly. I unbuckled my shorts and dropped them along with my boxers. We held firm eye contact while I waited for her reaction.

She grinned from ear to ear. "Wow ... it's actually pretty nice. I finally get a good look at what's been making me feel so good." We'd done some hand activities in bed, shit along the lines of what we'd done on the couch when I first moved in, because that was what seemed to get her the most excited. I used my cock to arouse her without penetration until she was bursting at the seams.

"I'm glad you like it," I joked awkwardly. Wasn't she the one supposed to feel insecure?

I gripped her hips to drag her closer, and she gasped at the feel of my cock rubbing against her. I kissed her deeply while kicking away my shorts.

"Bed," she breathed out when I slipped my shirt over my head.

"Abso-fucking-lutely." I pushed her down on the bed and began to crawl over her.

This was it.

We were going to finally have sex, and it was going to be fucking amazing.

We both jumped at the knock on the door. "Five seconds or I'm coming in," Daisy yelled.

"Jesus Christ," I groaned, looking down at Tessa lying underneath me.

"You've got to be kidding me," she said, slamming her hands down as I collapsed on top of her.

I rested my forehead on hers and sighed. "Babe, she's right. I'm not going to do this with a house full of people while they're standing out there waiting for us." She glared at me when I pulled away.

"I guess you're right," she said. I kissed the top of her nose while trying to talk my cock down and got up. "You know," she went on with a sly smile as I moved across the room butt ass naked. She leaned back on her elbows. "You have a pretty cock. Daisy and I used to Google penis pictures. I always thought they were anything but cute, but yours is definitely cute."

"Cute?" I repeated, raising a brow while pulling up my swim trunks. "Please babe, don't ever, and I mean ever, refer to my cock as cute again."

She laughed and pulled herself up from the bed. "Would you rather we name it?"

"Hell no."

"You sure? I could start brainstorming. Mr. Fun, Mr. Good Time, The Dragon of Excitement?"

"Come on, you pain in my ass. We're not naming my cock after some low budget porno." I opened the door, took one step out, and collided with Daisy's body. I narrowed my eyes at her. "Jesus, have you been waiting out her the entire time?"

"I told her not to interrupt you," Cora said. I looked behind Daisy to see the entire crew there. "But they wouldn't listen." She gestured to a grinning Daisy and Gabby. "Drown them in the ocean, not me."

"I didn't want them to get lost," Daisy argued. "They had to know where we're going."

Keegan laughed. "Babe, really?" He turned and pointed out the window. "The beach is *right there.*"

She gave him a dirty look and attempted to push him away, but her grabbed her waist to stop her and then kissed the top of her head. It was weird seeing her with someone other than Tanner, but I was happy the guy she was moving on with wasn't a douchebag.

Tessa's cheeks were bright red as she grabbed her beach bag and hitched it over her shoulder. I grabbed her hand while we followed everyone out of the house. The humid air felt suffocating when we first stepped out, but my mind was taken somewhere else as we walked down to the beach.

Tessa looked over at me eagerly. "So what do you think?"

It was my first time seeing the ocean. I'd never been on a real vacation before. Tessa and her family had invited me to join them on vacations before, but I didn't want them paying my way so I always made some bullshit excuse.

I peeled my sandals off, feeling the sand sink between my toes, and grinned. "Pretty damn good so far."

CHAPTER 31

TESSA

THE COOL LEATHER OF THE COUCH FELT REFRESHING ON MY sunburned skin when I collapsed onto it and sighed. "Thank god for air conditioning," I moaned out.

We ended up spending the entire day on the beach. My arms felt tender as I rubbed them, and I knew I'd be slathering on an entire bottle of aloe later.

Daisy fell down next to me and elbowed me in the side. "So you and Dawson, huh? I told you it'd happen eventually. I'm happy for you, but just make me one promise." She handed me a cold bottle of water before taking a drink of hers.

"What's that?" I asked.

"When you two get married and have adorable little babies, don't forget to name one after me."

I fussed with the wet tangles in my hair and laughed. "I think we have years and years to go through before we start talking kids."

She grinned. "Oh please, everyone knows it's going to happen. From the looks of it, that boy isn't planning on letting you out of his grasps anytime soon, and I'm sure you'd beat a girl down over him. So, yes, I'm waiting on my mini-Daisy."

She was right. I couldn't see myself without Dawson at my side. If there was one certainty I had in this chaotic life of mine, it was that Dawson would always be here with me. I wasn't sure if I'd even be alive if he weren't with her. He'd been my lifesaver and salvaged me from the destructive road I was traveling.

She lowered her voice. "How's ... uh ... everything else going?"

She knew I was going to therapy, but I didn't tell her everything. She didn't know about Reese or how I'd spiraled out of control with him. I never told her I paralyzed my suicidal thoughts by drinking or how I stupidly lost my v-card to a man that didn't give two shits about me.

It was at that moment that I realized I'd been so afraid that she'd moved on without me that I hadn't thought about how I'd been doing the same thing. We were growing up, doing our own thing, and creating our new lives that no longer involved Tanner. Gone was the two teenage girls who'd once laughed while talking about boys and did hideous make-up together. We were two young women getting over loss and finding our new ways.

I took a drink and swallowed it down slowly. "It's going okay. I haven't been going to therapy as much as I used to because my doctor says I'm doing better."

She took my hand in hers and squeezed it. "I'm proud of you, Tessa. You're doing great. I know when everything happened I was a shitty friend. I'm sorry. I wish I would've never left things how I did."

I shook my head. "You and I had different ways of dealing with our loss. Leaving seems to have been good for you. You would've never met Keegan, and who knows what would've happened if you'd stayed. You could still be sitting in your room heartbroken."

Her eyes watered as she nodded. "It also brought you and Dawson together. Tanner would've been happy."

"I hope it's good things being said about me over here." We both jumped at Dawson's voice as he came up behind us. His wet hair dripped onto the floor as he squeezed in next to me on the couch. I noticed his sunburned skin and knew I'd be sharing my lotion later.

"Of course," Daisy laughed. "We always say nice things about you."

He chuckled. "Right, I've heard way too many of your sleepover conversations to believe that."

My mouth flew open. "Seriously? You eavesdropped on our girl talks?"

A sly grin spread across his face. "Oh yeah." He grunted when I elbowed him in the side. "It was all Tanner's fault. He wanted to find out what Daisy was saying about him and *his skills*."

"We didn't talk about my brother's sex life, you freak," I replied.

"Yeah, I know, which made him nervous. He thought his performance was lacking because Daisy wasn't bragging about it."

I gagged. "Or she was trying to spare me the pain of gouging my ear drums out." Hearing about my brother's sex life was something I didn't ever want to hear, and I told Daisy that the first day they started dating. I looked over at Dawson. "Did I ever say anything about you?" I asked.

He nodded. "You talked about wanting to kill me and every

girl I dated on numerous occasions." He rubbed my shoulders and kissed me on the cheek.

"Yeah, he's definitely not lying about that," Daisy said.

"Pizza is here, bitches," Gabby yelled, walking through the front door with a stack of pizza boxes in her arms.

"How'd you get those?" Daisy asked.

"I borrowed Lane's car and took the long route so I could check out boys on the beach."

"I told you to quit doing that shit," Lane said, coming out of his bedroom with Cora behind him. He held out his hand when he reached Gabby and she dropped the keys in it.

"I didn't steal anything. I *borrowed* it to get us food." She held up the boxes higher. "So you're welcome."

He shook his head. "You're damn lucky I'm in love with your best friend."

"Oh, no, you're lucky my best friend is in love with you," she fired back, walking past him and into the kitchen. She dropped the pizzas down on the counter before kicking off her flip-flops and grabbing a handful of plates. "Now come on, after dinner we're pulling out the liquor and playing games. I need alcohol to hang out with all of these couples. Third wheelin' it sucks ass."

"If it's *Never Have I Ever*, it's not happening," Cora said, joining her in the kitchen and pulling out drinks from the fridge.

"That's a negative. There's always drama with that game," Gabby replied. "I nominate beer pong or flippy cup."

"That's because you always win at freaking flippy cup," Daisy groaned, grabbing a pillow and tossing it across the room. It came up short and smacked into a chair.

I could feel my body beginning to overheat. I hadn't touched a drink since I went to the hospital and was terrified to be around alcohol. I grew nauseated with envy and resentment. I was a teenager. I was supposed to be out drinking and having fun. This was my spring break, but I couldn't be that carefree girl anymore.

I was a different person. I'd grown up and my life had changed so much in the past few months. My best friends were my boyfriend and brother. I didn't go to parties. Hell, even the word *alcohol* made me feel even sicker to my stomach.

I looked down at the floor as tears laced my eyes. I'd been so excited about coming here that I hadn't even though about the fact there would be booze.

"Whatever you guys decide on it can't happen inside," Lane said. "My parents will have my ass if you knuckleheads fuck any of the shit up in this house."

Daisy turned around and looked at me. "What do you want to do?" she asked.

The room felt like it was spinning and the tears were growing faster. "I ...uh ..." I paused, not sure what to say before I pulled away from Dawson, jumped up from the couch, and fled the room. I shrieked when a hand stopped me before I slammed our bedroom door shut. I turned around to find Dawson's hand in-between the door and the frame, stopping me from closing it. I released my hold and walked backwards until I collapsed onto the bed.

He looked at me with worry in his eyes and squatted down in front of me to grab my hands and kiss them. "Baby," he whispered. "What's wrong?"

I peeked down at him. "Nothing is the same," I answered around sniffles. "Nothing is the same. I wanted to have fun. I've missed Daisy and have been excited about this trip since we first started planning it. She doesn't even know alcohol stares the living crap out of me, and I don't even know if I want her to. I'm afraid of being that outcast girl, but I can't start drinking again." I shook my head, my voice breaking. "I can't."

He started kissing my tears away. "It's never going to be the same, you know that. Daisy is still your best friend. If you talk to her, she'll understand. We don't have to drink and from now on

I'll try to make sure we're not around it, but it's bound to happen sometimes. It'll be hard at first, but remember it doesn't have control of you anymore."

I was a recovering alcoholic before graduating high school. That was just sad.

I shook my head a few times. "I no longer have a best friend," I cried out. "I'll all alone in this sober and lonely world."

"What about me?" he asked, holding my face in his hands. I stared into his eyes that were the same color as the ocean we'd been admiring earlier.

"What do you mean?" I asked, not breaking our eye contact.

"I honestly don't think you're losing Daisy as a best friend, but if you feel that way, what about me? I'd like to think I'm your best friend."

I ran my finger underneath my eye to capture any loose tears. "You're my boyfriend, you can't be both."

"And why the hell not?"

"Because best friends share secrets, laugh with each other, and have sleep-overs. Boyfriends can't do that."

He chuckled. "You kidding me? I know every single thing about you, your secrets, your annoying but cute habits, everything. You spend more time with me than you do anyone. I know what weird shit you like to eat, what you're allergic to, what shows you like to watch, and how your lower lip trembles when you see a homeless person standing on the corner begging for money. I know how your body tenses up when you're nervous, just like it did when they brought up drinking. And we pretty much have a sleepover every night. Baby, I know you, and that's what a best friends is – someone you can trust and someone you can confide in. You're my best friend. When something good happens or I need to talk to someone, I don't reach for the phone to call Cody or Ollie, it's you. You're my go-to. You understand me. You're my lover, my soul mate, *and* my best friend."

"Wow," I whispered, taking his words in as their truth sunk into me. "You're right. You are my best friend."

I melted into his touch when he kissed me again. Dawson seemed to always make my pain disappear. "Damn straight. Do you think we should make bracelets with our initials and paint each other's toe nails?"

I pushed his shoulder and laughed. "Sure, do you want pink or purple toenails?"

"It doesn't matter, just make sure you give me glitter so I can sparkle like your vampire boys."

I giggled and fell backwards onto the soft mattress. "I really don't want to go back out there. I'm embarrassed."

He took my sandals off and then started to massage my feet. "They don't think you're any of those things. If you want to stay in here, I can tell them you're not feeling well. It's no biggie."

"What about you?" I asked, leaning up on my elbows to look down at him. "I can't make you sit in here with me when you could be out there having fun. Just because I don't want to drink doesn't mean you can't."

He looks at me shocked. "Are you fucking kidding me? You think I'd have more fun out there?"

"Uh yeah."

"I don't give a shit about drinking games. I have fun when I'm with you, no matter what we're doing. I came here to spend time with you. I like the other people out there, but they're not my priority. I'd sit here and watch the paint dry if it's with you."

I frowned. "I still feel bad." This was his spring break too, and I was ruining it.

He brought himself up. "I want to spend time with you, period. Do you want me to go grab you some pizza?"

"I should probably go out there. I don't want to seem like a rude bitch."

I got up before he had the chance to argue with me, and he

followed me into the kitchen where everyone was sitting at the table.

"I saved you a seat," Daisy said, patting the chair next to her. I smiled in response and grabbed a slice while Dawson did the same.

My freak out didn't seem to change anything. They kept talking and didn't look at me any differently. No one asked why I'd ran off. That's when I understood why Daisy had fallen in love with these people. They understood. They didn't judge. They didn't pry into your business to know every detail when they saw you were hurting.

"I think we're going to hang back tonight," Dawson informed them. "We're both exhausted from the drive down."

Keegan nodded in understanding. "I get it, man. I was drained and your guy's drive was longer than ours. We have a whole week to hang out, and I'm sure we won't be doing too much tonight anyways."

"Yeah, we can all hang out tomorrow," Daisy said, smiling at me.

I smiled back, feeling much better, and finished off my pizza. Dawson and I helped clean up after dinner and stayed back when everyone else headed to the back patio.

"Where do you want to watch TV?" Dawson asked. "In the living or bed room?"

I circled my arms around his waist and rested my head on his chest. "I'm drained. I think the bed is calling our names."

He laughed and tucked me into his side while leading us back to the bedroom. I pulled down the comforter and climbed into the bed as soon as he turned on the light.

"You changing?" he asked, looking over at me as he rummaged through his bag.

I shook my head and let my hair down. "I'm going to sleep in these." I was wearing sweats and a tank that I'd thrown on after my shower. "I'm too exhausted to do anything else." I unsnapped my bra from underneath my shirt and tossed it across the room. It landed at Dawson's feet at the same time he slid his shorts off.

He glanced down at my bra before leaning down to grab it and holding it in front of him. "This one might be my favorite," he said, winking. "I've yet to see this one."

I laughed. "I don't think you're ever going to see or remember every piece of undergarment I own."

His eyes lit up with mischief. "Is that a challenge?"

I bit the bottom of my lip before allowing a slow smile to build across my face. "That just might be, Mr. Thomas."

He grabbed the top of his shirt and pulled it over his head, his hair getting messy in the process. My gaze promptly went to his chest as he pulled down the blankets and crawled in beside me.

"God, I could stay like this forever," I said, curling up to his side, and he kissed the top of my head. I winded my arm around his waist and peeked up at him while breathing in his cologne. "The beach, not hearing Derrick blaring his video games all night, this is perfection."

"Hey, I'm not complaining over here," he replied.

I took a deep breath and gave myself a silent pep talk for what I was about to do. "How about those rain checks?" I asked. I was trying to sound casual, but my heart was racing.

Tonight was going to be the night we finally had sex.

We were alone. We didn't have to worry about Derrick or my parents walking in on us. I could hear the faint sound of music playing outside, so we wouldn't have to worry about being quiet because it would drown us out.

I'd lost the number of times I'd attempted to get him to have sex. I'd tried everything and wasn't above using the power of persuasion with food, lip pouting, and even lingerie. But nothing worked. He insisted we needed to wait until I was ready, which always pissed me off, because I was the only one who'd known when I was ready – and I was.

I wanted to experience everything with Dawson and feel what he'd given all of those other girls before me. I ached for the experience of his naked body against mine while he was inside of me as we became one. My body throbbed with the want of him erasing the last, and only, guy who'd ever been that intimate with me. I needed him to kill Reese's mark there.

"I can do that," he whispered, his voice so low I barely heard him.

My mouth flew open.

Was this really happening?

"As long as you're certain that's what you want," he went on.

My pulse pounded, my nerves tingling, when I abruptly pushed up from him. A loud grunt emerged from his chest as I straddled his hips in one quick motion. There was no way I was giving him the chance to change his mind.

"Really?" I asked, unable to hold back my excitement. I was nervous. I was overwhelmed. I was happy. Panic and eagerness swept through me like a sea of emotions.

His eyes zeroed in on me as he smiled. "Yes, baby, really. And I think we've got a few rain checks to make up for."

I nodded in agreement and planted a knee to each side of him before grinding against him. His fingers latched onto my hips, and I yelped when he flipped us over so that I was on my back.

"You sure this is what you want?" he questioned again, hovering over me.

I grinned. "I'm positive."

He didn't argue. He actually didn't say anything. All he did was kiss me while I tried to catch my breath. I kissed him harder when he pulled my shirt over my head, and he kissed me harder when I rubbed his erection. I wiggled out of my sweats and panties, and he yanked the blanket away from us to throw it on the floor.

"Tonight I'm going to see all of you," he rasped out, his attention focused on my body. He gently glided a finger along my skin – like he was worshipping it. Every time he touched me it felt like the first time – like I was experiencing something new. I melted against the soft sheets, almost feeling weightless.

My head fell back when I felt a single finger glide to my inner thigh, drifting between my legs, and then slowly slide inside of me. He added another finger, curling the two together, and I gasped, my back nearly coming off the bed. I shut my eyes as everything around us evaporated until it hit me. My eyes flew open as I lost my breath when I looked down to see his head ducked in-between my legs.

The first lick was the most crucial. This was something new, a line we'd never crossed before, and it was incredible. He took one lick, paused, and then three in succession over and over again, like he was playing a game with his tongue and I was the prize.

I tensed up and slowly began rotating my hips in circles to meet every inch of his tongue until I couldn't take it any longer. I lost all of my inhibitions. I needed more. I craved more. My muscles tightened, begging to be released, and my entire body clenched as a wave of pleasure took me over.

He gave me a few more licks before pulling himself up and looking down at me with a shit eating grin on his face.

I cleared my throat. "Well that was nice," I finally said, chuckling awkwardly. "Uh ... thank you."

He busted out in laughter. "You're very welcome, I aim to please." His face went serious. "But really, did that feel okay?"

"Did you not just see me act like I was going to orgasm my brain out?"

He laughed again. "Just wanted to make sure. That's my first time, you know." His words drifted off as he looked away flustered.

"You've never gone down on a girl before?" I asked, my voice both shocked and perky. The thought of being his first at anything excited me. I grinned when he shook his head, but he didn't give me the chance to revel in my happiness. I gasped at the feel of him replacing his mouth with his cock.

"You ready?" he asked, holding it at my entrance.

I nodded nervously. He grabbed his erection and slid it back and forth against my opening. "Mother fucker!" he rasped, his hand suddenly stopping.

"What?" I asked.

"Fucking condom."

"I'm on the pill," I said quickly. I'd been on the pill for years for irregular periods.

"I know, but you never ..." He started to pull away, but my hands grabbed his ass to stop him.

"Quit stalling," I said, irritated. "I'm not changing my mind. I'm not letting you change your mind, so if you don't have sex with me right now, you're going to be dealing with one pissed off woman."

He didn't say anything. Instead he stared down at me, his face calm, and I thought I was going to lose it as he slowly entered me. It was uncomfortable at first, but he kept eye contact with me as a silent conversation and paced himself while sliding in. I adjusted to his size, and every stroke felt better than the last one. Five minutes ago, I thought his tongue had been the best experience ever, but there were no words for him being inside of me.

"Does that feel good, baby," he asked, leaning down to kiss me. His tongue darted into my mouth and matched the rhythm of his strokes. He moved in deeper and deeper until he completely filled every inch of me. I wanted him to stay there forever and never take this feeling away.

"God yes," I groaned. "Please don't stop."

"Never," he grunted. His mouth moved to my neck, biting it gently, and then he nibbled on my earlobe. I groaned at the sensations coming from everywhere. His mouth, his thrusts, his hands were making every part of my body explode simultaneously.

He covered my mouth with his when I moaned out in pleasure and let myself go. He picked up his pace, his strokes faster and rougher before his breathing deepened and he gave me the weight of his sweaty body.

He rested his forehead on mine and his mouth went to my ear. "That was amazing," he whispered. "That was so fucking amazing, baby, you have no damn idea."

"Oh, I think I do," I said, regaining control of my breathing.

He slowly lifted himself off me, walked into the bathroom, and came back with a warm washcloth. I winced as he began to wipe the sensitive area between my legs tenderly and then got back in bed.

"So now we can do this all the time now, right?" I asked, snuggling into him.

His chest moved as he laughed. "I've created a monster."

CHAPTER 32

TESSA

I LOOKED UP FROM MY LAPTOP TO FIND MY MOM PULLING out a chair across from me at the kitchen table and sitting down.

"I have something for you," she said.

"What is it?" I asked, setting my pen down next to my Calculus notes. It was the last week of school, finals ... or hell week. I'd changed my classes back to the college credit ones like I'd planned in the beginning before losing Tanner, so I'd been spending every second studying to catch up. I was positive I had the material down, but I could never be too prepared. I was going to be cramming until the teacher handed out the tests.

She rummaged through her purse, pulled out a large white envelope, and slid it over to me. My heart began to race as I looked down at the packet addressed to me. I looked at her in shock and then back to the envelope. No ... it couldn't be. I grabbed the envelope and examined it with my hands to make sure it was real.

"How did you get this?" I asked.

An eager smile spread across her face. "I called them, told them you never received your letter, and they were happy to send you another," she explained. Her crimson lips grew wider as she squirmed in her chair.

I used my hands to straighten the envelope, smoothing out every wrinkle before tracing the emblem in the left corner. Last time this was sitting on my kitchen table I'd thrown it in the trash. It did nothing but remind me of broken dreams. It reminded me that he'd never be there with me. I didn't want that future any longer.

I was still holding back from making plans after I graduated. I couldn't make up my mind, and my parents agreed that if I felt like I needed time they'd be okay with giving my a year off.

I took a deep breath. "Let's see what we've got," I muttered, gripping the envelope. I was about to open when I saw Dawson walk into the kitchen in his work uniform.

"I figured you'd be in here studying," he said.

He'd been picking up every shift he could, sometimes even working doubles while still going to school because he wanted to save up for his own place. I repeatedly reminded him he could stay with us for as long as he wanted, but he always shook his head and said that wasn't the future he wanted. I grew hot with fear every time we had that conversation. I knew Dawson would never leave me, but I still didn't understand why he felt the need to move out so badly. It wouldn't feel like home if he wasn't here.

I got a whiff of garlic and cheese when his lips smacked into my cheek and he sat down beside me. He dropped an order of breadsticks in front of me. "I figured you were too busy to remember to feed yourself," he said. "Time for a break, baby."

"You know me too well," I muttered, my eyes darting back to the envelope. "Thank you."

He scooted his chair in closer to me and snagged a breadstick. "So what's going on?" I grabbed the packet and showed it to him. He beamed as he read the name of the sender. "Awesome! That's where you've always wanted to go. The envelope looks pretty big, which means you definitely got in." He elbowed my side playfully. "Are you going to open it?"

I hesitated. The idea of traveling thousands of miles alone terrified me. The plan had been for Tanner and Daisy to come with me. But it wasn't the fear of going without them that was holding me back now. It was the fear of going without Dawson. Is this what I really wanted?

I shut my eyes before slowly opening them back up to find waiting faces. I was going to open it to please them, but I wasn't going. Knowing I got into my dream college was enough for me.

"I'm not sure if it's the right plan for me now," I said, sliding my finger along the opening of the letter.

"Why's that?" my mom asked. "That's your dream school, honey. You've talked about going there for years."

"You already showed her the envelope?" my dad asked, joining us. He rested his briefcase on the kitchen island, loosened his tie, and sat down beside my mom. Great, this was becoming too much. I didn't want all of these eyes on me when I told them I'd changed my mind. "I take it you haven't opened it yet?"

I shook my head. "You're right, it was my dream school, but my dreams and plans have changed." What if I got stressed out there and had nobody to help me? What if things got rough and I started cutting again? Or drinking? There's always drinking in college.

"Then what's the new dream?" Dawson asked.

"What do you mean?" I questioned.

"What's your new plan, babe?"

What were his plans?

The words were at the tip of my tongue, and they stayed there. I was too terrified to ask. His plan was to get his own place. We'd never discussed anything past that. I never brought it up because I was waiting on him to. I knew he couldn't afford college and his mom still wasn't talking to him, so she wouldn't be any help. We'd talked about our future together, our babies and our wedding, but we'd never talked about the near future. Our talks were only long-term plans.

Dawson grinned as he pulled something from his pocket. I gasped when he held it up into the air.

"This is my plan," he said, displaying the white envelope with the same logo on the edge. "As long as it's still yours."

"What?" I croaked out. "Why didn't you tell me?"

"I applied at the beginning of the year, but I wasn't genius enough to get an early acceptance like my brilliant girlfriend." He nudged my shoulder. "I got mine a few months ago. I applied for a few scholarships and student loans then started putting ten percent of each one of my paychecks into a savings account."

"That's why you've been working so much?" I asked, still in shock.

"I told you I needed my own place, but what I meant was our place."

He'd done this for me. He wasn't leaving. He was joining me. He was grabbing my hand and taking every walk, leap, and run with me. He'd never leave me alone.

I stared into his blue eyes while my imagination grew wild about the journey we were about so pursue together. Excitement grew at my fingertips as I gripped the envelope firmly. This was happening. We were doing this.

My dad clapped his hands together. "So what do you think kids? Open the damn things so we can figure out whether we need to plan a trip to the East Coast!"

Dawson ripped open his envelope, but I froze up. Reality hit me. What if he didn't get in? What if I didn't get in and he did?

He noticed my hesitation and stopped. "You don't have to decide right now," he whispered. "I'll give you time to think about it."

"No, I need to do this." I handed him my envelope and snatched his. "You're opening mine, and I'm opening yours."

"Ready?" he asked, and I nodded. "One, two, three." We both ripped the edges of the envelopes and frantically pulled out the packet of papers.

"Holy shit!" I yelped when I read the first line of the opening letter. "You got in!" I leaped up from my chair and started jumping up and down, but froze when I saw his face. "What?" His face was blank and unreadable. "What?" I repeated, panic making its way through me.

"I'm sorry babe," he began slowly, like he was looking for the right words.

"I didn't get in?" I asked, feeling the tears coming. Oh my god, I didn't get in.

"I'm sorry, but it looks like you're stuck with me forever," he yelled, grinning.

I smacked his shoulder. "You ass, you scared the shit out of me."

He got up from his chair to grab my face and gave me a quick peck on the lips. "I can't wait to take this journey with you," he whispered against my lips. "We're going to college, baby."

"There's so much to do now. We need to start planning when we're leaving. Is there a list of available classes because we're accepting late? I need to figure out whether freshmen have to stay in dorms or if we can get a place together," I began to ramble.

I snatched the envelope from his hand and began to scramble through the papers. He grabbed my arm, stopping me, and laughed. "Babe, we'll do that later. Now it's time to celebrate."

CHAPTER 33

TESSA

"Is this the last of it?" Dawson asked, stepping into my bedroom as I slid the tape gun across a box.

"Nope," I answered. I picked up a box and shoved it into his hands. He grunted, nearly dropping it in surprise, but squatted down to save it just in time.

"No?" He dropped the box in the hallway where the others were stacked and came back into the room. "There's like fifteen boxes out there."

"Just one more for shoes and handbags." I grabbed a few pairs of shoes sitting on my bed and tossed them into the last open box.

"You already have a box of shoes and handbags," he pointed out, jerking his head towards the hallway.

"You can never have enough shoes and handbags." I taped the box, settled it onto the floor, and collapsed onto my bed over the pile of clothes I'd decided against taking. "I can't believe we're leaving for college."

We'd graduated two months ago and then spent our summer getting everything in order to move. Dawson was working non-stop, so I was in charge of packing and planning. We were renting a small, studio apartment that was only a mile away from campus.

"These ones are pretty," he said, falling down beside me and tracing the bright pink marks on my arm.

I'd made a deal with my therapist on my last appointment. Whenever I felt like cutting, I'd grab a Sharpe instead and mark my body that way. It helped me with the urges and reminded me how far I'd come when I watched them fade. I'd started drawing on my wrist, my thighs, and my legs – giving them doodles of flowers, rainbows, and stick figures holding hands. Dawson would grab a marker sometimes and color inside the lines. It had seemed cheesy at first, but it was helping. I hadn't had a relapse since I'd left rehab.

"Thanks," I said. I pointed to the stick figures holding hands. "That's us."

He laughed, but I could tell something was wrong. "Impressive." He paused, and I waited for him to say something. "So guess who called me today?"

"Who?"

He scratched his head. "My mom."

She hadn't reached out to him since the day of the parole hearing. She never called and neither had he. He did send her a ticket to graduation. It pained me watching him scan the crowd every few minutes, hoping maybe she'd do the right thing, and show up. But she didn't. He tried to play it cool, like it didn't bother him, but I know deep down he was hurting. How could you *not* hurt when your parents abandoned you? Even if you despised them, you still felt the ache of being un-wanted.

He did reach out to his grandparents and had talked to them

on the phone a few times. They still lived in Illinois, and we planned on making a visit to them on a school break. A few weeks ago, I'd finally taken it upon myself to call his mom and tell her he was leaving. She didn't answer the call, but I'd left a voicemail. I didn't know what the outcome would be, but I prayed she'd do the right thing.

"And?" I asked.

He let out a heavy sigh and ran his hand over his chin. "She said her calling didn't change anything between us." I shut my eyes and shook my head. "She said she could never forgive me for what I did and we'd never be able to have a relationship, but she wanted to tell me goodbye and good luck."

The words, "Are you serious," were biting at the tip of my tongue, but I shut my mouth. I wanted to stomp over to his mom's house and scream at her for being so selfish. But I didn't want to make Dawson more upset, so I just nodded and let him continue.

"She said she was proud of me for graduating and getting into college," he went on. "That's something she'd never accomplished. And then she said she had to go."

I leaned into his side and kissed his cheek. "At least she called, that has to count for something," I said in an attempt to raise his spirits. "It sounds like she's slowly coming to her senses."

He shrugged. "I know she's my mom, but she's starting to remind me more and more of him. A relationship with her would be too hard for the both of us right now. Maybe we can try again in the future after the dust settles and she finally sees my dad behind his mask, but I can't forget that she choose him over me. I don't want a relationship with her right now either."

My heart broke for him as he went silent and stared at the wall. I rubbed his back while giving him his time.

He looked over at me before grabbing my face and kissing me softly. "I don't know what I'd do without you, babe," he whispered against my lips. I twisted sideways and winded my arms around his neck.

"And I don't know what I'd do without you," I said, kissing him again.

"You ready to do this?"

I grinned. "You know it."

He pulled himself up from my bed, and his hand shot out to pull me up. We walked out of my bedroom to find my parents and Derrick trekking down the stairs with boxes in their hands.

"Good thing we have a free moving crew," I said, grabbing a box and following them.

"That's what you think now, sweetie," my mom said, looking back at me "Until you get there and have to carry these boxes up three flights of stairs."

Shit! I hadn't even thought about that. "Okay, I think I've changed my mind about you guys coming with us," I said.

They'd went with us on the school tour and apartment hunting, but we told them we wanted to make this trip on our own. They'd already spent enough helping us get our apartment.

"Too late now," my mom said, laughing when we made it outside.

We loaded up the last of the boxes into my car, double-checked we had everything, and hugged everyone goodbye.

My life hadn't gone according to my plan, but I was beginning to be okay with that. I knew there still wouldn't be a day that I wouldn't miss Tanner, but losing him taught me a lot about myself. It made me see the survivor and strong woman inside of me that I could be on my own. He led me towards my life goals in spirit and brought Dawson to me to help along the way. Dawson and I healed one another and coped with our struggles.

We wanted to make every day count, and if something didn't

go according to plan, we'd find another. And another. And another. Until everything ended up being okay.

I stared out the passenger side window, the high of leaving wearing off, and focused my mind on what was about to come.

"You ready for our last goodbye?" Dawson asked, looking over at me.

I nodded, wiping away a tear, and took a deep breath as we drove through the entrance to the cemetery. "I am."

ABOUT THE AUTHOR

Charity Ferrell was born and raised in Indiana and still resides there with her future hubby and two Yorkies who run the house. She grew up riding her bike to the town's library and reading anything she could get her hands on. When she's not writing, you can find her reading, spending time with her family, online shopping, or plotting her next next book.

For more information:
www.charityferrell.com
charityferrell@yahoo.com

CPSIA information can be obtained
at www.ICGtesting.com
Printed in the USA
BVHW091502040522
636101BV00007B/373

9 781503 075979